Having worked full-time for nearly thirty years in the financial services sector, Robert has recently begun to spend more time writing. Starting as a hobby, he now hopes to pursue this as a career. After 'testing the waters' tentatively through self-publishing, Robert has recently completed his first book for full publication. Robert currently lives with his wife and pets near Edinburgh, Scotland.

To my wife, Angela.

Robert Archibald

MURDER AT ALPINE MANOR

AUSTIN MACAULEY PUBLISHERS™
LONDON • CAMBRIDGE • NEW YORK • SHARJAH

A CIP catalogue record for this title is available from the British Library.

ISBN 9781528910200 (Paperback)
ISBN 9781528959513 (ePub e-book)

www.austinmacauley.com

First Published (2020)
Austin Macauley Publishers Ltd
25 Canada Square
Canary Wharf
London
E14 5LQ

Chapter 1

December 20th

The two men sat staring at each other across the vast mahogany desk. At one side of the desk sat a laptop, open but currently being ignored. Next to it, a small pile of papers, a pen standing in a holder and behind the pen, a telephone.

Suddenly, a small buzz was heard and one of the buttons on the phone flashed.

Pressing the button quickly, the man behind the desk said, "I said I was not to be disturbed!"

"I'm sorry, Mr Rogers," the tinny voice said, "but…"

"I don't care!" Mr Rogers snapped. "No interruptions!"

He pushed the button again, terminating the intercom. He looked back at the man sitting opposite him. He was middle-aged, his short brown hair flecked with grey, hints of bags beneath his eyes, the jowls of his cheeks making his mouth look constantly downturned. A frown drew his eyebrows closer, creating wrinkles on his forehead. Everything about him was nondescript, even his clothes, an unremarkable, slightly wrinkled suit, a plain tie.

Jocelyn Rogers, on the other hand, was anything but nondescript. Almost seventy years old, his hair was white, his face showing the marks of time, however, he was immaculately dressed in the finest suit money could buy, tailor-made, naturally; his silk shirt probably costing more than the entire wardrobe of the man opposite him. His face had graced numerous covers of financial magazines, his business empire, which he had built from the ground up, employed thousands of people around the world and, it was safe to say, he was recognised everywhere he went. "Mr Thomas," Rogers finally spoke, "that is quite a tale. Pure fiction, of course, and if you repeat it elsewhere, you will hear from my lawyers."

Jack 'JT' Thomas stared back at Rogers, almost a hint of a smile tugging at his lips though Rogers could not be certain.

"I'm sure your lawyers are very... intimidating," he said.

"And effective," Rogers added. "Believe me, I only hire the best."

"Yes, I'm sure you do," JT agreed. "Unfortunately for you, them being the best won't change the facts. You murdered your former secretary, Elise Hampton, and you tried to cover it up."

"So you said," Rogers said, standing up and turning to gaze out the large window behind him. It offered a view of the city few other buildings could match, his being one of the tallest. Beyond the city, the sun was setting, casting a red glow across the sky. "Mr Thomas, do you have any idea how much money I am worth? How much of this city is mine? I have an empire, I have more money and power than most people could ever dream of, I have politicians at my beck and call. Anything I could ever want, I have. Why would I kill anyone?"

"The oldest reason in the book, money."

"Absurd!" Rogers scoffed. "I have more money than I know what to do with!"

"Yes," JT agreed. "And you wouldn't want to lose any of it, would you? Say, in a bitter divorce?"

"This is nonsense!" Rogers said. "Elise, rest her soul, was a troubled woman. She had a history of depression. The poor woman took an overdose. It was a terrible tragedy, nothing more."

"Elise's sister disagrees," JT replied. "She did not believe her sister killed herself, no matter what the police concluded. That is why she hired me."

"You may be some kind of famous private detective, Mr Thomas," Rogers sneered, "but I find it reprehensible that you are stringing this woman along, prolonging her suffering, rather than helping her accept the truth."

"Truth?" JT retorted, "Is that the truth about your affair with Elise, the truth that she didn't want to be 'the other woman' any longer? The truth that she thought you loved her and would leave your wife for her? That truth?"

Rogers stayed quiet, shaking his head.

8

"I have to admit, it was difficult," JT continued. "You swore Elise to secrecy and she never told anyone about the two of you, not even her sister. It was difficult to determine when the two of you were indulging in little private getaways, rather than the numerous business trips you embark on. I probably wouldn't have come close to piecing it together if it wasn't for one throwaway remark."

"Your fantasies notwithstanding," Rogers said, "as part of their investigation, the police questioned me. I had an alibi."

"Yes, you did," JT admitted. "One which, doubtless, was not scrutinised too closely. I'm sure your friends in high places would have been all too eager to accept your story, the way they accept your campaign contributions, right? And, I suppose, the police had no reason to suspect you were lying."

"That's because I wasn't!" Rogers stated emphatically. "And you can't prove otherwise."

"You like animals, don't you?" JT asked.

"What?" Rogers was taken by surprise. "Yes, of course. I donate to numerous animal charities; fund a conservation park in Kenya, campaign to ban hunting. What has that got to do with anything?"

"Yes, everything I researched about you, everyone I spoke to, all said the same thing," JT carried on. "In business, you are cut-throat Your Empire has been built on making tough, unpopular decisions; if something wasn't turning a profit, you'd cut it loose, downsize, whatever, even if it cost people their jobs. The only sentiment you have ever shown in your business dealings is when it comes to animals. Everyone agrees."

"That is not a crime," Rogers said.

"No, not at all," JT agreed. "In fact, it's very commendable. Sincerely, I wish more people in your position shared your attitude."

"What does this have to do with anything?" Rogers demanded; his impatience showing.

"Ah, yes, I nearly forgot," JT said apologetically. "It was when I was interviewing everyone the police had spoken to, just double-checking things, you understand, that I picked up on something that had not been mentioned previously. An innocent, harmless remark that, of course, could have no bearing on Elise's death."

"Which was?" Rogers asked.

"The cat," JT answered.

"I'm sorry? The cat? What cat?" Rogers demanded.

"Elise's cat," JT replied. "Do you recall, when the police phoned your office to say they had found her dead in her home, your secretary, the nice lady sitting out there just now, took the call, didn't she?"

"So?" Rogers asked. "Of course she would take the call, it's her job to take calls!"

"Yes, of course," JT agreed. "Do you remember what you said to her when she told you?"

"Of course," Rogers snapped. "I told her to inform the police that I would be happy to help them in any way possible. And..."

"And?" prompted JT.

"And I also instructed her to make sure the police got the appropriate animal-care services to take care of Elise's kitten."

"The cat," JT said smugly.

"I fail to see what relevance this has on anything," Rogers said angrily. "I'm afraid I am going to have to ask you to leave."

JT sat still, looking almost bored. "Why do they always resort to this sort of bluster?" he asked rhetorically.

"If you do not leave, I will have Security remove you," Rogers threatened.

Ignoring Rogers, JT stood up, walked behind the chair he had been sitting on and leaned his arms against it. "How did you know about the cat?" he asked quietly.

"W-what?" Rogers stammered. "I don't know... I mean, the police must have said to my secretary and she told me..."

"No and no," JT interrupted. "I have checked and double-checked. Neither the police nor your secretary were aware Elise had a cat, until you mentioned it. In fact, it was only after your mentioning it that the cat, the kitten, was found hiding in the linen closet."

"Well, Elise must have told me," Rogers said.

"She told you about her little, black kitten?" JT asked.

"It's not black, it's ginger," Rogers said before he could stop himself.

"Oh, yes, you're right," JT agreed. "Ginger. My mistake. How did you know?"

"Um… ah… well, Elise obviously told me and I just remembered," Rogers said, suddenly sounding less sure of himself.

"Hmm," JT murmured. "You want to hear a funny story?" Before Rogers could answer, he continued, "Elise did not own a kitten, ginger or otherwise. One of her neighbours does, a six month old ginger kitten called Spot of all things. It seems this neighbour had some kind of family emergency and had to leave town for a few days. She asked Elise to look after Spot while she was gone. Now, here is the funny part; it was the day of Elise's murder that she was asked to look after little Spot."

Rogers stared at JT, the colour drained from his face, his mouth dry.

"So, tell me," JT carried on, "how did you know about the kitten? The only way you could have known was if you saw Elise that night, which you denied happened." JT let his statement hang in the air as Rogers fidgeted in his seat.

"You know, I have to hand it to you," JT said after a moment. "Most people in your situation would have tried to be too elaborate, offering up lots of useless theories that would steer the police away from them. Not you. You kept it simple, didn't you? Give yourself an alibi then sit back and watch the police reach the wrong conclusion, not getting involved, not drawing attention to yourself. If only you hadn't made that careless remark."

"It doesn't prove…" Rogers began, unconvincingly.

"Just one little thread," JT said. "Give it a pull and, suddenly, your whole story begins to unravel."

Rogers sat silently, glaring at JT, his jaw twitching. JT could almost see the cogs of Rogers' brain spinning, desperately trying to furnish him with a convincing explanation with which to refute everything he had just heard.

Casually leaning across the desk, JT flicked the switch on the intercom and said, "Okay, he's all yours."

The double doors to the office were pushed open and two uniformed police officers hurried in, followed by a small woman holding an electronic organiser. Her brown hair was pulled up and tied in a bun and a pair of spectacles hung on a chain around her neck. She wore a skirt which hung just below her knees and shoes which could be kindly described as 'sensible'. Her suit jacket was buttoned tightly, like the blouse beneath it. The whole ensemble gave the impression of an elderly librarian, though in fact she was not yet thirty.

As the police officers were handcuffing Rogers, JT turned to the woman and said, "Well, Marie, another successful conclusion."

"Yes, Mr Thomas, um, boss," she stammered meekly, eyes down.

"You don't understand," Rogers wailed as he was dragged out the office, past the bewildered look of his current secretary. "First, she wanted a promotion. Personal Assistant! But that wasn't enough, she wanted more. She said if I didn't leave my wife, she would ruin me. I couldn't let that happen!"

"Quick, someone call the Cliché Police! Get them to send a couple of officers from the Mid-Life Crisis Department!" JT shouted sarcastically over his shoulder. "Can you believe that guy?" he said to Marie.

"Um, no, ah, not really," she murmured.

Marie Watson fumbled her spectacles on and looked at the electronic organiser. She had worked for JT for several years now and, although he often despaired at her lack of confidence and introverted nature, JT had to admit that she was absolutely top-notch when it came to keeping track of his business dealings, appointments and all the mundane day-to-day trivia that he had absolutely no interest in.

"Right, first thing tomorrow," JT told her, "you can inform the client of our success, provide her with a final bill and remind her payment is due by end of week."

Marie tapped on the organiser then, without looking up, asked, "Is that it?"

"I believe so," JT answered. "Unless you think I've overlooked something."

"No," Marie murmured. "It's just... well... our client's sister was murdered. It seems a bit... cold treating it like a... a... a business transaction."

"Come on, Marie," JT replied. "You know me well enough by now to know sentiment doesn't come into this. It is business, pure and simple."

"I know," Marie said. "It's just such a tragedy...."

"Stop!" JT said abruptly. "What you see as a tragedy, I see as a business opportunity. Come on, how much sympathy can you have for Elise?" Without waiting for an answer, he carried on. "I mean, how naïve was she? Did she really think for one moment that someone like Rogers would risk losing half his fortune in a bitter divorce just to be with her? Honestly, she is as big a cliché as Rogers. So, no, I have no sympathy for her but I am glad there are people like her because it is really good for business."

Marie was quiet, absently picking at bits of fluff on her skirt with her free hand.

"Right," JT said. "Now that we have had this heart-to-heart, again, what's next?"

Looking again at the organiser, Marie touched the screen to bring up JT's current itinerary, after a moment, she said, "Um, this was the last on-going case. Now that this is wrapped up…"

"Yes!" JT said, genuinely happy, "Christmas vacation!"

"Um, about that…" Marie began.

"No, we have already discussed this," JT spoke over her. "Like me, you have no family. I won't have you spending Christmas alone."

"But you have family," Marie said meekly.

"Technically, yes," JT admitted. "However, it's not one I have any wish to spend time with."

"But…"

"So, it's settled, then," JT carried on as if Marie had never uttered a word. "You will accompany me to Alpine Manor for the Holidays."

Marie sighed and nodded thinking maybe JT was right. Surely it would be better than being alone. Wouldn't it?

"Besides," JT added, "I have been thinking that some of my more interesting cases would make fantastic novels. Or, I might start my biography. Either way, I'll need you there to transcribe my notes."

Her shoulders sagging, Marie quietly followed JT out the office. As she passed the secretary, she glanced over, exchanging a sympathetic look with the woman sitting at her desk. As they waited for the elevator to take them down, Marie wondered which one really had the worse boss.

She sighed again as, oblivious to her thoughts, JT stepped into the elevator, a contented smile on his face.

Chapter 2

December 23ʳᵈ

Alpine Manor was located about three hours' drive from the city; sitting in a remote, secluded location that you would be unlikely to stumble across by accident. The original structure had been built over one hundred and fifty years earlier by an eccentric oil baron, a hundred room mansion that brought new meaning to the word opulent. It was rumoured that, because of the size of the manor, the original family had lived and died there without having set foot in every room.

That, however, did not stop subsequent generations from adding to the structure and renovating parts of it; continually working in an obsessive quest to keep Alpine Manor the most luxurious residence anywhere, even putting the most expensive, classiest hotels to shame.

This cycle continued for over one hundred years until, after a series of poor investments, the last of the original family line was forced to sell the manor for far less than its true worth in order to satisfy creditors and avoid prison. Unfortunately, this man, overcome with humiliation, could not live with his failure and, so another rumour goes, spent his last day wandering through the vast building, making sure he visited each and every room, before, finally, committing suicide in one of the more remote rooms resulting in his body lying undiscovered for three days.

Now owned by a multi-national consortium, Alpine Manor was redeveloped and extended even more. It now served as a country retreat where, during the summer months, you could indulge in outdoor activities such as tennis and horse-riding; as well as benefiting from the indoor facilities it offered which included a heated swimming pool, gymnasium, spa, ballroom/dining room, cinema and a games room for younger guests.

"But, hopefully, there won't be too many younger guests," JT said, finishing his lecture.

"It sounds… creepy," Marie murmured, giving an involuntary shiver.

"Creepy?" JT retorted, puzzled. "I would say they are irritating, not creepy."

"What? Who?" Marie asked.

"The younger guests," JT answered, "Children."

"No, um, I meant, the last of the original family committing suicide," Marie responded.

"Oh, that," JT said, shrugging. "It's probably just a story concocted up by some PR-type to give the place a little colour. You know, make it more interesting."

Marie thought there were other ways this could have been achieved without resorting to that kind of tale but kept this opinion to her-self. If JT had a particular opinion about something, there was little point in arguing. Once his mind was made up, he was like the proverbial immovable object that had yet to encounter an irresistible force.

Glancing out the window, she watched the countryside pass by, unending stretches of open land and tree-covered hills as they neared the end of their journey. Having left the main highway a few miles back, the road they were now on was down to two lanes and still covered in a thin layer of snow, not that this made JT drive any slower.

"We should be there in about ten minutes," he announced, looking at his watch.

"Good," Marie answered, looking up at the dark grey clouds overhead. "I think it's going to start snowing again soon."

"Nonsense," JT retorted. "I checked before we left. The forecast is for a frosty but snow-free Christmas."

"Forecasters sometimes get it wrong," Marie offered.

"They are trained meteorologists," JT replied. "They know more about the weather than you."

Not 'us', Marie thought to herself. "Yes, boss," she agreed quietly.

"Besides," JT continued, "if they make the occasional mistake, well, they are only Human, right? Nobody's perfect, after all." *Was this a rare moment of modesty?* Marie wondered.

"That's how I keep catching the bad guys," JT finished smugly, dispelling Marie's thought as if a pin had been stuck in a balloon.

"Yes, boss," she repeated, still looking out the window so JT could not see her rolling her eyes.

They lapsed into silence which suited Marie. If JT was not talking to her, it meant he was not issuing orders, belittling her or boasting about his mental prowess. Maybe, she thought fancifully, the festive season would bestow a Christmas miracle and turn JT into a nice person. Mind you, she doubted there were enough Ghosts of Christmas to achieve that feat. Perhaps she would meet a rich, eligible bachelor at Alpine Manor who would sweep her off her feet and take her away from the life of drudgery she felt she was currently living. Yes, her own Prince Charming who would find her beneath the mistletoe.

"What are you smiling about?" JT asked, glancing across to Marie.

"Um, nothing," Marie muttered, the small smile disappearing from her face as quickly as the fantasy disappeared from her mind.

As the sky above them darkened even more, small white flakes started drifting lazily down. Within seconds, the size of the flakes had increased, although their rate of descent remained the same. Effortlessly, the car continued along the road, leaving two trails where the wheels cut through the surface snow. JT flicked a switch and the car's window wipers slid back and forth across the windscreen, dealing with the flakes of white before they had a chance to accumulate. Ahead, caught in the beam from their headlights, a sign stood on one side of the road, large letters announcing, 'Alpine Manor, 2m', and an arrow pointing to a turning in the road opposite it.

"Ah, our journey nears its end," JT announced as he slowed the car before turning onto the new road. This road, narrower than the previous one, cut through a forest with tall fir trees on either side blocking the view of the fields, what little daylight there was struggling to fight its way through the canopy of branches and pine needles.

For a moment, Marie allowed herself to gaze at the trees, the green and white colours seeming to encapsulate perfectly the romantic, child-like feeling of Christmas. In that instant, it was easy to forget all the nastiness in the world, all the suffering, the greed and selfishness, and instead, feel the warmth of magic and wonder, happiness and kindness; and believe that maybe miracles do happen.

"I bet the tourists lap up this 'winter wonderland' look," JT scoffed. "Probably one of the reasons they are so happy to part with their hard-earned cash to stay at this place."

"Don't you like it?" Marie asked hesitantly, "I mean, don't you think it looks kind of, um…"

"Don't say 'magical'," JT interrupted. "You think it's a coincidence that there are so many fir trees here?" He snorted derisively and then continued, "They were planted here, oh, about seventy or eighty years ago. With the amount of snow that usually falls here, someone figured it would be a good idea to give the place a more 'Christmassy' look. Trust me, the only magical thing about this is how it increased their profits!"

The soft, fuzzy feeling that Marie had been feeling just a moment before fizzled away. JT's blunt words like a fire hose dousing the tiny embers of joy.

"Oh, right," she murmured, before lapsing into silence, her gaze returning to the passing trees.

After a few minutes of silence, JT said, "Well, here we are."

Marie looked but could not see anything other than trees until the car turned again onto another road, asphalt giving way to gravel, the tyres crunching their way through the snow. The trees thinned and disappeared behind them as the gravel track stretched in front of them revealing more fields, and straight ahead, the looming structure of Alpine Manor.

In front of the hotel, a large fir tree stretched upwards. The road formed a large circle around the tree, allowing vehicles to drop people off at the entrance and carry on round the circle until they were heading back out the way they had come in. For those arriving in their own vehicles, there was a valet service provided so guests could get out at the entrance and their cars were driven and parked in the large car park located about one hundred metres behind the main building.

JT stopped the car outside the main entrance and climbed out the car, Marie following his lead. A young, uniformed man approached JT.

"Good afternoon, sir," he said with a broad smile. "Welcome to the Alpine Manor. Will you be staying with us?"

"Yes," JT said holding up his car keys. "You'll find the luggage in the back. Don't scratch her, mind?"

"Of course, sir," the parking attendant said, the smile held firmly in place. Taking the keys, he handed JT a small, plastic disc in return. "Anytime you require your car brought round, please just pass this to the front desk and it will all be taken care of." He held his hand out expectantly.

"Oh, right," JT muttered absently. "Take care of that, would you, Marie?"

With that, he mounted the steps that led to the hotel's main entrance, a large revolving door constantly turning at a steady space, big enough to allow someone to step through whilst pulling two suitcases behind them.

About ten feet along from this was another door, this one comprised of two glass halves which slid apart as soon as anyone approached it. As JT stepped into the revolving door, Marie appeared at his side, slightly out of breath after dashing up the steps to catch up with him. They stepped out the other side into a very large foyer, Marie stopping in her tracks as she gazed around her. Down each side of the foyer, there were several small, round tables, with four small armchairs surrounding each one. At some of the tables, people sat, some drinking tea or coffee and talking, others sat alone reading newspapers. A door along one wall had a sign above it reading 'Bar' and people were going in and out, some carrying their beverages to one of the small tables in the foyer rather than stay in the Bar area. It's probably quieter out here, Marie thought to herself.

On the opposite wall, there was a large bookcase filled with reading material that the guests could avail themselves of, both fiction and non-fiction, as well as a revolving stand filled with magazines and newspapers. Several large paintings hung on the walls, depicting picturesque scenes of quaint coastal villages, tranquil meadows and other similar images. In between the paintings, stylish lights, designed to resemble Victorian gas lamps, cast a gentle orange glow. In the centre of the large foyer stood an equally large Christmas tree, tinsel and twinkling lights providing a multitude of colours, the base of the tree littered with what Marie presumed were fake presents. High overhead, a large, crystal chandelier hung from the ceiling, the lights reflecting off the numerous crystal prisms, refracting and bathing the foyer in additional light.

Beneath them, the thick carpet seemed to envelop their feet, making Marie feel like she was standing on a bed of marshmallows.

"Well, are you just going to stand there with your mouth hanging open?"

Startled, Marie turned to JT who was staring at her impatiently, his arms folded across his chest. He may have been tapping his foot but Marie doubted she would either see or hear it through the thick carpet.

"Um, sorry," she mumbled, following JT who resumed his journey to the front desk. "It's just… just…"

"I know, right?" JT answered, "I have to admit, even I'm impressed."

"But…" Marie began and then stopped, uncertain whether or not to ask. She recalled the conversation in the car, JT's dismissive remarks regarding the hotel's owner's cynical attempts to cash-in on the 'festive' image. Finally, she took a breath and blurted out, "But how can you afford to stay here?"

"Ah, you probably detected my disdain for this place from our earlier conversation," he answered. "Well done, I'll make a detective of you yet." Marie could not tell if JT was being serious or sarcastic so stayed quiet. "You're right, of course," he added. "The rates for the rooms here are, well, let's say, not designed for your average person, even a world-renowned private investigator such as myself. However, one of the benefits of being a world-renowned private investigator is you get employed by people who can afford the rates here. And sometimes, these clients are so grateful that, as well as paying for my services, they provide me with additional compensation."

"You mean, this is a freebie?" Marie almost cried out in surprise.

"Quiet!" JT hissed. "Are you trying to draw attention to yourself? People will think you don't belong here."

"I don't!" Marie protested softly. "This place will be full of rich, important people. I'll stand out like a sore thumb."

"Nonsense!" JT retorted. "Just follow my lead and you'll be fine. Also, perhaps it would be better if you say as little as possible."

Leaving Marie feeling embarrassed and insecure, JT stepped up to the desk. Sitting behind it, a young woman, possibly in her early twenties, sat typing at a computer. She wore a name badge which said 'Emma' and as she turned to greet JT, her long black hair swung across her blazer, obscuring the badge. She had long, perfectly manicured nails, coloured in a bright crimson nail polish which complemented her lip stick. As her lips parted in a smile, perfectly white teeth could be seen.

"Good afternoon and welcome to Alpine Manor," she said in a sing-song voice. "How can I help you?"

Standing just behind JT, Marie took all this in and despaired. The receptionist looked like she had stepped from the pages of a fashion magazine; hair, make-up, teeth all perfect. Marie, who was probably about the same age as her, felt like a complete mess, her drab clothes and lack of make-up probably making her look about twice as old as she was.

"Yes," JT said. "I have a reservation. The name's Thomas."

Emma turned back to her computer, her fingers gliding across the keyboard, clicking and clacking at high speed leaving Marie bewildered, wondering how she could do so with such long nails. "Yes, here we are," Emma announced, turning back to JT. "Is it yourself and your wife, sir?"

"My wife?" JT asked, confused.

"Yes," Emma said, looking over JT's shoulder. "Oh, sorry, your daughter?"

Glancing back at Marie, JT stifled a grin. "Wife? Definitely not! And, also, not my daughter."

"How old do you think I am?" he asked in what Marie thought could have been a flirting tone. "Don't let the colour of my hair fool you, I'm still in my prime." Marie started feeling queasy. "No, this is my assistant, Miss Watson. I arranged for her to use the adjoining room."

"Of course, Mr Thomas," Emma said, her smile dazzling Marie, leaving spots dancing in front of her eyes when she turned away. She reached across the desk, an electronic card between her shiny red fingernails. "You are in Suite 307, on the third floor. There is an elevator just there or you can take the stairs. We will have your bags brought up. I hope you enjoy your stay with us. And, please let me know if you require anything."

"Thank you," JT answered, taking the card and letting his fingers linger for a few seconds on Emma's hand, "I will."

On one side of the desk, he could see the bottom of the staircase, the wide, carpeted stairs disappearing as it spiralled upwards; on the other side, the elevator. He headed for the elevator with Marie close behind.

"I think she likes me," JT remarked.

"Perhaps you remind her of her father," Marie said innocently.

"Jealousy does not suit you," he remarked. "Mind you, neither does that outfit you're wearing...."

A ping announced the arrival of the elevator and JT stepped forward. He turned to see Marie had not moved.

"Come on!" he said abruptly. "We don't have all day."

"Um, I think I will stay down here a while," Marie said. "Maybe just... soak in the atmosphere for a bit longer. If that's all right?"

"Yes, fine, whatever," JT answered, already losing interest in the conversation. "Remember, Suite 307."

The elevator doors closed leaving Marie feeling lonely and worthless. She chastised herself for thinking this might actually have been a good thing. She knew JT well enough to know better. Why did she let herself be bullied into accompanying him? Wiping at her eyes, determined not to cry and embarrass herself further, she turned and walked over to the rack of magazines and newspapers. Finding a newspaper she regularly read, she took it and sat down at an empty table.

"Would you like something to drink?"

The voice startled her and she turned to see a waiter standing beside her table, an empty tray in his hand after delivering drinks to a nearby table.

"Oh, um, could I maybe have a coffee, please?" she asked.

"Certainly," the waiter replied.

"How much will that be?" Marie hurriedly asked as he turned to go. "I mean, um, I just want to be sure I have enough cash on me just now."

"Oh, not to worry, madam," the waiter answered with a smile. "Everything can be charged to your room, if you prefer."

"Really?" Marie asked. "In that case, please bring me a cup of the most expensive coffee you have, my good man."

She smiled to herself as the waiter departed. She would stay here for a while, have a cup of coffee, or two, and read the newspaper. Some time away from JT could only be a good thing.

With her jacket draped over the back of the chair opposite, Marie sat, finally starting to feel a bit more relaxed, the pleasant aroma from the coffee drifting past her as she sat with the newspaper opened on her lap. It had been nearly thirty minutes since she sat down, now steadily sipping her way through her second cup of coffee and turning the pages of the paper, glancing at headlines, reading fully those stories which caught her interest.

When she had ordered her second coffee, the waiter, whose name she learned was Toby, sat the cup in front of her, flashing her a brilliant smile. As Marie thanked him, he started chatting away. Marie knew that he probably treated all his customers the same way, men and women, being friendly and welcoming; it was a vital trait in the hospitality business, after all. Still, for all that after being put down again, by JT, Marie could not help but feel pleased by the attention Toby showed her. So what if she were being silly? There was no harm in allowing herself to enjoy their conversation and imagine he was flirting with her. After a few minutes of idle chit-chat, Toby left her alone, giving her another dazzling smile. That was when Marie realised who he reminded her of; with his short, dark hair and brilliant smile, he was not dissimilar to Tom Cruise. Thankfully, Marie thought as he walked away, he's a bit taller.

Now, with her glasses perched low on her nose, she studied the crossword puzzle in the newspaper. After some intensive digging, she had managed to locate a Biro deep within the bowels of her handbag. She had become so used to using her electronic organiser for so much; she rarely had to use a pen anymore. Luckily, the one she found still worked.

She took another drink from her cup and noticed she had almost finished it. Then, as if in answer to some unspoken message, Toby magically appeared beside her table.

"Another?" he asked, a twinkle in his eye.

"Oh, why not?" Marie answered with a smile. "I am actually enjoying it here."

"Yes, a lot of our guests like to relax here," Toby informed her. "I think they like to sit and watch the other guests coming and going. That can be quite entertaining," he said conspiratorially, leaning closer to Marie and giving her a friendly nudge. "You just sit there, soak up the ambience and I will be right back."

Alone again, Marie left the newspaper lying on her lap but now found herself distracted by the passing guests. From where she sat, in one direction she could see the entrance and, beyond that, the snow now falling quite heavily, and the other way she had a clear view of the reception desk, the far-too-perfect looking Emma busily working away, her far-too-perfect smile and far-too-perfect teeth greeting everyone who approached her.

Marie had never considered herself a 'people watcher' but, she had to admit, it was strangely compelling. As she watched people, young and old, couples and families, she found herself wondering what their stories were. Where did they work? What were their hopes and dreams? Were they happy? Sad? And, did any of them look at her with similar thoughts? If so, what conclusions would they reach? Marie wondered.

"Here we go," Toby said, startling her out of her reverie. "Enjoying the view?" he asked good-naturedly.

"Oh, um, I'm sorry," Marie stammered, blushing.

"Hey, no problem," Toby assured her. "I do it myself."

"It feels a bit… voyeuristic," Marie admitted, "but kind of compelling."

"Yep," Toby agreed, sitting down beside her. "It beats reality television, let me tell you." He chuckled to himself.

"I suppose you'll see all sorts passing through," Marie suggested.

"True enough," Toby replied. "Also, there are quite a few regulars."

"Really?" Marie asked.

"Oh, yes," Toby said. "There are some people who just can't seem to get enough of this place. Take him, for instance." Toby pointed to man, impeccably dressed, who had just stepped into the foyer, shaking snow from his coat. He removed his hat to reveal a shock of white hair. As he ran a hand through his hair, he glanced around, eyes narrowed, a frown creasing his forehead, almost scowling. "That," Toby whispered to Marie, "is Sir Henry Fitzroy."

"He looks so… serious," Marie said.

"Yes, he always does," Toby replied. "Not sure what his story is but he has been staying here since before my time. All I know is, he is former military something-or-other, inherited the family fortune, worth a packet, he is." They looked away quickly as Sir Henry, unaware of their conversation, strode past them and made his way to the reception desk. "Her over there," Toby resumed once Sir Henry had passed, pointing now to an elderly lady sitting at another table, sipping from a tall glass of green liquid. "That old sweetheart is Mrs Beryl Lambert, another long-time guest here. She lost her husband about forty years ago although, from what I hear, he left the old dear quite well off, thanks to some very shrewd investments."

Marie thought it was stating the obvious that the guests here would all be 'well off' to say the least but she did not want to mention this in case it got Toby enquiring about her status. Of course, she had nothing to hide, or be ashamed of, but still…

"Anyway, I better get back," Toby said, standing suddenly. "Don't want my boss giving me grief. Well, no more than normal. See you later."

As he walked away, Marie wondered about Toby's story. Was he and everyone else who worked here envious of the wealth of the guests who stayed here? Did they feel, as she did, out of their depth in this kind of group? It was their job to cater to their guests' needs but did any of the guests look down on them, treat them with contempt, because of their roles?

There was a shriek of excitement drawing Marie's attention back to the revolving door where a family had just entered, a middle-aged couple with two young children, a boy and a girl, and it was the girl who had squealed with delight on seeing the Christmas tree. She ran up to it, the dark colour of the carpet hiding the damp footprints she probably left in her wake, and stood looking up to the star atop the tree, almost touching the chandelier.

"Santa!" she cried happily, "Santa!"

The girl's mother hurried forward and took her daughter's hand, coaxing her away from the tree. Meanwhile, the boy, perhaps a couple of years older, stood back, sulking, arms folded across his chest. The father, who was stamping loose snow off his shoes held a phone to his ear. Speaking loudly, Marie heard him say, "I don't care… No, you listen, the deal was for… If you even think of backing out, I will drag you through the courts…. What? I… Look, the reception out here is lousy… I said, the reception is lousy…"

He had raised his voice to the point where he was almost shouting. "Just sign the damned document before the 31st!" he said loudly, ending the call and shoving the phone in his pocket. "God damn back waters!" he grumbled loudly as he passed Marie and reached his wife and daughter. Marie could see the woman's lips move as she started to speak but her husband cut her off. "I told you I was too busy to take this vacation. The deal is in danger of falling apart and I'm not there to hold it together. And my god-damn phone doesn't work here!"

He continued grumbling as the four of them reached the reception desk. Marie noted that Emma's smile did not falter once even though she could tell from the body language that the man was still complaining. Plastic surgery, Marie decided. Either that or she is a robot. Marie sat for another half hour gazing at the guests that wandered past. A couple of times she heard Emma greet a guest with, 'Welcome back', so Toby was right; there were quite a few regulars.

Finally, Marie steeled herself, retrieved her jacket and made for the elevator hoping there was enough caffeine now flowing through her veins to allow her to deal with more caustic barbs from JT.

As the elevators slid open, Marie stepped forward and entered, finding herself standing between two young men dressed casually, carrying sports bags, hair damp, the smell of shampoo and aftershave assaulting her nostrils.

"Which floor?" one of the men asked.

"Um, three?" Marie answered nervously.

"You don't sound too sure," the man joked as he pressed the button.

"Um, yes, I'm sure," Marie said.

As the elevator ascended, the men returned to their conversation. Marie heard words like 'trust fund' and 'Forbes rich list' and 'Porsche' and wondered again what she was doing in a place like this. A ding announced the elevator's arrival on the third floor, the doors sliding open.

"After you," one of the men said, letting Marie pass.

"Oh, is this your floor, too?" she asked.

"Well, any higher and we'll be in the rafters," he answered with a smile.

"Oh," was all Marie could manage as she stepped out the elevator feeling foolish.

The two men turned and headed along the corridor, the same, plush carpeting as in the foyer absorbing the sound of their footsteps and voices as they disappeared out of sight. Marie glanced at the opposite wall and was thankful to see signs indicating the direction of Suites 301 to 320. Going in the opposite direction from the two men, she walked along the corridor glancing at door numbers as she went. Like the foyer, the corridors were illuminated by old-fashioned looking lights. She turned a corner, followed the corridor further and stopped at the door numbered 307. Taking a deep breath, she knocked timidly on the door and almost screamed as it was immediately pulled open.

"Ah, there you are," JT said. "I wondered if you had maybe gotten lost, or something."

"No, um, I, erm, just had a coffee," Marie answered.

"Well, don't just stand there, come in," he said, stepping aside to let her enter.

The room Marie stepped into was large, extravagantly furnished with a couple of small sofas, a glass coffee table a bureau against the wall, a wall-mounted television with a rug on the floor behind the coffee table. Further back, the rest of the room sat slightly raised, a table and chairs sitting next to a mahogany cabinet. Then, there was a pair of glass sliding doors which looked like they led onto a small balcony but as the daylight had now totally disappeared, Marie could not be certain. All she saw was the room reflected in the glass although she could make out the snow falling, the large flakes falling fast past the window.

Off to one side, a door led into a bedroom. Marie could just see one corner of the bed and noticed that one of JT's suitcases sat on it. His other case and Marie's luggage was sitting in a pile in the middle of the main room.

"Um, where…?" she asked nervously, her eyes darting to the bedroom door.

Following her gaze, JT quickly said, "No, don't worry. Like I said, you get the adjoining room."

"Adjoining room?" Marie asked.

"Yeah," JT said, nodding to the other side of the room where there was another door. "These Suites have adjoining rooms to accommodate extra guests. That's where you'll be sleeping."

"Right," Marie said, barely concealing the relief she felt, "of course."

"Well, don't just stand there," JT said, waving towards the room. "Get unpacked, freshen up and we'll go down to the bar for a drink before dinner."

"Um, okay, right," Marie replied picking up her suitcases and dragging them into her room.

Kicking the door closed behind her, she studied her accommodation. While not nearly as elegant as the main suite, Marie was still happy with what she saw; a large, comfy bed, two small armchairs with a table between them, a cabinet at either side of the bed, and a dresser where a small television sat. There was a wardrobe for her clothes and another door which led to the bathroom.

Okay, she thought to herself, let's freshen up and find out what delights JT has planned for me.

Chapter 3

JT and Marie entered the bar, a large room with a tall window at one end showing a view of the front of the building. Now, the view consisted of a constant flurry of large snowflakes falling, weaving about, some of them hitting the window leaving small trails as they slowly melted. "Quite the blizzard out there," JT remarked casually.

"Um, yes," Marie agreed.

There were several tables and booths all around, stools along the front of the bar, all the furniture various shades of mahogany, muted lighting giving the place an almost cosy feel. In one corner, there was a Christmas tree, a smaller version of the one in the foyer, the lights around it twinkling and blinking at random intervals. On the wall to one side of the bar was mounted a large television, currently showing a satellite news channel, the volume muted but subtitles allowing anyone watching to know what was being said. From speakers somewhere presumably mounted on the walls, although Marie could not see them, music could be heard, the volume loud enough to make it discernible but not enough to be a nuisance.

A few of the tables were occupied, people talking and laughing, everyone seemingly having a good time. One of the bar staff was wandering between tables, gathering up empty glasses, wiping and polishing the tables as she went.

JT stopped at the bar, Marie just behind him, and the barman approached.

"Well, hello, again," Toby said with his dazzling smile. "I was hoping I'd see you again. Didn't think it'd be so soon."

JT, surprised, was about to respond when he realised Toby was looking past him to Marie.

"Um, hi, er, I mean, hello," Marie stammered feeling herself blush.

"Hi," Toby said to JT, extending his hand. "I'm Toby. I had the good fortune to meet your daughter earlier."

"Oh, um, er," Marie began, flustered.

"I'm her boss," JT said coldly, ignoring the outstretched hand. "Jack Thomas. Perhaps you've heard of me." This was offered as a statement rather than a question.

"Jack Thomas?" Toby said, scrunching his face in concentration. "Jack Thomas.... Jack Thomas... Nope, sorry, doesn't ring any bells."

"He's a private investigator," Marie offered quickly.

"Oh, really?" Toby asked, "What kind of things do you investigate?"

"I'm sorry," JT answered with a sneer, "that's private."

"Good one," Toby said laughing. "So, what will it be?"

"I'll have a vodka," JT replied, "A double."

"And the usual for you?" Toby asked Marie, flashing her a smile.

"Um, yes, ah, yes, please," Marie muttered.

With that, JT turned and found a booth as far from the bar as he could, dropping into the seat, Marie hurrying to catch up.

"The damned cheek!" JT fumed before Marie had even sat. "As if I'm old enough to be your father!"

"Well, actually," Marie started to say.

"And not a word from you!" JT interrupted. "You may find it amusing. I certainly do not."

"I was only going to say...."

"Nothing is what you are going to say," JT said pointedly.

They sat in silence until their drinks arrived. Marie was relieved to see it was the woman who brought them over, Toby giving her a small wave and smile from behind the bar when she glanced in that direction. Not that she would not have been happy to see Toby again but the last thing she wanted was JT to be in a foul mood since she was going to be stuck with him for the next twelve days. Looking outside, the snow still falling heavily, she feared she really would be stuck, unable to leave even if she wanted to.

Raising his glass to his mouth, JT downed half his drink and sat back with a contented sigh.

"That hits the spot," he said. "Just what the doctor ordered."

Only if the doctor was trying to sell you a new liver, Marie thought, sipping at her coffee.

"So," JT said, "here is what I had in mind." Marie steeled herself. "I figure if that Christie woman can sell a few books about a fictional detective, my cases would be very marketable. Obviously, we would need to change a few names, we don't want to be sued, after all, but the framework is already there."

"Um, okay," Marie said uncertainly.

"So, what I want you to do is take one of my cases, I thought maybe the Fulham kidnap case or the Starlight jewel heist, and… Dramatize it," JT explained.

"Um, okay," Marie repeated.

"Now," JT continued, "I should point out, the Alpine Manor prides itself on the fact that you can't get a phone signal out here and they don't allow their guests Wi-Fi access. They actively dissuade guests from using any kind of electronic devices, in fact. They want their guests to be social, not glued to a tiny screen obsessing over social media, tweeting or whatever it is that seems to obsess everyone nowadays."

"You mean…?" Marie asked.

"Pen and paper," JT declared with a smile.

"But…"

"Now, don't worry," JT said reassuringly. "I brought a lot of my case files so you should have all the material you will need."

"But…"

"So, I thought you could start after dinner," JT continued. "Read over the cases, have a think about how best to, ah, fictionalise it. What do you think?"

"Um, okay, I guess?" Marie murmured.

"I knew you would think it was a good idea," JT said, sitting back happily, totally oblivious to the resigned look on Marie's face.

"Um, what are you wearing?" JT suddenly asked.

Caught off guard, Marie opened and closed her mouth without saying a word. Glancing down, she absently fingered her cardigan. "Um, this?" she asked. "It's, um, my, er, favourite cardigan."

"Yours or your grandmother's?" JT retorted, "I suppose, if you dress like that, it'll stop people asking if you're my daughter. No, they'll think you're my mother."

Marie felt her face redden as JT emitted a tiny laugh, unaware, or unconcerned, of the discomfort she was feeling.

"So, where were we?" he asked, almost to himself. "Ah, yes," he continued before Marie had a chance to speak. "I was thinking, after dinner you could start reading through some of the case files just to get a feel for things then, tomorrow, you can start making notes on which case or cases you feel are most suitable and start writing."

"But tomorrow's Christmas Eve!" Marie protested.

"And can you think of a better place to spend it?" JT asked, waving his arm around. "Isn't this place magnificent? Now, no need to thank me. You deserve this just as much as me. Well, obviously not as much as me, after all, I do all the real work, but, still, I don't mind sharing. It's not every boss who would be so generous to his employees, you know."

"No, boss," Marie muttered. "I mean, yes, boss. Um, thank you?"

"You are welcome," JT said as he motioned for another drink.

Ten minutes later, JT and Marie walked through to the ballroom/dining room, JT carrying his third drink, his cheeks starting to glow a pinkish red though his gait was steady.

They were greeted as they entered and, after giving their room number, were directed to a table.

All the tables were round, accommodating up to eight people, covered in white, gold-trimmed cloth, cutlery and glasses gleaming under the lights. Each table had a centrepiece which consisted of a tiny artificial Christmas tree surrounded by miniature parcels. Finally, there were four small candles, already lit, the tiny flames flickering and dancing about any time somebody walked past. As Marie glanced around, she was amazed at the size of the room. Even in a mansion as this building had originally been, she figured this had to have been several rooms knocked into one. Several pillars, no doubt needed for support, were spaced around the room, all decorated with tinsel and twinkling lights. Above, four chandeliers provided illumination for the vast room and, at the far end, there was a small dance-floor in front of a stage, currently empty, with a Christmas tree at either side.

JT dropped into a seat with a contented sigh, the vodka sloshing in his glass. Marie sat down carefully, staring at all the cutlery before her, thinking there was more there than she had in her own kitchen. Trying not to panic, she took a breath and reminded herself to just work from the outside in. At least there weren't chopsticks, she thought with a sigh.

People were still drifting in but already more than half the tables were fully occupied. At their table, two people were already sitting there, a man and a woman engrossed in conversation. They looked across at JT and Marie as they sat, smiling and saying hello, introducing themselves as Peter and Lucy Tenor. They looked to be in their late forties, Peter's receding hairline fast approaching the bald spot in the centre of his head. This was counter-balanced by a thick, bushy moustache and beard which, like the hair on his head, was dark coloured but flecked with grey. Lucy had long, wavy hair, chestnut coloured. Marie noticed the roots were starting to show then immediately chided her-self for thinking it. There were slight wrinkles around Lucy's eyes, although make-up managed to hide most of them. As she reached across to shake Marie's hand, Marie noticed a diamond bracelet, sparkling, hanging on Lucy's wrist, as well as the rings on her fingers.

Peter, slightly overweight, his waistcoat straining slightly to contain his girth, also shook hands; a Rolex watch revealed itself as his shirt sleeve rolled back slightly as he extended his arm.

Again, Marie could not help but wonder what she was doing there. She definitely did not belong in the same world as these people with their jewels, fancy clothes and wealth. As she wondered this, Peter was explaining about his job in the City, Lucy's role as doting wife and mother (the two children, Peter Jnr. and Lucille spending Christmas in Aspen with the rest of their private school classes), and how he felt the country club he was a member of was letting its standards drop, admitting any old riff-raff nowadays.

Eventually, he seemed to run out of steam and said, "But enough about us, tell us about your-selves."

"Actually, I'm from what you might call 'new money'," JT said causing Marie to almost choke as she sipped at her coffee.

"Really?" Peter asked. "Well, I won't judge!" He laughed a little at this joke, Lucy smiled politely.

"Oh, yes," JT continued, ignoring the urgent look from Marie. "Yes, my family was lucky enough to get in on the ground floor of the, uh, dot-com boom. Yes, it was amazing what a few fortuitous investments reaped. Then, they dabbled in property, before the Crash, of course," JT rambled on, "Definitely blessed with the Midas touch when it came to property."

"And now?" Lucy asked. "What do you do?"

"Heh," JT snorted. "I live off the fruits of my family's good fortune, travel, you know, the usual. But, um, as a sort of hobby, I actually dabble in detective work. Just to relieve the tedium, you understand."

"Really?" Lucy asked. "How marvellous!"

"What kind of detective work?" Peter asked. "Not investment fraud, I hope!" He laughed loudly.

"Oh, just this and that," JT answered vaguely. "Most recently, I actually investigated a suicide which turned out to be murder."

"Gosh!" Lucy said. "How terribly exciting. And does your daughter help in your investigations?"

Clearing his throat and fighting to keep the smile on his face, JT replied, "Marie is, er, my assistant, not my daughter."

"Oh, I do apologise," Lucy said.

"Assistant, eh?" Peter said, giving JT a knowing wink. "Heh, we should all be so lucky!" Lucy smiled tightly at her husband's joke although Marie could not help but wonder if there was some underlying tension.

"Really," JT said, both men ignoring the women with them, "if I was going to be like that, I wouldn't pick someone who dresses like my mother!"

The loud guffaws drew looks from nearby tables although everyone was too polite to let their gaze linger more than the merest fraction of a second. Marie felt her face flush and fought the urge to stand up and leave. That would only draw more attention, she decided. No she thought, best to sit quietly and wait until they tired of her as a conversation piece and moved onto something, or someone, else. At that moment, another four people joined the table, another middle-aged couple and two younger people, late teens or early twenties, Marie guessed. They seemed to be together and Marie wondered if they were a family.

Peter immediately introduced himself and his wife, then JT and Marie. The new arrivals were Philip and Theresa Sonnerson, their daughter Sophia and her fiancé, Rupert. Philip was slim, clean shaven, hair short, almost military-like, and had a tiny scar just below his left eye, a wound from his army days, he explained. His wife, Sophia, was also slim, with long, brown hair, her long finger nails painted a light purple colour, matching her lipstick. They were both tanned although Marie could not tell if it was real or the result of time spent under a tanning lamp. Sophia, on the other hand, was unremarkable, a plain-looking young lady with curly, brown hair, a freckled face and a slight gap between her front teeth. She wore no make-up and her clothes were simple. It's hard to imagine they are all related, Marie thought to herself. Rupert, in fact, seemed more like Philip and Theresa, dressed smartly, a tidy haircut, similar to Philip's, well groomed.

Marie noticed that Sophia barely spoke as the introductions were made, other than a mumbled 'hello' which she uttered while staring at the table. For whatever reason, she clearly did not want to be there and was making little effort to conceal the fact. Marie sympathised with her. Perhaps their mutual discomfort would offer them a connection. Anything would be better than having to listen to JT ramble on about his family's 'new money' all night.

"So," Marie began, looking across to Sophia, "are you looking forward to spending Christmas here?"

"I guess," Sophia mumbled, barely looking up.

"Yes," Theresa added. "It's really exciting. Sophia and Rupert tying the knot on New Year's Eve! Isn't that fabulous?"

"Congratulations," Marie said although Sophia still barely glanced up.

"Yes," Rupert joined in, taking Sophia's hand. "It will be marvellous, won't it, darling?"

"Uh-huh," Sophia mumbled, pulling her hand away.

"How did you meet?" Lucy asked, joining in the conversation.

"Rupert is an old friend of the family," Philip answered. "Good, reliable military chap, like myself. Sophia is a very lucky girl."

Marie did not have to be a detective to see that Sophia looked far from lucky at that particular moment.

"Jolly good show!" Peter cried. "Nothing beats a good wedding, eh?"

"Ours was certainly one to remember," Lucy said, smiling at the memory.

"Been married long, have you?" Philip asked.

"No, no," Peter answered. "I suppose you could say we were late to that particular party, eh?"

"Peter and I met about six years ago, wasn't it?" Lucy said, "Married the following year. A bit of a whirlwind!"

"Well, I'm sure Lucy will forgive me saying this, but neither of us was getting any younger," Peter said with a small chuckle. "No sense dilly-dallying and risking letting a good thing slip away." He gave Lucy's hand an affectionate squeeze.

"This man saved me from the life of a spinster," Lucy said, leaning across and kissing Peter's cheek.

"And all I had to do was give up the care-free life of an eligible bachelor!" Peter joked.

"But, enough about us," Lucy said, turning to Marie. "What about you, dear? Any nice young men lurking in the background?"

"If there are, they must be lurking too far back because I can't find them," Marie answered, forcing a smile.

"Never give up," Lucy said. "It took me a while, but I found my true love."

"Um, yes, sure," Marie said.

"Maybe what you need is for this slave-driver to stop working you so hard and give you some time off," Theresa suggested playfully.

"Oh, well, that would be…" JT started to say.

"And, of course, with your family money, you could treat her to a holiday, somewhere exotic, the Caribbean, maybe?" Peter said winking at JT.

"I'll… certainly think about it," JT said, forcing a smile and desperate to change the subject. "So, ah, Philip, you served in the military?"

As Philip regaled them with tales of his military career, Marie smiled to herself at JT's discomfort a moment earlier. Even if he was as rich as he was pretending, she doubted the old skinflint would consider paying for her to go on holiday. He barely paid her enough to cover her normal living expenses, let alone anything as extravagant as a holiday! Maybe Lucy was right and there was some nice, young man out there just waiting to find her. Perhaps Toby… She immediately chided herself for entertaining such foolish fantasies. The idea that someone who worked in a place like this, meeting the sort of people who stayed here, would be interested in someone like her, beyond ridiculous, Marie thought sadly.

Still, sometimes magical things happened at Christmas…

Chapter 4

While JT was being more than slightly creative with his financial history, at a nearby table another group of people was making introductions as the last two seats were occupied by an elderly couple. As the couple took their seats, slowly lowering themselves down, each leaning on a walking stick, another man at the table spoke.

"Good evening," he said in a cheerful manner. "The name's Weathers, Harold Weathers. Call me Harry." He was middle-aged, with an unruly thatch of ginger hair and a bushy moustache which seemed to cover half his face. He wore a tweed jacket, with a cravat. He spoke in a clipped, refined accent. He motioned to the woman sitting next to him. "This is the wife, Pru. And, next to her, that's Tim and Sally." The two children were dressed in a very formal manner, Tim in a suit, shirt and bow tie, Sally in a black dress with flecks of silver through it.

"Evening," the elderly man replied, with a slight wheeze. "I'm Stanley and this is my wife, Gemima."

The couple looked to be in their seventies, Stanley's head covered in a thin wisp of grey hair, his face lined with wrinkles, his eyes large behind the thick lenses of his glasses. Gemima had silvery white hair, tied back in a small ponytail, make-up giving her cheeks a reddish tinge, her lipstick the colour of her hair. Like her husband, she wore glasses, although the lenses were much thinner, which were currently hanging on a chain around her neck. Like the Weathers', they were dressed smartly if somewhat old-fashioned, Stanley wrapped in a thick cardigan while Gemima had a woollen shawl draped across her shoulders.

The remaining two women sitting at the table, feeling compelled to introduce them-selves, greeted the new arrivals and gave their names as Magenta and Scarlet, sisters in their twenties who, Magenta explained, were spending Christmas at Alpine

Manor because their father was away on a business trip and they found that sort of thing such a terrible bore.

Magenta, with short black hair, and minimal make-up, smiled as she told everyone this. Scarlet had blonde hair which hung down to her shoulders and wore lipstick which matched her name. Both ladies wore sleeveless dresses, Magenta displaying a sparkling necklace and bracelet which glinted in the light. Scarlet wore a chain around her neck with a silver pendant hanging from it.

"My, what… unusual names," Gemima said. "I mean, I'm probably just… um, that is, er, they are probably not unusual for the younger generation."

"It's okay," Scarlet said, easing the older woman's obvious embarrassment with a disarming smile.

"We imagine our parents used a paint colour chart for inspiration. Really, we got off lucky."

"Yes," Magenta agreed. "I could have been called Fuscia or, goodness, Beige!"

Everyone at the table laughed at this, except for the two children who both looked bored.

"And is your mother away with your father on his business trip?" Gemima asked.

"Our mother… passed away," Magenta said with a wistful look in her eyes.

"Oh, my dears," Gemima cried. "Oh, I'm so terribly sorry."

"Please, don't worry," Magenta answered. "It was several years ago and she had been quite unwell. Actually, it was after that that Father threw himself back into his work. I suppose he didn't know what else to do, how to deal with it."

"We have tried to be there for him," Scarlet added. "Although he has somewhat shut us out since Mother died."

"Oh, you poor, dear, brave girls," Gemima said, reaching across the table and giving their hands a gentle squeeze.

"Well, what about you two?" Harry asked suddenly, looking to Stanley. "What's your story?"

"Nothing exciting, I assure you," Stanley said, taking a cloth from his pocket and rubbing at his glasses.

"It's exciting to me!" Gemima protested. "We are celebrating our fiftieth wedding anniversary."

"Congratulations!" Pru said. "Isn't that marvellous, Harry?"

39

"I'll say!" Harry nodded. "I don't think this one could put up with me for that long!"

"Ignore him," Pru said. "He's just being silly."

"Well, this calls for a celebration, I reckon," Harry said. "Hang on a sec," he said as he caught the eye of one of the waiting staff.

"Yes, sir?" the young lady asked as she stepped over to their table.

"I know there are complimentary drinks for us," Harry said, motioning to the bottles of wine sitting in coolers, as well as two carafes of water, "but I wonder if you could fetch a bottle of your finest champagne? And charge it to my room."

"Oh, we couldn't let you do that," Gemima protested, blushing.

"Nonsense!" Harry retorted. "This is a special occasion and we should be celebrating! Now, that's settled, so champagne it is."

"Of course, sir," the woman said. "I'll see to that immediately."

"But our anniversary is not until tomorrow," Stanley said as the woman walked away.

"Well," Harry said bullishly, "it's tomorrow in some part of the world and that's good enough for me!"

Hurrying through to the bar, the waitress, Vanessa, passed another employee, dressed in the uniform of the hotel; white shirt, maroon waistcoat with the Hotel's logo in gold, and either black trousers or skirt.

"Hey, Candace," Vanessa said to the woman who was carrying a tray full of drinks.

"Hey, Vanessa," Candace replied. "Looks like it's gonna be a busy night!"

"Yeah," Vanessa agreed. "See you later."

Candace disappeared with her tray. Vanessa stopped at the bar and was greeted by Toby.

"What'll it be?" he asked, flashing her a smile.

"Champagne," Vanessa replied. "The good stuff," she added.

"Champagne?" Toby repeated. "What are we celebrating?" he asked, leaning his elbows on the bar, looking into Vanessa's eyes.

"We are not celebrating anything," she told him bluntly. "It's for one of the tables."

"Oh, Vanessa, why do you tease me so?" Toby asked playfully. "You know, we could get a drink later, just the two of us."

"Your 'charm' won't work on me," Vanessa answered. "I've heard all about you."

"Don't listen to the gossip," Toby said. "You know it's only you I'm interested in."

"I'm sure you say that to all the girls," Vanessa retorted dryly.

"Only the good looking ones," Toby said with a grin.

"Well, consider me flattered," Vanessa said. "Now, the champagne…?"

"Right," Toby said. "Well, you can't blame a guy for trying. Okay, the good stuff is down in the cellar. Keep an eye on the bar for me, will you? I'll be right back."

Vanessa watched Toby hurry off and sighed to herself. She was glad she had been warned about him, she thought, otherwise she might have fallen for his charms.

Marie sat quietly as conversations carried on around her. With the arrival of the second course, she pretended to take a greater interest in the food on her plate, slowly and methodically eating the food before her, taking great care not to put too much food on her fork, leaning close to her plate so if any food fell from her fork it would land back there. Looking at the people around her, she felt as if everyone was wealthier and, somehow, more refined than her and she was determined not to draw attention to herself if she could avoid it.

JT obviously thought the same otherwise he would not have concocted that ridiculous story about his family's wealth. Was ingratiating himself to these people so important to him that he felt he had to lie? Marie could hardly wait for the meal to be over so she could escape back to her room. What if someone started talking to her? What would she say? Would she have to concoct some sort of elaborate lie to help maintain the fiction JT had invented?

As JT shoved a forkful of food into his mouth, he said, between chews, "Come on, Marie, try to look like you're enjoying yourself!"

"Um, sorry, it's just, er," she stammered, then faltered into silence.

"Listen," JT whispered conspiratorially, leaning across so no one else could hear, "if you're worried about my little pretence, it's okay. You are still my PA. If anyone asks for details, just keep it vague. You know, you organise my schedule, and so on. The usual stuff, just on a grander scale."

"But…" Marie began.

"Look, it's a bit of fun," JT whispered, more harshly this time. "I know what these people are like; if you don't have money, they think you're beneath them. Well, not me! I won't have them looking down on me so let them think I'm rich! It's only for a few days, anyway."

"Of course," Marie said quietly, "whatever you say."

Soft music played in the background, just loud enough to be heard over the drone of conversations but not loud enough to be intrusive. Staff milled to and fro, bringing drinks and clearing plates away and, when their services were not required, they waited discreetly off to the side.

Soon, they were wheeling trolleys through carrying a selection of desserts; the best part of any meal, thought Marie.

As a plate was placed in front of her, the Black Forest Gateau drizzled in cream; Marie decided that this would make the whole evening worthwhile.

Stanley sat back in his seat resting his hands on his ample girth. "My, the food is truly exquisite. Thankfully, I no longer need to worry about my figure. Not like you ladies," he said, smiling at Magenta and Scarlet. "Not that you need worry," he quickly added after getting a stern look from his wife. "You are two very attractive young ladies, whereas I, on the other hand, am just a rotund octogenarian." He dabbed at his mouth with a napkin.

"Don't worry," Gemima said, taking his hand in hers. "If you're rotund, it just means there is more of you to love."

Stanley leaned across and caressed Gemima's cheek. "Oh, my dear," he said, "you are too kind to me." Suddenly, he grimaced, slightly. "Unfortunately, I have been a bit unkind to my ageing body, overdoing the rich foods. Excuse me, my dear," he said as he struggled to his feet knocking his napkin onto the floor. Grabbing his walking stick, he made his way slowly to the Bar where the toilets were located.

Magenta stood up next, declaring, "I think I need to powder my nose, before the coffee is served, Scarlet?"

Scarlet stood also and, carrying their handbags, they walked away.

"Will your husband be okay?" Pru asked Gemima as she watched Stanley shuffling along.

"Yes," she answered with a faint smile. "The years have taken their toll, certainly, but there is still life left. It just requires more medication to maintain it, that's all."

"My, you two are simply amazing!" Harry beamed. "I think we should get one last bottle of champagne as a nightcap. What do you say?"

"Well," Gemima began but was cut off by Harry.

"Good, we're agreed," he said. "Ah, there's the filly who helped us out earlier," he murmured catching Vanessa's eye and beckoning her over. "Another bottle of champagne," he said without preamble, "on my tab."

"Of course," Vanessa said, nodding. "I'll see to that right away."

"Now, if you ladies will excuse me," Harry said, standing up. "I need to, er, step out for a moment."

Without another word, Harry hurried out the large room.

"Is anything the matter?" Gemima asked.

"Oh, nothing, I'm sure," Pru answered vaguely. "He has probably just remembered some business call or other that cannot wait."

"Men," Gemima said sympathetically.

"Surely Stanley is not like that!" Pru said.

"No, not now," Gemima admitted. "But, when he was younger, well... I know it was different back then, we didn't all carry mobile phones with us, or have computers and such, but Stanley took his job very seriously, worked very hard." She paused, letting her mind drift back. Then she pulled herself back to the present. "Still, it was all worthwhile. We have had a long, happy life and are making the most of our retirement years."

"Good for you," Pru said kindly. "You deserve it."

Beside her, the two children fidgeted, Tim pulling at his collar, Sally picking at crumbs of food on her dress.

"I'm bored," Tim suddenly announced. "Where's Daddy? Can I go and look for him?"

"Hush, Tim," Pru said sweetly. "Your father will be back in a moment."

"Your children are adorable," Gemima said. "How old are they?"

"Tim is eight, Sally is five," Pru said, beaming with maternal pride. "What about you and Stanley? Any family?"

"No," Gemima answered softly. "No family."

For the next two hours, Marie forced herself to sit and nod politely if anyone spoke to her, responding by saying as little as she felt she could get away with and not be considered rude. JT was engaged in an animated conversation with Peter Tenor, the clear liquid sloshing about in his glass as he waved his arms to and fro. At one point, on noticing this, Marie got so engrossed in following the glass's path and marvelling at the lack of spillage that it was almost hypnotic. She had to force herself to look away. Lucy Tenor, Marie noticed, seemed almost as bored as she herself felt. It seemed as though Peter had forgotten she was there, too busy talking with JT to pay his wife any attention.

Meanwhile, the Sonnerson party all seemed to be having a good time. All, that was, except for Sophia. Mr Sonnerson seemed to be very fond of his soon-to-be son-in-law and Mrs Sonnerson was constantly fussing over him. Sophia, on the other hand, sat quietly, eyes staring down at her lap having barely spoken five words since before the food was served. Also, she had barely touched her food, instead just shoving the food around her plate with her fork. As bad as some of the company might be, Marie had to at least admit the food was excellent.

Then, Sophia stood and excused herself, mumbling something about going to the Ladies' Room. Marie decided on impulse to follow her. When she thought about it later, she could not explain what made her do this. Certainly, she was bored and looking for an excuse to get away from JT for a while but she could have done that at any time, really. She hoped at least part of the motivation was concern for someone who seemed terribly unhappy although curiosity was also a factor, if she was honest with herself.

Leaving the Ballroom, Marie spotted Sophia passing through a door to the toilets. Hurrying past other guests and staff who were milling about, Marie passed through the same door.

Inside, one wall was lined with six stalls, the doors all open. Opposite, the wall was lined with mirrors and, below them, six small porcelain sinks, a mixer tap at each one activated automatically when you held your hands beneath it, a soap dispenser glued to the wall just above it. Three hand driers were on the wall opposite the door as well as a paper towel dispenser. A circular bin stood in the corner, its metallic surface gleaming, whilst another, slightly smaller, bin stood beside it, its lid closed over with a label on it identifying it for the use of feminine hygiene products. Above them, there was a shelf with a selection of lotions and creams for the guests' use. Sophia was standing leaning against one of the sinks, staring into the mirror. Marie stopped in her tracks, expecting the young woman to look up, move, do something to acknowledge someone else had just walked in, but she stood transfixed,.

Suddenly feeling less sure of her-self, Marie debated what to do; if she turned and left, and Sophia recognised her, she might question her back at the table and what would she say? How could she explain? On the other hand, to carry on seemed just as awkward.

Finally, Marie decided the best course was just to leave. With luck, Sophia would not say anything, assuming she was even aware of Marie's presence. Marie reached for the door handle.

"I'm sorry," Sophia mumbled. "Please, don't leave because of me."

Startled, Marie was silent. Then, she said, "Um, sorry, I didn't mean to intrude. It's just, er, um…"

Sophia turned and stared at Marie, her eyes seeming to bore straight through her head.

"Um, I should go," Marie said at last.

"No, please!" Sophia's tone, previously flat, lifeless, suddenly sounded urgent. "Did you follow me in here?"

"Um, well," Marie stammered. This was not going how she imagined. Instead of being seen as some caring person showing concern for another, she now felt like a stalker, some kind of weirdo who follows complete strangers into hotel toilets.

"It's okay if you did," Sophia said.

"It is?" Marie asked, barely hiding the surprise she felt. "I'm… that is, er, I…" She stopped, cleared her throat and began again. "Yes, it's true, I was following you. It's nothing inappropriate, honest, I was just concerned for you."

"You were?" Sophia asked.

"Yes," Marie answered, determined to finish now that she had started. "At the table, you looked so sad, lost. I… I know it's not any of my business, but are you all right?"

Turning back to stare into the mirror, Sophia bit her lower lip, a frown creasing the smooth skin of her forehead.

"Am I all right?" she repeated softly and then laughed derisively. "I suppose the obvious answer is, no, I am far from all right."

"Is there… anything I can do to help?" Marie asked hesitantly.

Taking a deep breath, Sophia turned and faced Marie. Clasping her arms, she blurted, "That's the nicest thing anyone has said to me in absolutely ages! Thank you!" Then, she embraced Marie, hugging her tightly. Stepping back, she smiled at Marie, a small smile that didn't seem to reach her eyes, then hurried past her and out the door leaving Marie standing alone, confused.

When Marie returned to the Ballroom, most of the tables had at least some empty seats. The dance floor was now filled with people dancing to a festive song, some people were wandering between tables striking up conversations with other guests, staff wandered back and forth carrying drinks and collecting empty glasses and one or two others had obviously stepped outside for a short time, probably to smoke, Marie thought disapprovingly, as they returned to the Ballroom with small, tell-tale traces of melting snow still noticeable on them.

Returning to her table, Marie noticed that, currently, only JT and Peter remained, still discussing who knew what. JT was struggling to remain upright in his chair, having to straighten himself up every few seconds before sliding back down again. And still, Marie noted, all without spilling a drop!

"Ah, there you are!" JT cried, his cheeks flushed, his eyes glazed. "I was… I was… was jush telling Peter what a… what a… I wash just pelling Teter…"

"Um, I think you've maybe had enough?" Marie said tentatively.

"Nonshense!" JT slurred. "I'm ash shober as a… as a… well, I'm not drunk!" Marie glanced at Peter who was sitting in his chair, head lolling forward, snoring.

"Um, JT, boss?" Marie said. "You know he's asleep, right?"

JT shot a glance at Peter and snorted. "Lightweight!" he said. "And it was his round!"

"Look, come on," Marie said, taking JT by one arm, removing his glass and sitting it on the table, and pulling him to his feet.

He stumbled against her as Marie tried to steady him, his breath fogging her glasses and making her feel light-headed as the toxic fumes assaulted her senses. Shaking her head to clear the fog which threatened to descend upon her, Marie put her arm around JT's waist, managed to lift one of his arms and put it across her shoulders, and steered him out the Ballroom.

JT stopped and took his wallet out his pocket, pulling out a couple of notes which he then proceeded to drop as he attempted to count them.

"What are you doing?" Marie asked impatiently.

"I wash… I was… jush going to tip the star baff," he answered.

"I don't think this type of establishment expects that," Marie replied. "Look, just don't move!" She dropped to her knees and scooped up the money and, inadvertently, a napkin, and stuffed everything back into JT's wallet. Returning it to him, she said, "Okay, let's go."

Watching Marie and JT, Sophia was standing, holding onto Rupert as he guided her slowly round the dance floor. Next to them, Philip and Theresa were also dancing slowly. Rupert noticed Sophia staring over his shoulder and glanced back.

"Who are you looking at?" he asked, trying to keep his tone light.

"That woman at our table," Sophia answered. "She's… nice."

"Nice?" Rupert repeated. "Seemed a bit dull to me. Dressed like an old maid, too."

"Well, I like her," Sophia said.

"Well, good for you," Rupert answered sarcastically. "Is that going to be another guest at the wedding, then?"

"Don't be silly!" Sophia retorted. "Anyway, what if it were? It's Father who is paying for all this, after all."

Rupert stopped moving, gripped Sophia's arms and whispered harshly, "Yes, that's right! Your dearest Daddy is shelling out quite a lot to get you off their hands. Between the job at his company, with a guaranteed seat on the board to follow, and the stocks, he is practically paying me to marry you!"

"All you care about is money!" Sophia snapped, wiping at her eyes.

"And all they care about is getting a grandson to carry on the family name!" Rupert shot back. "And since no one else would have you, I guess this is a win for everyone!"

Sophia swung her hand at Rupert's face but he was too quick, catching her arm and gripping it tightly as her face contorted in frustration. He quickly shoved her arm down before anyone had a chance to notice. With an insincere smile, he murmured, "I do so love your passion, dear."

They stepped closer to Philip and Theresa, Philip looking across and saying loud enough for Sophia to hear, "Look at that, Theresa. Young love! Reminds me of when we were young."

"Now, Philip," Rupert said disarmingly, "I don't know about you but your beautiful wife is still young."

"Oh, Rupert," Theresa said, smiling. "You're such a dear boy. Sophia is very lucky."

"Yes, isn't she just?" Rupert replied before leading Sophia away.

At the front desk, Jane Franks was sitting filing her nails. Now in her fifties, her dyed hair and judiciously applied make-up were the only weapons left in her arsenal to try and make her look even just a few years younger. Slightly overweight, her uniform jacket was slightly tight when buttoned up. She could apply at any time for a new jacket in a bigger size but she was determined to start another diet in the New Year and the daily struggle to squeeze into her current uniform would hopefully serve as motivation to stick to it this time.

At this time of night, no more guests were expected. The revolving door, which was never locked, was still operating for any guests, or staff, who wanted to step outside for a smoke. Jane was on duty for another hour, until midnight, at which time the night shift was supposed to take over.

Outside, the snow had been falling heavily for several hours now, the blanket of white getting deeper and deeper. The road was invisible, any tyre tracks long since buried under the falling snow.

Luckily for the staff, there were rooms set aside for their use in case they were working double shifts or, like tonight, where the weather made it too dangerous to travel. Unfortunately, this resulted in most of the night shift staff being unable to reach the hotel, except for a small number who were already staying in the staff accommodations.

Jane glanced at the time displayed on the computer screen on her desk. Since she was stuck there anyway, she had agreed to cover the desk for a few hours more, then Emma would relieve her. To be honest, other than being tiring, it was not too much of an inconvenience. Like most of the people who worked there, Jane had no plans for Christmas, no husband or children to rush home to, which was why she was happy working over the Holidays.

She stifled a yawn then looked up when she heard voices approaching. Watching, she saw a young lady, dressed like an old librarian, stumble past, practically carrying an older man who looked, to say the least, slightly the worse for wear. She watched as they made it to the elevator and, after a moment, stumbled into it, something terribly funny making the drunk man laugh so hard he was almost bent over double.

Shaking her head, Jane sat back, turned her attention back to her computer and tried to log onto the Internet. After a few attempts, she gave up, tried her smart phone and had the same lack of success. She picked up the handset of the telephone on her desk and listened for a dial tone but all she heard was intermittent crackling.

"What's up?"

Startled, Jane saw Toby standing in front of the desk, carrying a crate of beer.

"Oh, I didn't see you there," Jane said, replacing the handset. "I think the phone lines are out."

"Probably the blizzard," Toby offered.

"Yes, it looks like we are snowed in for the night," Jane said.

"Well," Toby said smoothly, "if we're stuck here a while, we will have to think of some… fun way to pass the time."

He gave her a wink, a beaming smile and continued on to the bar.

Feeling her cheeks redden, Jane smiled to herself. Oh, he's a right Jack-the-Lad, that one, she thought to herself. If only I was thirty years younger…

Behind the bar, Vanessa was serving another drink when Toby appeared with the beer. Since the meal had finished, gradually more and more guests had drifted through to the bar so that, now, every table was occupied, people were standing around, and there was a line of people at the bar.

Toby sat the crate on the end of the bar and was about to step behind it when, over the steady buzz of conversation, he heard a slightly raised, angry voice.

Rupert had been leading Sophia through the crowd of people, heading for the bar, when Sophia decided she had had enough for one night.

Turning, she made to leave but Rupert grabbed her arm and pulled her back towards him. "Right, enough!" he snapped. "I will not tolerate any more of your…"

"You won't tolerate?" Sophia demanded.

"Keep your voice down!" Rupert ordered her.

"Are you worried I will cause a scene?" she asked sarcastically.

"All right, if that's what you want…."

"Excuse me, is there a problem here?" someone said.

Rupert turned at the sound of the voice and found himself facing Toby.

"Not at all," he said calmly. "This is a private matter so if you will excuse us…"

"I'm sorry, I can't do that," Toby said, staying where he was. "The lady looks upset. Are you all right, love?"

The question was directed towards Sophia but Toby kept his gaze locked on Rupert.

"Right, listen up... Toby!" Rupert sneered, peering at Toby's name badge. "Why don't you be a good little boy, run along and stick to serving drinks, there's a good chap. I will, in return, refrain from making a formal complaint to the manager of this establishment about the conduct of its staff."

"Listen, just say the word..." Toby said to Sophia, reaching past Rupert to remove her arm from his grip.

"Unhand my fiancée!" Rupert shouted, pulling Toby back around and raising his fist.

Before he could swing his arm, however, Toby had already reacted. Leaning in to block Rupert's raised arm, he swung his other fist into the side of Rupert's face.

There was a dull thud then Rupert staggered back, lost his balance and fell back onto his behind, blood streaming from his nose, Toby standing over him gently rubbing the knuckles on his fist.

Silence descended and all eyes turned to the altercation in their midst.

"I will make you pay for this!" Rupert snarled, struggling back to his feet. "You will regret this, I promise you."

Fighting to hide her smile, Sophia ran to Rupert's side. "Come on," she said softly to him, patting his arm. "I'm sorry, it was all my fault. Please, let's go."

She led Rupert away, stealing a glance back over her shoulder and mouthing 'thank you' to Toby.

"Okay," Vanessa called out from behind the bar. "That's tonight's floor show over. Now, who's going to order another drink? Or should I just call last orders now?"

There was a sudden flurry of activity as several voices spoke at once requesting more drinks. Toby hurried behind the bar to help serve.

Shuffling towards the elevator (if there had not been an elevator, Marie would have probably just left JT in one of the comfy chairs in the foyer), Marie tried to ignore the disapproving glances being directed their way from some of the other guests.

At the elevator, an elderly couple were standing waiting, the panel at the side lit up to indicate it was on its way down.

"Marie," JT said in a drunken whisper, which meant he practically deafened Marie as he shouted in her ear.

"What?" she hissed sharply as the couple gave them a wary glance and took a step away from them.

"Think of… think of a…," JT mumbled.

"A number?" Marie asked.

"No, no, no," JT answered. "Think of a… a… think of a colour!"

"What? Why?"

"Because… just because," JT retorted.

"Okay," Marie said, sighing. "Right, I'm thinking of a colour. Now what?"

"You… you know… what… you know what… that is, right?" JT asked.

"No," Marie answered. "What is it?"

"It's… it's a… it's a pigment of your imagination!"

He started laughing loudly, wiping tears from his eyes, gasping as he repeated the punchline to himself.

At that moment, a small ding announced the arrival of the elevator. The elderly couple stepped aside and waved Marie in. As she turned, JT still propped beside her, she waited for the couple to enter.

"It's okay," the man said, "we'll catch the next one."

Too embarrassed to argue, Marie pushed the button for their floor and the doors closed, JT still laughing.

With difficulty, Marie managed to guide JT from the elevator to their room, propping him against the wall as she reached into his pocket looking for the room key card.

"Why, Mrs Robinson," JT smirked, "are you trying to sheduce me?"

He laughed again, loudly, as Marie tried to quieten him, suggesting some guests might be trying to sleep. Finding the card, she swiped it through the electronic reader and heard a faint click as the door unlocked. Shoving the door open with one foot, Marie reached in and switched the light on. Looking back at JT, she suddenly considered just leaving him there, perhaps hanging the 'do not disturb' sign on him then she thought about the other guests, or the staff, who might have the misfortune to encounter JT in his highly inebriated state.

Reluctantly, she dragged him into the room, letting the door swing closed behind her. Puffing and panting, wiping sweat from her eyes, Marie made her way towards JT's bedroom.

"Oh, Mrs Robinshon," JT murmured again.

As they crossed the threshold and entered the bedroom, Marie used an elbow to switch the light on then guided JT to the edge of the bed. As he stood swaying, Marie looked around and reached down to pull the cover back when she felt JT fall into her. She turned, reaching up to try and steady him but he kept falling and, his weight too much for Marie to manage, knocked Marie onto the bed, landing on top of her his arms sprawled outwards, his feet hanging over the edge of the bed. Beneath him, Marie fumbled until she managed to roll out from under him, sliding off the bed and landing on the floor with a mild thump.

"Ouch!" she muttered.

Standing up, she noticed JT was asleep, muffled snores rippling the bedding. She managed to turn his body slightly and made sure his head was on its side (Marie did not want to have to deal with JT vomiting in his sleep and choking himself to death), then backed out the room, switching the light off as she went, pulling the door closed behind her.

She leaned against the door, emitting a long, slow sigh and then hurried to her room before JT awoke. Sitting on the edge of her bed, Marie kicked off her shoes and let herself fall back and lay staring at the ceiling for several moments. Eventually, she pulled herself up, and decided that, once in bed, she would spend a short time reading over some of JT's case notes. If JT was going to spend their time here intoxicated, Marie would have a lot of time to herself so she may as well use it productively.

Over the next hour or so, Jane sat behind the desk idly flicking through the pages of some 'celebrity' magazine that Emma had left lying about, gazing at photos of famous people with their designer dogs, famous people on the beach, famous people at movie premiers. Yes, really famous, she thought to herself, so famous I don't recognise any of them. She did concede she might recognise some of the women once they were dressed properly, then suddenly felt quite old.

There was little else for her to do; steadily the guests were leaving the bar to return to their rooms, Toby could still be seen going back and forth from the bar to the cellar though he never came across to talk to Jane; a couple of guests, and one or two staff, dared to venture out into the blizzard to have a quick smoke, huddling against the side of the building to try and get a modicum of shelter. Unless the phone rang, which seemed highly unlikely given the adverse weather, or a guest came down to the desk for some reason, there was nothing for Jane to do. Except for the 'celebrity' crossword in the magazine…

Chapter 5

December 24th

JT stirred then grabbed on tightly to the bed. Who was spinning it round and round? How was that even possible? And who was banging on drums??

With a groan, he slowly opened his eyes and stared at the ceiling. He waited a moment until the spinning slowed then stopped. Unfortunately, the banging continued.

"Ohhhh," he groaned.

"Boss? You awake?" followed by another tap at the door.

"Keep it down!" JT moaned, then groaned loudly.

Pushing the door open, Marie stuck her head round. "I've made coffee, black," she said. "Um, just, er, when you feel ready to get up."

JT slid his feet onto the floor, stood up, swayed, fell back onto the bed, stood up again, more slowly this time, swayed a bit less and, once he was sure he was not going to fall down, shuffled towards the door. His hair was sticking up, his clothes were rumpled, his eyes bloodshot, his voice thick.

"What time is it?" he asked.

"Seven," Marie answered brightly.

"Seven?" JT almost shouted, immediately regretting his raised voice as he clutched his hands to the side of his head. "Seven?" he repeated. "Why in God's name are you waking me up at seven?"

"I got up at six," Marie answered, "like normal," she added. "I've showered and am ready for breakfast but I thought you might need a little... pick-me-up before heading downstairs."

"Breakfast is served until ten," JT muttered, pushing past Marie and falling into the nearest chair. "Besides, I'm not that hungry."

Marie fetched him a cup of coffee. "Here," she said, "just the way you like it; black, four sugars."

"I take my coffee white, no sugar," JT protested weakly, trying to wave Marie off.

"Yes, under normal circumstances," Marie agreed, forcing the cup into JT's hands. "However, these are not normal circumstances. This will give you a little boost." JT reluctantly sipped at the coffee and pulled a face. "Don't be such a baby," Marie chided him.

JT tried to give Marie a disapproving look but found he could not muster the energy so he settled for thinking dark thoughts about her cardigan unravelling.

"What are you smiling about?" Marie asked.

"Nothing," JT said quickly, raising the cup to his mouth and taking another sip. "Just, ah, enjoying this coffee."

"So, I read over some of your case notes last night," Marie said.

"My God, woman, don't you ever sleep?" JT asked, incredulous.

"Five hours and I'm good," Marie responded.

"You're not normal," JT muttered. "You're probably not even Human. Are you a robot?"

"Anyway," Marie continued, ignoring JT's sarcasm, "I've started jotting down some notes just to, um, get a flavour of how you work. I thought we could discuss it at breakfast?"

"Ugh!" JT groaned again. "Will you please stop talking about food?"

Emma sat at the front desk, her long hair tied in a ponytail, her long nails painted pink, with matching lipstick and eye shadow. Outside, the blizzard continued; a couple of staff were out with shovels trying to keep the entrance clear but seemed to be fighting a losing battle as, around them, the snow was now about thirty centimetres deep and rising.

The phone lines were still out so Emma had been instructed to make a sign, which she displayed on her desk, apologising to the guests, explaining there was currently no phone service due to adverse weather. At least, the hotel had its own generator so they would not have to worry about power cuts and they had stocked up for the Holidays so would not run out of food or drink anytime soon.

The kitchen staff had been working since six, preparing the food. In the Ballroom, the tables had been set for breakfast and the guests could help themselves to a cooked breakfast, or cereal and pastries, toast, fruit, tea, coffee or fruit juices.

Candace, on her way to the cellar to collect more cartons of juice, stopped at the front desk. "Good morning, Emma," she said brightly, even though she had worked a double-shift the previous day.

"Oh, hi, Candace," Emma answered. "How is the breakfast crowd?"

"Just warming up," Candace replied. "It's still early, probably get busier soon."

"Yeah," Emma agreed, "it's been quiet out here, too." She looked past Candace towards the entrance. "Still snowing, too. Looks like we'll be stuck here awhile."

"Huh," Candace snorted. "So much for the weather forecasters. Last I heard, they predicted 'a light flurry of snow and only a 5% chance of a white Christmas.'"

"You don't think it'll clear up, then?" Emma asked with a smile.

"Fat chance!" Candace shot back with a laugh. "Anyway, I best be getting along. Toby must have slept in so I'm having to make the cellar run."

"I would offer to call his room but," Emma said sweetly, pointed to the sign on her desk and shrugged her shoulders.

"Heh, don't worry about it," Candace said. "If he doesn't show up in the next half hour, I'll go knock on his door!"

"He might be a heavy sleeper," Emma said.

"Believe me," Candace said with a wink, "I'll knock loud enough to wake the dead." With a laugh, she left Emma and headed for the cellar.

Candace opened the door and reached for the light switch before descending the steps down to the cellar. A flick of the switch and the light at the top of the stairs flickered on then, a second or so later, a similar light located at the bottom did likewise.

Candace had taken two steps when, looking down, she noticed something at the bottom of the stairs, like a pile of discarded clothes. Another couple of steps and she realised it was a person.

From behind her desk, Emma heard the shrill shriek and looked around. There was nobody around at that moment and she was about to put it down to a gust of wind, or something equally innocuous, when Candace appeared in the doorway, ashen and shaken.

Emma immediately rushed round her desk and hurried across to the panicked woman. "What's wrong?" she asked. "You look like you've seen a ghost!"

Candace tried to speak but could not find the words. She just burst into tears and buried her face in Emma's shoulder.

JT had finally been persuaded to take a shower. Standing under the hot water, he eventually felt slightly better and, after what seemed an eternity, emerged from the bathroom, a towel wrapped around his waist, his hair slicked back, rivulets of water running down his face and body.

"There, isn't that better?" Marie asked.

"Marginally," JT admitted grudgingly.

"Well, throw some clothes on, then, and we can go down for breakfast," Marie said. The mention of food made JT realise that the healing properties of a hot shower only extended so far. He felt his stomach give a slight lurch, rebelling against the idea of consuming food, and felt bile rise in his throat. "On second thought," Marie said, noticing JT's greenish complexion, "maybe you should just stick to coffee."

"Maybe I should stick to bed!" JT retorted, going into the bedroom and slamming the door shut behind him.

"You're not a morning person, are you?" Marie called after him. After putting up with him the previous night, she was actually enjoying this, seeing JT suffer. Marie smiled to herself.

Suddenly, a loud rap at the door startled Marie. As she went across to open it, JT shouted from the bedroom, "Tell whoever it is, unless someone's died, they'll have to come back later to change the sheets." As he dressed, he continued muttering to himself, "Not even eight o' clock yet and they expect us to be out the bloody room! Is this a hotel or a prison?"

As he buttoned up his shirt he looked about until he located his shoes. Slipping them on, he sat on the bed and leaned down to tie the laces. Standing back up, he ran his hands back through his hair so that it was pressed flat against his head.

"I hope you told that maid to bugger off and come back at a sensible time!" he said angrily as he stepped out the bedroom. He stopped in his tracks when he saw a man with Marie, dressed very formally, shoes shining, a bow tie tied crisply round his neck. His hair was flattened against his head but JT thought that was more likely down to some kind of gel rather than just having stepped from a shower. He had a small, neat moustache which, like his hair, was dark but flecked with white.

"Good morning," he said, the words clipped, perfectly enunciated.

"Good morning to you," JT said warily, shooting a glance at Marie.

"My name is Haddington-Smythe," the man said, extending his hand. "Gerald Haddington-Smythe, manager of the Alpine Lodge."

"Well, I'm pleased to make your acquaintance," JT answered. "Tell me, do you visit all your guests before breakfast, or just me?"

"Um, boss," Marie said nervously, "there's been, ah, an... incident."

"Yes," Haddington-Smythe said quickly before JT could ask more questions. "One of our people, that is, an employee here, was found a short time ago. Dead."

"I'm sorry to hear that," JT said, not sounding sorry at all. "What do you want from me?"

"Well, knowing your particular... vocation," the manager said carefully, "I thought, perhaps, it would be prudent to avail ourselves of your presence and have you take a quick look over the... scene."

"My vocation?" JT repeated. "You mean my dabbling in private detective work to relieve the boredom of coming from 'new' money? Made in the dot-com and property boom, you understand." Marie hung her head in her hands and tried to stifle a groan.

"Um, Mr Thomas," Haddington-Smythe began, paused, then continued, "I am fully aware of the guest who is allowing you to stay here at their expense. As a 'thank you' of sorts for services rendered, if I understand correctly. You do not need to adopt any pretence with myself, I assure you."

"Oh, right," JT muttered, wondering how many people he had already fed that tale to and what they would think if they found out the truth.

Seeing the frown on JT's face, Haddington-Smythe added, "Rest assured, I will not disabuse anyone else of any... ideas they have formed about you from anything you may have told them."

"Right. Thanks, I guess," JT replied. "Let me grab my jacket."

Moments later, the three people exited the elevator in the foyer and Haddington-Smythe led them to the door at the top of the cellar entrance.

"Do you suspect foul play?" Marie asked, the first any of them had spoken since leaving the suite.

"Shh!" the manager said quickly, although there were no guests about at present. "We do not want to distress the guests."

"I doubt they would be as distressed as whoever's lying down there," JT muttered under his breath earning a narrow-eyed look from the manager.

They stopped in the doorway, the manager stepping aside to let JT and Marie precede him down the stairs. At the bottom, they saw the body lying in a heap, a woman kneeling next to him. "This is Dr Stepford," Haddington-Smythe said when they reached the bottom. "A regular guest here, she was kind enough to examine the body."

"Pamela, please," she said, standing up to shake their hands. She looked like she had dressed in a hurry, her mousy brown hair unkempt, with no make-up. She looked to be in her late thirties. "It was just a cursory exam," she explained. "Gerald asked that I try not to disturb anything before you had a chance to look at things."

"Good," JT said. Pamela stepped back as JT circled the body slowly and then knelt down, leaning close to look at the head and face. He then let his gaze take in the whole body, slowly working his way from the head to the feet then back again. Something caught his eye, a tiny blemish on the cuff of one of the shirt sleeves. He carefully took the cuff between his thumb and forefinger and rubbed at the blemish then held his hand up to study the fine, beige-like powder.

"Who is it?" Marie asked from behind him.

"Toby," the manager answered. "He's… was…"

Marie gasped. "Yes," she said quietly. "I met him yesterday. He seemed like a very nice man."

"Yes, he was very… popular," replied the manager delicately.

"Popular, how?" JT asked immediately.

"With, ah, some of the, er, lady guests," the manager answered, coughing to cover his embarrassment.

"Well, he was friendly," Marie admitted. "You don't think….?"

"Let's not speculate," JT interrupted. "Doctor, what do you think?"

"Cause of death seems to be a broken neck as a result of a fall down these stairs," she answered.

"Yes, but was he helped along the way?" JT murmured, glancing back up the stairs, frowning. Finally, he stood up and faced Haddington-Smythe. "I'm sorry," he said. "Like the doctor said, he seems to have died from a broken neck. He could have tripped at the top of the stairs and fell, he could have been pushed. Unfortunately, there is no way to tell how this happened."

"What course of action would you recommend?" the manager asked.

"For the moment, unless you know of a specific reason why someone would want to kill him, say, a jealous husband, then my best guess is this was an accident."

Haddington-Smythe clenched his jaw and rubbed at the side of his head as if trying to massage it. "Well, for all the… 'friends' this young man made over the years, there were never any problems, no jealous boyfriends or husbands looking for retribution."

"No problems that you were aware of, at any rate," JT responded.

"Hmm…"

"So, what should we do?" Marie asked.

"Are the phones still out?" JT asked, looking at Haddington-Smythe.

"Yes," the manager answered. "We have no way of contacting the emergency services and it would be foolhardy for any of us to attempt a journey, even if we were able to clear a path for a car."

"You can't leave him here," Pamela said. "Do you have any outbuildings not currently in use?"

"Yes, I'm sure we do."

"It's not ideal," Pamela continued, "but if we wrap the body up and store it in one of those buildings, it will serve as a fridge of sorts. It's the best option until the snow eases up and we can re-establish contact with the outside world."

"Of course," Haddington-Smythe agreed hurriedly. "I will see to it immediately and hopefully the guests will not need to know of this."

He hurried back up the stairs, Pamela following him.

"What do you think?" Marie asked JT.

Without answering, he slowly ascended the stairs, pausing on each one, pressing down firmly, looking for any tell-tale signs of a loose floorboard or anything else that just seemed... out of place. He stopped at the stair second from the top, pressed his foot down and listened as the floorboard creaked, then felt it wobble.

"This one here," he said to Marie who was following him, "it feels loose. That could be what caused him to fall." There was also another tiny beige mark on the handrail where Toby must have brushed against it.

"So, you think it was an accident?" Marie asked.

"More than likely," JT murmured. "I think it might be a good idea to try and track his movements last night, you never know, someone might have seen something."

"I can't believe someone here would commit murder," Marie said, casting a final look at the body at the bottom of the stairs.

"Well, let's get some breakfast!" JT declared happily.

"What?" Marie could not hide her surprise. "Half an hour ago, you looked worse than poor Toby. The mere mention of food turned you green. And, now, suddenly, you're hungry?"

"What can I say?" JT asked innocently. "An unexpected corpse, a possible murder, seems to be an ideal hangover cure."

"I seem to have lost my appetite," Marie said.

"Nonsense!" JT retorted. "Breakfast; most important meal of the day!"

Haddington-Smythe returned to his office where Candace was still sitting, crying. Emma had to return to the front desk so, now, Vanessa was trying to comfort the distraught woman.

"Um, how are we... doing?" Haddington-Smythe asked awkwardly. Honestly, what was it with hysterical women, he thought to himself. It was bad enough in the old days but now, with all this touchy-feely get-in-touch-with-your-emotions nonsense, it was ten times worse. Yes, Toby had caught a bad break, poor chap, but life goes on, doesn't it? And it is not as if Candace was particularly close to Toby. If it was not for the infernal snow, I could at least send her home, restore some normality back to this place.

"She's had quite a shock," Vanessa answered, squeezing Candace's hand comfortingly. "Shh, it's okay."

"Er, perhaps she would be better after a lie down," the manager suggested, trying to make it sound like an act of kindness when all he wanted was his office back.

"Do you think that doctor could, you know, maybe... prescribe her a sedative?" Vanessa wondered.

"I highly doubt you would be able to reach a Pharmacy," Haddington-Smythe responded bluntly. "However, I shall enquire if she has anything she might be able to offer help calm Candace down. You get her back to her room, I'll send Doctor Stepford up momentarily."

Standing up and stepping away from Candace, Vanessa lowered her voice to a whisper. "Listen, Mr Haddington-Smythe," she began nervously, "I think there is something you ought to know about."

"Yes?" he responded.

"Last night," Vanessa explained, "there was an... altercation between Toby and one of the guests."

"What kind of altercation?"

Vanessa quickly related the events of the previous night. Haddington-Smythe listened without interrupting. Finally, when Vanessa was finished, he said, "Yes, I can see how that could look bad. You were right to tell me, of course. I will relate this information to our Mr Thomas and see what he makes of it."

Vanessa turned and gently coaxed Candace to her feet and led her out the office. Haddington-Smythe fell into his chair behind his desk and reached for the telephone before he remembered they were currently out of order, even the internal lines. He rose to his feet and left to find Dr Stepford, then JT.

In the Ballroom, half of the tables were now occupied. All the guests were allocated the same seating arrangements as for dinner (Mr Haddington-Smythe felt this made life easier for guests who were less keen to socialise) so Marie and JT sat down in the seats they had been occupying the previous night. JT sat a tray down on the table; a bowl of cereal, yogurt, a plate of toast with butter and jam, a glass of fruit juice and a steaming mug of coffee. Everything was squashed together to fit onto the tray. By contrast, Marie was carrying a mug of coffee and nothing else.

Presently, the only other people at the table were Sophia and Rupert. Sophia had a cup of tea in front of her, Rupert had a cooked breakfast which he was attacking with delight. With his fork halfway to his mouth, he nodded a greeting to the new arrivals. Sophia showed no sign she saw them, her eyes fixed on her teacup.

Marie said, "Good morning," and Sophia glanced up and gave her a brief flicker of a smile. As Sophia toyed with her cup, her sleeved pulled back slightly and Marie noticed a purple bruise. "Are you all right?" she asked with concern.

Quickly pulling her sleeve forward, Sophia murmured, "Oh, yes, er, I'm just a bit clumsy, that's all."

"Clumsy?" Marie queried doubtfully.

"Yes," Rupert interrupted. "Honestly, poor Sophia here can be frightfully clumsy, isn't that right?" Sophia nodded but remained silent. Rupert continued, "Yes, just last night, on our way back to our room, she tripped. The old girl could have done herself a terrible injury but, lucky for her, my reflexes would put a cat to shame. Without thinking, my arm just shot out and I caught her before she hit the floor. Unfortunately, I don't seem to know my own strength. Got a grip like a vice, eh, Soph?"

Marie tried to keep her face neutral and not show the scepticism she was feeling. Perhaps if she had a chance to talk to Sophia alone, she could find out what really happened.

"So, that's quite the appetite you have there," Rupert said to JT, changing the subject.

"Breakfast; most important meal of the day," JT repeated from earlier, spreading some butter on a piece of toast and biting a bit off, crunching it between his teeth.

"I am somewhat surprised," Rupert said. "I thought, perhaps, after last night, you might have been sticking to the coffee like your young friend there."

"Nonsense," JT answered. "I'm right as rain."

"Hah, Lucy would need to see you to believe you," Rupert said with a smirk. "She was in, briefly, earlier, getting some coffee for her hubby who, she says, looks and feels like death warmed up!"

"Strange," JT said. "We didn't have that much to drink."

Marie, who was sipping at her coffee, nearly spat it out in shock and then her attempt to avoid this caused her to start coughing and spluttering.

"Are you okay?" JT asked.

The coughing subsiding, her face scarlet, tears running down her cheeks, she gasped, "Fine, it, um, must have gone down the wrong way."

Haddington-Smythe had entered the Ballroom and was hovering about discreetly hoping to catch the attention of JT or Marie. He noticed the young lady seemingly choke on something, a fit of coughing briefly interrupting whatever conversation had been underway.

As JT turned to his companion to speak to her, Haddington-Smythe found himself in his direct line of sight. He took a couple of steps forward and JT looked up, noticing the manager. Haddington-Smythe gestured with his head towards the door and headed towards it. Entering the bar, he stepped off to the side and, a few seconds later, JT appeared and walked across to him. "There is something I have just been made aware of which I believe you should know," the manager began. Quickly, he repeated what Vanessa had told him about Toby's altercation with Rupert.

"Hmm, interesting," JT said quietly.

"Yes, isn't that what you chaps refer to as a good motive?"

"Indeed," JT agreed. "If this were a murder mystery, it would be too obvious, a red herring. However, sometimes, in life, the obvious answer is the right one."

"So, you think he killed Toby?" Haddington-Smythe asked.

"Possibly," JT admitted. "But it is too early to jump to conclusions. I'll have a little chat with Rupert, see what I can learn. In the meantime, can you check with your employees, find out who saw Toby last night, when, where, so we can try and pinpoint when he had his… fall."

"Of course," the manager said, nodding eagerly. "I say, this is rather exciting, is it not?"

"It can be," JT answered. "Yes, it definitely can be."

With that, he returned to his table while Haddington-Smythe went to question the other staff to try and get a picture of Toby's movements the previous night.

"Everything all right, old boy?" Rupert asked as JT sat. "You rushed off in quite a hurry." JT thought quickly; basically, he had two approaches to choose from. Go for subtlety, approach the problem carefully from the edges, picking and feeling his way to the answer. Alternatively, he could employ the direct approach, ask Rupert outright about the previous night's incident, see how he reacted. JT preferred the direct approach only when he was sure of the facts. At the moment, there were still too many unknowns to be certain of anything. If he played his hand too early, Rupert might clam up and JT would learn nothing. So, the subtle approach it is, then, he thought.

"Hmph!" JT answered, trying to sound irritable. "I saw the manager wanting to have a word, thought it was maybe to do with a room upgrade. Turns out, there was a complaint last night about my 'state of drunkenness', if you can believe that!"

"Really?" Rupert said. "Not very festive."

"I'll say!" JT grumbled. "Apparently, one of the staff, some young upstart goes by the name of Toby Something-or-other, said I was being rude and obnoxious."

"Toby?" Rupert asked, frowning. "Why do I recognise that name…?" Suddenly, he clicked his fingers. "Yes!" he said, "That's the name of the chap who stuck his nose into my business."

"Really? What happened?"

"You know how it is," he answered, giving a knowing look to JT. "Sometimes couples have little tiffs and the old girl needs put in her place."

"I hear you," JT said. Marie had to play along, even though she wanted to reach across and slap Rupert.

"So, there we are, having a little… disagreement," Rupert explained, "when, out of nowhere, this pup decides to butt in, be the dashing hero, a knight in shining armour, whatever. I told him to push off and he got shirty with me. Next thing I know, he's taking a swing at me, catches me completely off-guard, you know, and lays me flat out. Dirty pool, old boy."

"Gosh, did you make a formal complaint against him?" Marie asked. She did not know the real facts but she was pretty sure Rupert was embellishing.

"Well, one has to be the bigger man, doesn't one?" Rupert said magnanimously. "Season of goodwill and all that, after all."

"That's decent of you, turning the other cheek like that," JT said. "In your position, I'm not sure I could be so generous, Christmas or not. What I would like is maybe just five minutes alone with him, that way we could resolve our… issues between ourselves. Yes, just five minutes…."

"I suppose I can see the appeal in that," Rupert admitted. "If nothing else, the reputation of my old school boxing instructor would be vindicated. Old Parsons took great pride in making sure us boys could take care of ourselves in the ring. In a fair fight, what?"

"You know what?" JT said. "I think he's nothing but a hustler, making up bogus complaints about the guests, hoping we'll pay up so he'll shut up! I think we should both go right now and confront the manager, together," JT said, pushing his seat back and getting to his feet. "If you tell him what happened with you, it'll help to prove this kid is out to cause trouble."

"Well, erm, if it's all the same, old chap, I'd just as soon give it a miss,"

"What?" JT said, outraged. "After what he did to you? Why?"

"I would just… that is, ah, well…" Rupert stammered.

"So, you're letting me get hung out to dry?" JT snarled.

"No," Rupert protested. "I mean, um, I…"

"You realise," JT said, "if he gets away with this, he'll probably come after someone like you next, another easy mark."

"No he won't," Rupert said. "Why would he? It's not as if…."

"Hang on," JT said, frowning. "What aren't you telling me? How can you be so sure he'll leave you alone? Unless…"

"Unless?" Rupert repeated nervously.

"Oh, you crafty dog, you," JT said grinning. "Oh, I should have known. All that talk about turning the other cheek, season of goodwill, you're just being modest, right? I bet you went back for him after you took your wife back to your room, maybe had a quiet word with him, if you catch my drift, perhaps gave him a demonstration of your boxing skills just to put him in his place, made it clear what would happen if he messes with you, am I right? I must say, I'm impressed." JT leaned across the table and whispered conspiratorially, "I take it you stuck to body blows, after all we wouldn't want people asking how he got black eyes, right?" JT winked at Rupert and sat back smiling.

"Body blows?" Rupert said, sounding anxious. "Black eyes? What are you...? Wait, is he saying I attacked him? That is an outrageous accusation. I haven't laid eyes on him, let alone fists, since we left the bar last night. Is he saying I attacked him? It's absurd, I tell you! I don't believe in violence! I'm a pacifist!"

"But, what about Parsons?" Marie asked innocently.

"Damn the old fool!" Rupert snapped. "He was nothing but a bully!"

Rupert's face had turned bright red and, as he made this last comment, his voice had gotten louder to the point where he was practically shouting, spittle flying from his mouth. "Come on, Soph," he said. "I seem to have lost my appetite!"

"But..." she began.

"Now!" he snapped, grabbing her arm and pulling her to her feet, knocking the table and tipping over her cup in the process. As they hurried off, JT stared after them, frowning. Marie also watched them.

"Pacifist, huh?" she said softly. "Parsons would be proud."

Chapter 6

Rupert's outburst had attracted a lot of attention, people glancing across trying to see what all the fuss was about. A member of staff had appeared and was trying to clean up the mess; the previously white table cloth now had a large, brown stain where the tea had spilled.

"I say," a voice called out from a nearby table. JT turned and saw an old man waving them across. "Why don't you join us? We have a couple of spare seats and I am sure no one will mind, under the circumstances."

Picking up his tray, JT led Marie to the table and they took the empty seats. Quickly, introductions were made. "I'm Stanley," the man said, "and this is Gemima, my wife. This is Harold and Prunella (their children declined to join them for breakfast hence the spare seats), and these lovely young ladies are Magenta and Scarlet."

"Thank you for this," JT said.

"Don't mention it," Stanley answered. "I have to ask, mind you, what did you say to get that gentleman so riled up?"

"Oh, nothing much," JT replied. "He was telling me he had a spot of bother with an employee last night. I wondered if he had, well, had a little 'heart-to-heart' with him afterwards, if you catch my meaning?"

"What an odd reaction," Stanley said, "Strange fellow."

"Which employee?" Magenta asked suddenly.

"Who was it?" JT asked, turning to Marie, brow furrowed in concentration as if he was trying hard to remember. "Tony…?"

"Toby!" Marie said, clicking her fingers. "Yes, Toby. He was working behind the bar last night when it happened."

"Oh, my!" Magenta gasped, her hand rising to her mouth, a shocked expression on her face. "Oh, goodness!"

"Oh, nothing to worry about," JT said casually, picking up another piece of toast, looking at it for a moment, then returning it to his plate. "From what I hear, Toby put our friend, Rupert, in his place."

"You don't understand," Magenta said, brushing a strand of hair from her eye. "I was talking to a woman from Housekeeping earlier, she said there had been some kind of accident last night and that Toby's body was found this morning!"

"Oh, um, gosh, that's, er, terrible," Marie stammered, shooting a nervous glance at JT. So much for being discreet, she thought. Mr Haddington-Smythe would not be pleased to hear that the news had already started to spread among the guests.

"Yes, that is… terrible news," JT said. "Um, well, ah, I'm not as hungry as I thought. Think I'll just go back to my room. Marie?"

"Yes," Marie said quickly, getting to her feet. "Um, yes, ah, we can go and, er, plan our day."

They hurried out, Stanley staring at their backs. "People are acting mighty strange today," he murmured.

"Magenta," Gemima asked, "what else did you hear?"

"Oh, Gemima," Stanley scolded. "Surely you're not going to indulge in idle gossip."

"Now, Stanley," Gemima responded, "this is important. That poor young man is dead and here it is, the day before Christmas. I don't see this as gossiping so much as a display of sympathy for that boy and any family he has left behind."

Magenta, who had been drinking a glass of orange juice, dabbed at her lips with a napkin, then said, "I don't know much. I just happened to bump into someone earlier, I think she said her name was Valerie, or something. Anyway, she said one of the staff was found dead this morning. The manager was trying to keep it all hush-hush, I think, but I got the impression she was just desperate to tell someone and I happened to be there."

"Did she say what happened?" Gemima asked.

"It seems he fell down some stairs, broke his neck," Magenta replied.

"Oh, my, how awful!" Gemima said. "What a tragedy."

"I know," Scarlet offered. "He was quite cute."

"Scarlet!" Magenta said sternly. "This is hardly the time for jokes."

"Well, he was!" Scarlet protested, pouting at her sister.

Harold and Prunella had sat listening to this exchange without offering any comment. Finally, Harold said, "Actually, I also heard something this morning."

"Harold, I don't think…" Prunella began.

"Listen, Pru, it's not like we are betraying State secrets," Harold said, determined not to be left out. "I, er, overheard a couple of people talking. At the time, of course, I had no idea who they were talking about, but, now, well, I think it must have been this young man whose body was found earlier."

"Oh, do tell us," Magenta said. "Gosh, this is exciting, isn't it?" Seeing the looks from Gemima and Stanley, she quickly added, "I mean, it is a terrible tragedy, naturally, but, well, one feels like they're caught up in a good old-fashioned whodunit!"

"In that case, you will find this very interesting," Harold said. Pausing for dramatic effect, he took a breath, then said, "Apparently, he was a bit of a ladies' man. And none too discreet about it, from what I hear."

"Now, really, I must protest!" Stanley said firmly. "That is most definitely gossip and I find it highly inappropriate, under the circumstances. Don't you agree, Gemima?"

"Yes, I do," Gemima said. "Whatever… failings this young man may have had is irrelevant now and I don't think we should indulge in this kind of… of… of gutter-talk!"

"Okay, okay," Harold said, putting his hands up in surrender.

"Well, I disagree," Scarlet said defiantly. "Just because someone is dead, why should they be treated as if they were perfect? If this man…"

"Exactly!" Stanley said. "'If' being the key word. None of us here knew him, knew anything about him. We do not know if these… stories have any basis in fact. It would be wrong to repeat them."

"I think it's a bit late for that," Scarlet replied innocently. "Whoever was talking earlier has probably repeated it to half the people in the hotel by now."

Gemima shook her head sadly. Magenta shot a glare at Scarlet who pretended not to see it. Harold and Prunella seemed suddenly focussed on their coffee as an awkward silence settled around the table.

Gerald Haddington-Smythe wiped at his brow with his handkerchief. He was back in his office facing JT and Marie. "This is terrible," he moaned, wringing his hands together. "Absolutely terrible."

"People were going to find out sooner or later," JT said, trying to be pragmatic.

"Later would have been preferable," the manager muttered, "I have been practically accosted by several guests already demanding to know what is happening. It seems half the hotel knows."

"And they are probably telling the other half as we speak," Marie said.

"Not helping," JT chided her. "Okay, listen," he said to the distraught man before him. "Just stick to what we know which is, he died after an unfortunate accident."

"Why did this have to happen to me?" Haddington-Smythe wailed.

"I feel your pain," JT said, not sounding in the least sympathetic. "Look, it's Christmas Eve, there is the fancy dress ball tonight, I doubt anyone will be that bothered about this."

"What?" Marie asked.

"I said, I doubt anyone will be that bothered," JT repeated.

"No, the bit about a fancy dress ball," Marie said. "What fancy dress ball?"

"Oh, did I forget to mention it?" JT asked. "Oops, sorry."

"I hope you don't expect me to go," Marie said.

"Don't worry, you'll be fine," JT assured her.

"But, um, I, ah, don't have a costume," Marie protested weakly.

"Well, not since you wore your 'old maid' outfit to dinner last night," JT said sarcastically. "It's okay, the hotel provides costumes."

"But…"

"Right, that's settled," JT said. "Listen, Mr Haddington-Smythe… actually, can I just call you Gerald because Haddington-Smythe is quite a mouthful and very time consuming."

"Yes, fine, whatever," Haddington-Smythe waved his hand in a 'just get on with it' motion.

"Right, Gerald, it's business as normal as far as everyone is concerned. Right?"

"Apart from the dead body," Marie said. "And being snowed in with no way to get in or out of here."

"Still not helping!" JT muttered through clenched teeth. "So, Gerald, anyway, just carry on as normal. I will continue to work on piecing together Toby's movements last night. Okay?"

The manager sighed and nodded. "Fine," he said. "Perhaps you should talk to Vanessa. She was working with Toby last night."

"Right," JT answered. "Will do."

The Alpine Lodge had been upgraded and extended many times over the years. Now, as well as the original building which contained the bar, ballroom, and most of the guest rooms, the original cellar had been greatly enlarged. As well as a cellar, there was now a gym located beneath the building. Extensions to the original structure created additional rooms for guests and staff, there was an indoor swimming pool and tennis court, spa centre and a library for the guests' use, as well as a 'social room' where guests could sit and chat, read, or play games.

Another outbuilding contained all the skiing equipment kept for the guests' benefit for anyone who fancied a bit of cross-country skiing. At the moment, the weather was still too hazardous for anyone to contemplate that kind of activity so the building was locked. It was in here that Toby's body had been carefully covered and left until the weather conditions permitted access to the hotel.

There was also a smaller building containing the hotel's generator meaning that they did not have to worry about power outages caused by the inclement weather.

Magenta and Scarlet had booked an appointment at the spa for facials. As they made their way to it, they passed Stanley and Gemima who were entering the library.

"You know, if this is a whodunit," Scarlet said, a wicked gleam in her eye, "my suspect would be old Mr Lewinski, in the library, with his moral superiority."

"Oh, Scarlet," Magenta chided, "don't let the old fool get to you. You and I both know there is no harm in a little gossip. I mean, where would our favourite reality TV shows be without it?"

"I swear, Magenta, if I ever get that old, I might have to kill myself."

"You can be such a drama queen," Magenta said, laughing.

"Seriously," Scarlet added. "The first sign of a grey hair and that's it for me!"

"I hope all this excitement doesn't give you wrinkles," Magenta teased. "After all, it was exciting enough before, wondering if we could pull it off, now, it's even more thrilling!"

"No wrinkles, my sweet Magenta," Scarlet purred. "Adrenaline keeps me young."

Rupert had stormed back to his room, fuming, pulling Sophia along behind him, muttering angrily under his breath. His cheeks burned as he relived the humiliation from the night before, when that uppity barman stuck his nose where it did not belong. He could not be sure but he thought he caught Sophia smiling as he had got back to his feet and, he was sure, everyone had a right good laugh at his expense after he left. It was obviously too much to hope for that people would be too polite to mention the incident. Now, as if his humiliation were not sufficient, the barman was going to try and cause more trouble for him?

He stopped outside his room, noticing the cleaning trolley, the door to his room open and the sounds of a vacuum cleaner coming from within. The vacuum stopped and a woman appeared in the doorway, tall, thin, short, spiky light-coloured hair. She was wearing protective gloves and, in one hand, held some kind of cleaning spray. Her ears had several piercings and there was also one above her left eyebrow. Her face was pale making the dark lipstick and eye shadow stand out even more. Just above the collar of her top, Rupert could see part of a tattoo.

"Your room?" she asked in an accent that Rupert guessed was Eastern European, though he could not be more precise.

"Yes," he answered impatiently, "My room. Our room," he amended, remembering Sophia standing just behind him. "Are you almost done?"

"Yes, yes," she answered. "Almost done. How you say, all span and spick."

"Good," Rupert muttered.

"My name is Valentina," the woman said, pointing to the name badge she wore. "You remember, eh? Valentina. If manager ask, you say, Valentina clean good?"

"Yes, yes," Rupert agreed. "Fine, whatever."

Valentina went back into the room and returned a few seconds later pulling the vacuum cleaner along behind her. She retracted the cable, sat the machine beside her trolley then took a couple of fresh towels off the top of the trolley. Walking back into the room, she looked back and saw Rupert and Sophia following her in. As she deposited the towels in the bathroom, she called out, "You hear of excitement this morning?"

"Um, excitement?" Rupert said distractedly. Surely, his outburst at breakfast had not become common knowledge so quickly.

"Yes, yes, excitement," Valentina said, emerging from the bathroom. Lowering her voice, she whispered, "Dead body found. In cellar."

"What?" Rupert asked, sounding surprised. "What are you on about? What dead body?"

"You no hear?" Valentina asked. A glare from Rupert was all the answer she got. Undeterred, she continued, "Yes, body found in cellar. Dead. Barman Toby."

Beside Rupert, Sophia stiffened. "What happened?" she asked nervously.

"No really know," Valentina answered. "He maybe fall down stair, break neck, dead."

"That's, um, that is… I mean, er, what a shock," Rupert stammered.

"Yes, shock for Candace, she find Barman Toby," Valentina carried on. Gently coaxing her toward the door, Rupert ushered her out, as she continued to offer her sympathies for Candace and Barman Toby.

Closing the door behind her, Rupert leaned against it, feeling beads of sweat popping out on his forehead.

"My God," he muttered. "They'll think I had something to do with it, won't they?"

"Where did you go last night?" Sophia asked, fear in her voice.

"What?" Rupert asked, startled.

"Last night," Sophia said. "After we returned to our room, after our little 'tiff', you stormed off. Didn't come back for almost an hour. Where did you go? What were you doing?"

"You don't honestly think…?" Rupert fell into a stunned silence. Finally, he stepped past Sophia. "Get your things," he said. "We're leaving."

"What?" Sophia said. "Don't be silly! We can't…."

"You will do what you are told, or else," he said darkly. "Am I making myself clear?"

"But Mother and Father…"

"I will think of something," Rupert said. "Just, get your things."

Absently rubbing her bruised wrist, fear in her eyes, Sophia started gathering all her things together.

In the next room, Philip and Theresa had just stepped out when Valentina was ushered out of Rupert and Sophia's room.

"I clean?" she asked.

"Oh, yes, dear," Theresa said. "We are going down for coffee so you just carry on."

"I clean good," Valentina said confidently. "You be sure to tell manager, Valentina clean good."

"Yes, of course," Philip answered, not really interested in what Valentina was saying but just agreeing to try and keep her happy.

"You hear of excitement today?" Valentina asked before they could escape. "Dead body in cellar. Poor Barman Toby."

As they exited the elevator on the ground floor, Philip was saying, "I just think we have to concede there's a possibility she might be wrong."

"But, Philip," Theresa argued. "How could she get something like that wrong?"

"Look," Philip replied, "I don't mean any offence but, well, obviously the Queen's English is not her first language. She may have simply got her… wires crossed."

Theresa looked doubtful but did not argue the point. She was sure that if it were true, other people would be talking about it.

"Gosh, look at that!" Theresa said, seeing the snow outside. "It must be three feet deep!"

"At least," Philip agreed, "Good thing we weren't planning on going anywhere."

Getting a couple of coffees from the bar, they returned to the foyer, found a table close to the Christmas tree and sat down.

"This is simply going to be the best Christmas ever!" Theresa said happily, "Sophia is such a lucky girl."

"I'm lucky, too," Philip said, "Rupert has a good business head on his shoulders. He will be good for the company. It will be in safe hands once I'm gone."

"Oh, you do fret over your company so," Theresa said, "Are you not happy your daughter is getting married?"

"Yes, of course," Philip hastily agreed, "Still, I admit I was worried for a bit, you know. Running a company is not the kind of thing a woman can do, certainly not as well as a man."

"Philip, are you ever going to join the twenty-first century?" Theresa asked.

"Mock me, if you will," Philip replied. "You'll see, Rupert will prove me right, mark my words."

The elevator door opened on the ground floor. Within it, Rupert and Sophia, coats and scarves already draped round them, stood with their luggage. Sophia exited first carrying her small holdall, followed by Rupert who had a large suitcase in each hand and another, slightly smaller suitcase, nestled under one arm. He was breathing slightly heavier under his burden.

They made their way to the front desk drawing quizzical looks from people nearby. Stopping in front of the desk, Rupert dropped the suitcase from under his arm, it making a thudding noise as it landed on the floor.

Perplexed, Emma looked up and said, "Can I help you, sir?"

"We are checking out," Rupert stated bluntly. "I'll sort the bill out; you have someone bring my car round."

"But, sir…?" Emma began but was immediately cut off by Rupert.

"Listen here, I'm not in the mood for twenty questions, all right?" Rupert said harshly. "Now, I don't suppose you are a rocket scientist," he sneered, "but I think even you can follow a couple of simple instructions!"

Fed up with his tone even before the personal insults started, Emma struggled to stifle the smile that was threatening to light up her face. Pausing briefly to maintain her composure, she eventually replied, "Well, of course, sir, I can prepare your bill for you. We have your credit card details already so, providing you have no queries, this should only take a moment."

"Good," Rupert said. "Now, have someone bring my car round."

"That, sir, will not be possible," Emma answered sweetly.

"Now, you listen to me, young lady," Rupert said through gritted teeth. "I don't know what game you think you're playing but I'm not in the mood. If I have offended you, well, sorry. There, I have apologised. Now, have someone fetch my damned car!"

"As I said, sir, that is not possible," Emma repeated; then pointed over Rupert's shoulder.

Turning, he looked to the view at the front entrance and saw the thick blanket of white which covered almost everything. As he looked, he saw two men outside with shovels in a vain attempt to clear some kind of path but the snow, still falling heavily, was covering the cleared area almost immediately.

"But… but… but," Rupert stammered.

"That is an awful lot of 'buts', sir," Emma said innocently. "Do you like 'buts'?"

"What…?" Rupert spluttered. "What are you talking about? We need to leave. Now!"

"I understand, however, as you can clearly see, it is not possible at the moment," Emma responded.

"I demand to see the manager!" Rupert practically yelled.

On hearing the raised voice, Philip looked up and beyond Theresa and spotted Rupert and Sophia at the desk, luggage in hand, looking like they were planning on leaving.

"What on Earth…?" he said almost to himself.

Theresa turned to look at what had distracted her husband and was stunned by what she saw.

"Philip," she said, turning back, "what is going on?"

"I have no idea, but I intend to find out," he answered, pulling himself out of his seat and striding purposefully over to the desk, Theresa scurrying to keep up with him.

"Now, what's all this?" he asked, startling Rupert.

"We, ah, need to leave," Rupert mumbled. "Um, something… important has come up, ah, requiring my, erm, attention…."

"Rupert, I don't know what kind of joke you think you are playing, but have you looked outside?" Philip demanded.

"Sophia?" Theresa said to her daughter, "what is the matter?"

"Look, it's... nothing!" Rupert answered. "I... we... we have to go, that's all."

"Sophia," Theresa said pleadingly, "look at the weather. It's not safe to travel."

While this discourse was taking place, Emma had discreetly slipped out from behind her desk and hurried to Haddington-Smythe's office.

"Arctic explorers would be reluctant to travel in that!" Philip told Rupert forcefully. "I don't know what has gotten in to you, lad, but if you are determined to go, so be it. However, Sophia will be staying with us."

"Now, Philip," Rupert said, trying to sound reasonable.

"Excuse me, what seems to be the problem?"

Everyone turned and saw Emma had returned with the manager in tow.

"Are you the manager?" Rupert asked immediately.

"Yes, sir, Mr Haddington-Sm..."

"Whatever," Rupert interrupted. "We, my fiancée and I, are checking out. This lady here," he pointed to Emma, "is being quite unhelpful."

"I tried to explain why they can't leave," Emma said.

"Sir," Haddington-Smythe said calmly, "surely you appreciate the adverse weather conditions make it impossible for you to get your car."

"Call me a taxi," Rupert said.

"Sir, the phone lines are currently down," the manager explained. "However, even if they were not, I fear you would find it impossible to persuade anyone to attempt to drive out here."

"I have to leave," Rupert said desperately.

"I believe you were booked to stay over the Holidays," Haddington-Smythe said. "If I may ask, what has prompted this... urgent need to depart?"

Rupert looked at the manager then at the faces of everyone else. How could he explain so they would understand?

"He heard about the body discovered this morning," Sophia blurted out.

"Damn you!" Rupert snarled.

"I don't understand," Theresa said, bewildered.

"Explain this insanity," Philip said sternly.

"I… I…I…" Rupert opened and closed his mouth, lost for words.

"Rupert fought with the man," Sophia said. "Last night."

"Is this true?" Philip asked.

"It… it… it wasn't me," Rupert whined. "It wasn't me."

"What wasn't you?" Haddington-Smythe asked, clearly as bewildered as everyone else.

"I didn't kill him!" Rupert said harshly. "You're going to try and pin it on me, well, I won't let you!"

Realising that people nearby were starting to pay more attention to what was going on, Haddington-Smythe cleared his throat and said, "Perhaps we would all be more comfortable in my office?" He turned to Emma and whispered, "Get the detective, please. He'll want to hear this, I shouldn't wonder."

"Yes," Philip said harshly. "I think that would be best. Let's go!" He grabbed Rupert roughly by the arm and, Haddington-Smythe leading the way, they all entered his office, except for Emma who remained behind at her desk, allowing herself a smirk of satisfaction when she pictured Rupert's panicked expression, like a deer caught in a car's headlights.

Chapter 7

Haddington-Smythe's office, while not considered small, was not designed to accommodate more than a few people so, at the moment, it was a bit claustrophobic. Sitting behind his desk, Haddington-Smythe looked across; Rupert and Sophia occupied the only two other chairs in the office, at the other side of the desk from the manager; Philip and Theresa stood just behind Sophia, their body language making it clear they were there to support their daughter; JT and Marie were off to the side, JT leaning against a cabinet upon which sat a coffee maker and, behind two glass doors, several cups and saucers.

"I think you better explain what is going on," Haddington-Smythe said to Rupert. "We can't have scenes like that or it will upset the other guests."

"I'm… that is… I apologise," Rupert mumbled. Clearing his throat, he continued, "After what this man said to me earlier," he pointed towards JT, "implying I had, somehow, been involved in an altercation with that young man…"

"Another altercation," JT said.

"Excuse me?" Rupert said.

"I think you meant to say, I implied you had been involved in another altercation," JT explained. "Or, do you deny last night's incident?"

With a heavy sigh, Rupert nodded. "Fine, another incident. Happy?" he sneered. "Well, I… thought this Toby chap was looking to cause trouble for me. Then, I learned his body had been discovered this morning and I suppose I panicked. After last night's… scuffle, well, people would naturally jump to conclusions. I thought the best course of action was just to make a… discrete exit."

"That was discrete?" Marie asked.

"How did you learn of it?" JT asked.

"One of the maids, if it is still politically correct to call them that," Rupert said sarcastically. "Valentina, she said her name is. Valentina clean good," he said in a mock imitation of her accent.

"That's who told us!" Theresa cried.

Haddington-Smythe studied the man before him and said, "I am sure you will appreciate that leaving here at the moment is quite impossible." Rupert nodded. "Um, as for the other matter, er, well, it seems Toby simply fell down the stairs. There is no hint of foul play."

"There isn't?" Rupert asked.

"No," JT added. "It is all very… cut and dried."

"Well, that is quite a relief," Rupert said mustering a small smile.

"I am curious," JT said slowly. "Why did you assume Toby was murdered?"

"Um, I, erm, well, he seemed too young and… healthy to, um, just drop dead, you know?"

"Even so, why assume you would be suspected?" JT persisted.

"Well, after last night…" Rupert said.

"And, after that incident, you never saw him again?"

"Of course not!" Rupert exclaimed. "Soph and I went back to our room and never left until we went down for breakfast earlier. Isn't that right, Soph?" Rupert said, giving his fiancée a hard stare. Sophia was silent for several seconds. "Soph?" Rupert said more forcefully.

"Um, yes, that's right," Sophia finally said. "We, er, were there all night."

"See?" Rupert said triumphantly. "As I said."

JT stayed silent although a tiny frown creased his forehead and Marie could tell he did not believe Rupert's entire story.

"Well, that settles everything, then," Haddington-Smythe said, sighing with relief. "Now, please return to your room. Let us all put this matter behind us now and try to enjoy the festivities coming up, eh?"

"Can I stay with you?" Sophia asked her mother.

"Sophia?" Rupert said, surprised.

"Sophia, dear, whatever is the matter?" Theresa asked.

"Nothing," Sophia murmured. "It's just… with everything that's been going on… I think I am just a bit… stressed. I'm sorry, Rupert, I just think… I need to be with my parents for a little while. You understand?"

"Er, yes, yes, of course," Rupert said, forcing a smile. "Of course, you must do what is best for you, darling. Will you be well enough to attend the ball this evening?"

"I… I will see how I am feeling later," Sophia answered then, carrying her holdall, let her parents lead her out of the office.

"Well, gosh, I feel a bit of an ass," Rupert said, giving a little embarrassed laugh, "Definitely not one of my prouder moments, what? Well, ah, I should get all this back upstairs. Good morning."

Once he had left, Haddington-Smythe looked to JT and asked, "Surely you don't think he could be responsible?"

"Hmm," JT murmured. "At the moment, we still have nothing to suggest foul play. However, if it was indeed murder, well, I don't know. He doesn't really seem the type; assertive to the point of bullying Sophia, but from all accounts, when Toby confronted him, his bluster was easily dealt with. More of a coward, really."

"I think he was lying about his whereabouts last night," Marie suggested. "It looked like he was coercing Sophia."

"I agree," JT said with a nod. "But that does not necessarily relate to this matter. Marie, find Vanessa, get the story of last night's little bust up, and find out exactly when it was she last saw Toby."

"Right, boss," Marie replied.

"And what are your plans, Mr Thomas?" Haddington-Smythe asked JT.

"I think I better have a chat with Valentina," JT said. "Find out exactly what she knows and how she knows it."

Candace awoke in her room. Dr Stepford had offered her a sleeping pill which she had refused but did accept the small brandy which, though foul-tasting, seemed to settle her nerves and calmed her down enough so that she dozed for a couple of hours.

Now, in the quiet, dark room, the memories came flooding back. She felt a wave of sadness wash over her as she pictured Toby's body lying at the bottom of the stairs then, perhaps selfishly, wondered why it had to be her who discovered him there. If only it had been someone else who went down to the cellar…

That was when the thought struck her. It hadn't occurred to her earlier, she had been too upset to think clearly but now, calmer, she remembered. Was it important? She did not know but decided the best course of action was to inform Mr Haddington-Smythe and let him decide.

JT tracked Valentina down on the third floor, still working her way through the rooms. There was also another member of housekeeping working that floor but, as he neared her, JT saw her name badge said 'Debbie'.

Debbie smiled a greeting at JT as he walked past, stepping round her cart. Along the corridor, there was an open door and, from within, the sound of a vacuum cleaner struggling to drown out the wailing screech of a dying banshee. Cautiously sticking his head round, JT saw Valentina, earphones in, singing at the top of her voice as she worked. JT winced as the cleaner attempted to hit a high note almost bringing tears to his eyes. He was not sure what she was singing along to but he was fairly confident that the original song sounded nothing like Valentina's interpretation. Quickly, he rapped loudly on the door. Getting no reaction, he did it again, harder.

"Oh!" Valentina said, startled. She removed her earphones and reached down to switch off the vacuum cleaner. "Sorry!" she said with an embarrassed grin, "I no hear you. Is your room?"

"No, no," JT assured her. "No, I was wondering if I could speak to you for a minute."

"Um, no want boss, Mr Smythe, catch me no working," the cleaner replied nervously.

"It's okay," JT said. "Mr Haddington-Smythe knows I am here. He is happy for me to ask you a couple of questions. All right?"

"Sure, I guess okay, if Mr Smythe say so," Valentina said, sitting on the edge of the bed. "Um, what questions about?"

I understand you have been telling some people about the death of Toby, is that right?" JT began.

"Oh, yes!" she said, excitedly. "Poor Barman Toby, his body found in cellar. Very exciting!"

"How did you hear about it?" JT asked.

"Another cleaner she see Candace all upset, crying, being taken to room to rest," Valentina answered. "She overhear Candace muttering about poor Barman Toby, how she find his body in cellar."

"And she told you?" JT asked realising then how quickly the news probably spread round the staff and guests.

"Yes!" Valentina beamed.

"And you told?" JT prompted, though he suspected he knew the answer.

"Um, just, er, one or two peoples," Valentina said hesitantly.

"Valentina, please," JT said, "it is important you tell the truth. You won't get in trouble, I promise."

"Okay, um, well, er, maybe more than one or two peoples?" she said.

"How many more?"

"Um," Valentina seemed to be deep in thought as she tried to recall how many people she related the gossip to. "Um, perhaps fifty peoples?"

"Thank you," JT said with a sigh. "Well, it's not unexpected, I suppose," he murmured to himself. Then, to Valentina, he said, "There is probably no point in asking you to keep quiet now since it seems to be common knowledge. However, please think carefully. If you, or your friend, hear anything that might relate to this matter, I need you to tell me immediately. Do you understand?"

"Yes," Valentina said, sounding relieved. "I tell you immediately."

Marie found Vanessa serving coffee in the ballroom. Waiting until she had served the guests and was heading back to the bar, tray under her arm, Marie stepped up beside her and gave a discreet cough. "Um, excuse me," she said. "Do you mind if we talk?"

"Oh, you're with that detective fella, aren't you?" Vanessa asked.

"Um, yes," Marie replied with a nod.

"Is this about Toby?" Vanessa asked, though she knew it was.

"Yes," Marie answered. "Is there somewhere we can talk?"

"Tell you what," Vanessa said. "You go and find a seat out in the foyer. I will get us a couple of coffees and be right back."

"Oh, great, thanks," Marie said.

A few minutes later, Marie looked up from where she was sitting and saw Vanessa sit the tray down bearing two steaming cups of coffee. Falling into the seat opposite, Vanessa sighed.

"It's funny," she said, looking around. "The day before Christmas, sitting beside this beautiful Christmas tree, outside looking like a giant Winter Wonderland, all these people here for a good time, to relax and have fun and… and it feels… empty now. Does that make sense?"

"Yes, I think I know what you mean," Marie said. "Listen, JT, my boss, asked me to ask you a few questions. I hope you don't mind."

"Wasn't it an accident?" Vanessa asked.

"Yes, but… but, I guess, JT is just making sure," Marie responded.

"About him," Vanessa said. "I hope you don't mind my saying, but he seems a bit… arrogant? Like, I dunno, like he thinks he's better than everyone."

"When it comes to things like this, he usually is," Marie admitted. "But, er, he, um, maybe doesn't realise how he comes across when, ah, he's preoccupied with a case."

"Look, you don't need to defend him to me," Vanessa said. "It's just my opinion, that's all."

"Um, right, okay," Marie mumbled.

"I'm just surprised you can put up with him," Vanessa added. "I doubt I could. It would probably drive me to murder." Vanessa paused then said, "Sorry, poor joke."

"Um, well," Marie said, hoping to steer the conversation back on track. She did not feel comfortable having this kind of conversation about JT with a stranger, with anyone, really. Probably because Vanessa was right, Marie admitted to herself. "Okay, I know you didn't find the bo… I mean, Toby," Marie stammered, "but you witnessed the altercation last night, I believe, between Toby and one of the guests?"

"Yes," Vanessa said leaning forward and cradling her cup of coffee in her hands. She raised the cup to her lips and sipped at the hot liquid. "That kind of thing, well, it doesn't happen in a place like this," she said.

"Tell me about it," Marie said. She had a pad on the table beside her cup, a pencil in hand ready to scribble notes.

"Well, um, let me think," Vanessa said. "I was serving behind the bar, the place was quite busy, a lot of the dinner crowd had drifted through. Toby, well, he was helping, as well. I think he had just taken drinks to a table when there were raised voices." Vanessa paused trying to recollect every detail. "At first, well, I didn't pay too much attention. Like I said, that kind of thing doesn't happen here. So, I continued serving. I guess Toby was closer, he must have seen or heard more. Next thing, I looked up and Toby was facing off against this other guy who was with a woman, although she looked none too happy about something."

"Go on," Marie pressed, still scribbling away.

"Well, by this point, more people realised something was going on so had stopped what they were doing to have a look," Vanessa said. "The other guy looked livid about something then he tried to punch Toby. Toby was too quick for him, though. Next thing, this other guy is lying in a heap. He jumps to his feet, leaves in a hurry, shouting threats at Toby and….well, I thought that was all there was to it."

"The other man," Marie said, "how would you describe his demeanour?"

"That's the funny thing," Vanessa said. "As angry as he looked, it also looked like he couldn't get away quickly enough. It's like, all his anger, all the things he said, it was just bluster."

"Did you see him again?" Marie asked.

"No," Vanessa answered. "After that, well, it wasn't too long before we closed up for the night. Everybody left, Toby and I closed up the bar and I said goodnight to him." Vanessa paused, swallowed. "I… I never saw him again."

"Right, um, well, thank you for your time," Marie said, putting her pencil down. "This must be very difficult for you."

"Did you meet Toby?" Vanessa asked.

"Um, yes, briefly," Marie admitted, blushing.

"Then you have an idea of what kind of person he is… was," she continued. "He could charm the birds out the trees, that one. A right Jack the Lad, know what I mean? And yet, for all that, he was well liked here. His playful flirting never offended

87

anyone; he was a hard worker, reliable. It's… it's hard to believe he's gone."

The urgent knock on his door startled Haddington-Smythe who had been trying to relax by practising his meditation techniques. With a frustrated sigh, he called out, "Come in."

The door was flung open and Candace stood there, breathing heavily after having practically run from her room down to the office.

"Candace, are you all right?" Haddington-Smythe asked. "Come in, come in," he said, suddenly hoping she had not found another body.

Candace threw herself into a seat and started talking rapidly. "I'm sorry, sir, I never thought about it. I should have realised but I was too shaken up by what I saw. It was only when I woke up before that it occurred to me. It's probably nothing, I know I probably sound hysterical, but I thought you ought to know, just in case it is important."

Raising his hands, Haddington-Smythe stopped Candace. Her face was bright red, her breathing fast. "Calm down, please, calm down," he said. "Okay, please, tell me, slowly, what it is you need to tell me."

"It's the cellar door," Candace said.

"What about it?" Haddington-Smythe asked.

"It was locked," she replied.

"Yes, it usually is," the manager said, stifling a sigh.

"No, you don't understand," Candace said. "And I never thought of it, either."

"Do explain, then."

"I had to unlock the cellar door this morning," Candace said. "If Toby was already in the cellar, why was the door locked?"

Haddington-Smythe opened his mouth to answer then realised he could not explain it. "Um," he said thoughtfully, "that is, er, a very good point." He sat back and ran the possibilities through his mind. Could Toby have been up to something underhand? Would he really have locked the door behind himself? It made little sense. Finally, he said, "Stay here."

He hurried out of his office and saw Marie sitting in the foyer. Vanessa had just stood up and was walking away, a sad expression on her face, leaving Marie alone. She was still scribbling notes when Haddington-Smythe appeared beside her.

"Oh, hello," she said.

"Where is your employer?" he demanded brusquely. "There has been a... development."

"Um, he was going to interview the cleaner," Marie reminded him. "He should be back any moment now. What is the problem?"

"I am not sure," he answered, distracted, looking about. "When Mr Thomas returns, please have him wait here. I will return momentarily."

He hurried off, leaving Marie sitting alone, puzzled.

JT was riding the elevator down to the ground floor, deciding he was wasting his time. Probably just as well, he thought. It's one thing for me to get a nice, juicy murder to solve, but I can't have Marie getting distracted. She needs to focus on my case notes.

The elevator door opened with its customary ding. JT strode from it and soon found Marie in the foyer. She quickly updated him on her encounter with Haddington-Smythe so JT sat down beside Marie to await the manager's return.

"You know, I was thinking," he said. "I think I need a catchphrase."

"What?" Marie asked, puzzled.

"My character," JT explained. "It might make him more interesting if he has a catchphrase."

"What kind of catchphrase?" Marie asked reluctantly.

"I don't know," JT said, frowning. "Have a think about it. Maybe once you've read enough of my notes, something will spring to mind."

"Um, okay, er, sure," she replied, once again wondering why she had agreed to come here. She was spared any more of JT's wild ideas by the return of Haddington-Smythe. He was accompanied by Dr Stepford.

"Please, come with me," Haddington-Smythe said quietly.

"What's going on?" JT asked, rising to his feet.

"Please, just follow me," the manager answered. "I will explain shortly."

He led them away from the foyer, along a corridor and stopped at a door at the far end.

"I apologise for this, but it is important we inspect the body immediately," Haddington-Smythe said, fishing a bunch of keys from his pocket and sliding one into the lock of the door. He turned it and pulled it open. Straight away, they were assaulted by swirling snow and a freezing wind. Raising his voice, Haddington-Smythe said, "The building is just across the courtyard. Please, follow me."

Stepping outside into the blizzard, Haddington-Smythe led the small group of people across the courtyard which was under about twelve inches of snow. It would have been worse but the layout of the building afforded a small degree of shelter so the snow here was taking longer to accumulate.

Trudging through the snow, their feet getting wet, crouched down, arms raised to shield their faces from the blizzard, the four people soon found themselves at another door. Haddington-Smythe already had a key in his hand. He fumbled for a second or two, the cold temperature making it difficult to move his fingers, until there was a slight click, barely audible, and he pushed the door open.

They stumbled inside and he closed the door behind them. Marie stamped her feet trying to shake the snow loose, then brushed at her hair and shoulders.

"Okay, care to explain?" JT asked, rubbing his hands together.

"Candace came down to my office," the manager answered.

"The girl who found Toby?" Marie asked.

"Yes," Haddington-Smythe explained. "She has calmed down a bit, now, and just remembered something which may be of importance."

He quickly filled them in on his conversation with Candace. At the end, JT asked, "So, if there are no keys on the body…?"

"Yes," Haddington-Smythe nodded. "I have spoken to the two men who carried Toby's body here. They assured me they removed nothing from his person. In fact, it was as quick as they could drop him here and get out."

"Dead bodies have that effect on some people," JT murmured.

"Well, let's get this over with," Dr Stepford said. "The sooner we do this, the sooner we can get a nice, hot drink to help thaw us out."

Haddington-Smythe and Marie stood back as the other two people uncovered the body, which was lying face-down.

"Here, Pamela," JT said, "help me turn him."

Once they rolled the body over, JT carefully checked through every pocket, then patted the body all over to make sure there was nothing else there. He turned to Haddington-Smythe and confirmed, "There are no keys here."

"But, if the door was locked," Marie said, "then someone must have taken Toby's keys and locked the door."

"Yes," Haddington-Smythe agreed. "Toby would have needed to have his keys with him in order to gain access to the cellar."

"I guess that removes any doubt," JT said standing up. "There's been a murder."

A short time later, they were back in Haddington-Smythe's office. Candace was still there, waiting for the manager to return. He quickly thanked her and dismissed her, asking her to say nothing of what she had said to him. He was determined to keep this latest development under wraps. The last thing he wanted to do was cause a panic.

He sat down behind his desk as JT motioned to Marie to pour everyone a cup of coffee.

"Well, what do we do now?" Haddington-Smythe asked JT.

"Normally," JT answered, as Marie passed him a cup, "the police are called in, they stumble about for a bit, getting everything hopelessly wrong, I float around in the background, noticing things they don't, asking questions they overlook, then unmask, figuratively speaking, the murderer."

"Calling the police is not an option," Haddington-Smythe reminded them. "Can you not… investigate this matter?"

"Yes," JT responded. "However, you have to understand, with no police involvement, this would be entirely unofficial. People may be less inclined to co-operate. Certainly, the murderer won't feel under any pressure if it's just me sniffing about, unless we get some hard evidence linking someone to this crime. The other problem is…"

"We are all stuck here," Marie said. "If we start asking questions, people will soon realise it wasn't an accident. If they think they are trapped here with a killer, it could, um, cause a panic."

"Surely, you are not suggesting we do nothing?" Pamela asked, horrified.

"No, not at all," JT answered. "I just wanted to make sure Gerald was aware of the... problems this situation is likely to create."

Haddington-Smythe sighed and looked at the time on the monitor screen on his desk. "Lunch will be served soon," he said. "Later, it is the costume ball. Mr Thomas, please carry out your investigation as you feel best but, please, try to keep things as low-key as possible."

"Mum's the word," JT promised.

Oddly, Haddington-Smythe did not find this reassuring.

Chapter 8

There was a brief knock at the door and it was opened to reveal a middle-aged man standing there. "Sir Henry!" Haddington-Smythe exclaimed. Marie remembered what Toby had told her about him; a former military man, multi-millionaire, regular guest of the Alpine Lodge.

"Sorry to intrude, Gerald, old boy," Sir Henry said, looking at the other people in the room and not sounding sorry at all, "Wondered if I could have a word."

"Yes, yes, of course," Haddington-Smythe said, flustered. He quickly stood and ushered out JT, Marie and Pamela, muttering, "We will talk later," to JT as they left.

Closing the door behind them, Haddington-Smythe gestured for Sir Henry to take a seat.

"Coffee?" he offered.

"Come on, old boy," Sir Henry said with a knowing wink. "I'll take a snifter of the good stuff, if you know what I mean."

"Of course," Haddington-Smythe murmured. He reached below his desk, opened a drawer and removed a small decanter and two glasses. He poured some of the amber liquid into both glasses, giving Sir Henry a very generous measure. Passing the glass across, Sir Henry accepted it with a smile. Sir Henry raised the glass to his lips, drank from it and sat back with a contented sigh. He raised the glass so it was level with his eyes, studying the liquid as he sloshed it around the glass.

"Beats coffee any day of the week, what?"

Haddington-Smythe sipped slowly from his glass and waited for Sir Henry to come to the point. "Okay, old boy," he said, sitting the glass down. "What's this business with a dead body in the cellar?"

"Um," Haddington-Smythe managed, his brain working furiously. Yes, he had wanted to keep as much information as possible from the guests but this was Sir Henry Fitzroy, one of the Alpine Lodge's most prestigious guests. If Haddington-Smythe did anything to upset this man, he would be as well asking Father Christmas for a new job. "Well," he tried again. "Um, what, exactly, have you heard?"

"Well, the jungle drums have been beating furiously," Sir Henry replied. "The natives are a bit restless, you know? Everyone seems to be talking about some poor chap who was found dead in your cellar. Is this true?"

"Well, you see," Haddington-Smythe said, "there was, um, an unfortunate, er, accident." Taking a breath, he continued, "It was one of my staff, that young chap Toby, seems to have taken a tumble down the stairs, had the rotten luck to break his neck in the fall."

"I say!" Sir Henry said, then swallowed the remainder of his drink. He then seemed to study his empty glass for a moment.

"Um, would you like another?" Haddington-Smythe asked.

"Gosh, terribly civil of you, old boy," Sir Henry said offering his glass.

Once Sir Henry was enjoying his second drink, Haddington-Smythe said, "You understand, of course, we would have preferred to keep this matter under wraps. Didn't want to upset the jolly Christmas atmosphere, you see? Unfortunately, one of our girls found the situation… exciting, if you can believe that, and was telling anyone who would listen to her."

"Damned gossips!" Sir Henry said with a frown. "Foreign, I assume? I mean, we Brits know how to comport ourselves in these situations, what?"

Haddington-Smythe hoped a baleful grin would suffice as an answer. He did not want to debate with Sir Henry the merits of 'foreigners'. Whilst not too old himself, Sir Henry seemed to possess incredibly out dated values. He seemed to be a man out of time, more suited to the old, colonialism of the British Empire than he was to the twenty-first century. However, money bought you a lot of latitude and money was something Sir Henry had in abundance. If it kept Sir Henry happy, Haddington-Smythe would happily agree, quietly, with all his views.

"Well, I should not keep you," Sir Henry said standing up. "Just thought I would check in, get the low down on the scuttlebutt, what?"

"Of course, Sir Henry," Haddington-Smythe said, managing a small smile. "I would be eternally grateful, should anyone ask about it, if you could…"

"Don't worry, old boy," Sir Henry said. "I will quickly put them straight. Honestly, the way some of them are acting, you would think they were hoping it was murder!"

"Quite," Haddington-Smythe muttered.

Sir Henry downed the last of his drink, placed the glass on the desk and gave Haddington-Smythe a half salute then left the office.

Alone again, Haddington-Smythe sat back in his seat. He glanced down at the drawer where the decanter was kept but decided, as tempting as it was, he had better keep a clear head. In only a few hours, a dead body had been discovered, which had been a great subject of gossip, then it was discovered that it was not the result of an accident but, rather, foul play. Also, because of the freak snow storm, everyone was trapped in the hotel, there was no way to summon help and he had to try and keep the guests from finding out there was a killer in their midst less it cause a panic.

The ballroom was full, all the guests having turned out for lunch. By now, word had spread round everyone; the body in the cellar was the number one topic of conversation. For the moment, it was still being discussed as an accident. But, even then, a few guests did their best to try and paint a slightly more exciting picture of events, no doubt due to having seen too many Agatha Christie adaptations on television, not stopping to consider that this was real life and someone had died.

Sir Henry entered the ballroom and walked across to his table. Unlike most of the other tables, this one only seated four people, although it was nearly as big as the tables seating twice that number. There were a few tables like this, situated nearest the small stage, reserved for the most favoured guests. Even at the Alpine Lodge, where most of the guests were very wealthy, there was still an unspoken hierarchy; an elite within the elite.

Today, there was only one other person at the table; Mrs Beryl Lambert. The other two seats were normally taken up by a married couple, politicians, who had spent the past six Christmases at the hotel. Unfortunately, this year, shortly before they were due to arrive, they became embroiled in some sort of scandal (it had been extensively covered in all the tabloids, naturally, however, those guests better acquainted with the couple considered it too common to indulge in gossip so it was not spoken of) so had to cancel their trip.

As Sir Henry sat, Mrs Lambert, who had been sipping from a glass of sherry, smiled a greeting.

"Sir Henry," she said, very loudly. "You are looking well."

"Thank you," Sir Henry replied, equally loudly as Mrs Lambert was quite deaf. Regular visitors to the hotel were aware of this and thought nothing of her raised voice. In fact, truth be told, they expected it. It was considered part of the Alpine Lodge's character, as much as the décor, the scenic locale, the opulent furnishings. "And you, if I may be so impertinent, look quite exquisite today. Very youthful, in fact."

"Oh, Sir Henry, you are such a tease!" Mrs Lambert said, smiling. "Why, I am old enough to be your mother."

"Nonsense!" Sir Henry protested. They had had this conversation many times and, Sir Henry hoped, would have it many more. He liked and admired the old girl. In his mind, she represented the best of Britain, a Britain which seemed to have died out years ago, a victim of 'progress' and shifting attitudes.

"Did you speak to Gerald?" she asked.

"Yes, yes, I did," Sir Henry replied.

"Did he explain what all the tittle-tattle is about?"

"Yes, Beryl," Sir Henry answered. "Bad news, I'm afraid, old girl. It seems the tittle-tattle had a bit of substance to it, after all. That chap, Toby, had a bad fall, did himself a cropper."

"Toby?" Mrs Lambert repeated loudly. "My, how awful! He was such a charming young man, always said the kindest things to me. I saw him last night, you know."

"You did?" Sir Henry asked.

"Oh, yes," Mrs Lambert answered. "It was quite late on. You know, the old insomnia was up to its usual tricks. I couldn't sleep so I went for a walk, you know?"

Several tables away, Marie and JT both looked up at the same time, exchanged quick glances then hurriedly made their way across to Sir Henry and Mrs Lambert.

"Excuse me," JT said, interrupting their conversation. "I couldn't help but... overhear just now, you said you saw Toby last night?"

"What's that, my boy?" Mrs Lambert asked. "You'll need to speak up."

"I say," Sir Henry said. "This is rather impertinent, what?"

"Oh, we, um, do apologise," Marie stammered. "It's just, we..."

"Hang on," Sir Henry said. "I recognise you two. Weren't you just in Gerald's office a short time ago?"

"Yes," JT answered. "He has asked me to... clarify the events leading up to Toby's, um, accident. For insurance purposes, you understand."

"Oh, right," Sir Henry said. "Well, I suppose if old Gerald has asked for your help, then carry on, old boy."

"Right, er, thanks," JT said.

"And do sit down," Sir Henry added. "Can't conduct a conversation with you standing, it just wouldn't be civil."

JT and Marie sat down and JT repeated his question to Mrs Lambert. Sir Henry then repeated it again, loudly, and the look of confusion on her face vanished.

"Ah, yes," she said. "I was just saying to Sir Henry, I often have trouble sleeping and I find the best cure is to take a little stroll."

"What time was that?" JT asked, practically shouting. If she has anything important to say, JT thought, there is no way it will be kept 'low key' as Gerald asked. Everyone in the hotel will be able to hear her, the way she is shouting.

"Oh, it must have been about 1 o'clock," Mrs Lambert answered. "Yes, I had gone for a walk, as I said. Went down to the foyer, sat down for a few minutes and watched the snow fall. It is lovely, don't you think? Makes everything seem so clean and fresh. Then, I was returning to the elevator when I saw Toby coming up from then cellar."

"Did you speak to him?" Marie asked.

"Oh, no, dear," the old lady replied. "He was too far away. I did call out to him, by name, and wave and he waved back, locked the cellar door behind him then left."

"Are you sure it was Toby?" JT asked doubtfully.

"Well," Mrs Lambert hesitated. "I think so. I mean, it looked like him and there are not too many men who work here. Besides, if it wasn't him, why would he wave back?"

"Of course," JT said. "Just trying to be thorough, you understand."

He was about to motion Marie to stand when Mrs Lambert spoke again. "Funny thing is, I thought I saw him earlier but that is not possible if what Sir Henry says is true."

"Earlier? When?" JT asked.

"Oh, not too long ago," she answered. "In fact, I almost thought I saw him here just a short time ago." She looked past JT as she spoke, a thoughtful expression on her face. "It was a strange feeling," she continued. "Just for a second, out the corner of my eye, I could have sworn I saw him, but when I took a proper look, he wasn't there. And yet, I was so sure…"

She fell into silence. JT waited a moment in case she had anything else to add but, when it was clear that she had finished, he thanked them for their time and motioned to Marie. They stepped away from the table and Marie whispered, "What do you make of that?"

"Old, deaf as a post, probably blind as a bat," JT muttered. "And senile too, I wouldn't be surprised."

"Bats are not blind," Marie said. "It is a common misconception, but…"

"I don't think this is the time for an educational lecture on flying rodents!" JT said harshly.

"Um, sorry," Marie murmured. "So, er, what do you make of her story?"

"It may be true," JT conceded. "But, let's be honest, she is not the most reliable of witnesses, is she? Certainly, she could not have seen Toby today since he is dead."

"What about last night?" Marie persisted.

"Possible," JT said. "But, her 'sighting' today calls her credibility into question."

"So, we dismiss everything she said?" Marie asked.

"Not necessarily," JT said. "We just take it with a pinch of salt."

As JT and Marie returned to their own table, they passed the table where Magenta and Scarlet were sitting. Harold, Prunella and their two children were there also. Stanley and Gemima were just sitting down. Stanley was wheezing slightly as he sat, hanging his walking cane on the back of his seat, the buttons of his cardigan straining to contain his mass.

"What is all that fuss over there about?" Gemima asked once she was seated.

"I'm surprised you didn't hear," Scarlet answered. "They were positively shouting."

"They were discussing that poor wretch, Toby," Magenta said.

"Yes, it seems the old girl saw him last night," Harold added. "Of course, she also claimed she thought she saw him earlier. My guess is, she's batty!"

"Harold!" Prunella reproached her husband.

"Well, how else would you explain it?" Harold asked defensively.

"Maybe she sees ghosts!" Scarlet claimed in mock horror.

"Or maybe she's the killer!" Magenta joked.

"Now, now, ladies," Stanley said, then coughed. "Speaking as a member of the… older class, I must point out that being old does not mean you have lost your faculties."

"It was Harold who said she was batty!" Scarlet protested with a pout.

"Yes, you did, didn't you?" Stanley asked, turning to Harold. "Now, I know you probably think I am an old stick in the mud but I don't find these kind of 'jokes' particularly funny. In fact, they are rather cruel."

"You're right, of course," Harold said sheepishly. "I meant no offence."

"That's all right," Stanley said with a satisfied smile. "We'll say no more on the subject except if the lady thought she saw Toby earlier it must simply be an innocent mistake, nothing more." He wheezed and coughed again as Gemima poured him a glass of water

"What do you make of all that snow?" Scarlet asked to change the subject. "Isn't it simply marvellous?"

"Really, Scarlet, sometimes you act like a child!" Magenta said. "You do realise we are stuck here, don't you?"

"We were planning on staying past New Year's anyway," Scarlet said. "So, I don't mind being 'stuck' here now. We will have a white Christmas, for sure."

"Yes, I suppose we will," Magenta agreed.

"What about your children?" Scarlet asked Prunella. "Are they looking forward to Christmas?" The two children both nodded eagerly and started to tell Scarlet what they had asked Santa to bring them.

Back at their table, JT and Marie sat down. Rupert and Sophia were there, along with Philip and Theresa and Peter and Lucy. Sophia was sitting between her parents, keeping apart from Rupert who was looking embarrassed and ill at ease. Philip and Theresa were talking with Sophia and Peter and Lucy and pointedly ignoring Rupert.

"Um, I couldn't help but overhear," Rupert began.

"I'm sorry," JT said. "I appreciate the conversation was rather... loud, however, I cannot elaborate upon anything we discussed. Gerald, I mean, Mr Haddington-Smythe values discretion, I'm sure you understand."

"Er, yes, of course," Rupert answered.

Marie stared at Rupert. Now that it was officially a murder, she had to wonder about him. The way he treated Sophia showed him up for a bully and he would have been humiliated by Toby in the bar last night. He would have wanted revenge, Marie was certain, but he would not confront someone directly, unless he was confident of his physical superiority like with Sophia. Yes, Marie could easily imagine Rupert sneaking up behind Toby and giving him a good, hard push down the stairs. A cowardly attack from a cowardly man.

"Is there something you wish to say?" Rupert asked Marie, his voice tight. Marie continued to stare for a few more seconds until, finally, Rupert looked away.

"Now, now," JT whispered to Marie. "It's rude to stare."

"I wasn't staring," Marie whispered back. "I was giving him the evil eye."

"Well, that is probably rude, too," JT replied. "Rupert," he said, louder, "forgive my associate. It's the time of the year, you know. She is one of those types who gets down during the festive period. Don't understand it, myself. Anyway, how are you? I know this has been a difficult morning for you but, hopefully, things will improve."

"Well, uh, yes, it has been," Rupert agreed. "And it is kind of you to say that," he added, then glanced across to Sophia. "If only everyone were so understanding."

"No matter," JT said jovially. "I say, it's Christmas, a time of joy and goodwill. So, in the spirit of the occasion, let me buy you a drink."

"That's very decent of you," Rupert said, barely concealing his surprise. "Thank you."

Marie decided it was best to leave JT with his new 'friend' and, instead, focus her attentions on Sophia. She knew JT well enough to know he was only being friendly with Rupert to prise information out of him that he might not otherwise share if he felt he was being interrogated. Well, JT was welcome to him, Marie thought.

"Hi, Sophia," she said to the young lady. "How are you feeling?"

"Better," she answered. "I had a lie down and the rest seems to have helped. I had a blinding headache earlier but it has passed, thankfully."

"I'm glad to hear that," Marie said with a smile.

"Oh, I'm sorry," Philip said suddenly. "Sophia, why don't you swap seats with me, make it easier to have your chat, eh?"

"Oh, thank you, Mr Sonnerson," Marie said as he swapped seats with his daughter.

"Think nothing of it," Philip answered. "Now, I can sit beside this lovely lady," he said, squeezing Theresa's arm. And, please, it's Philip, I insist."

Now that they were sitting together, Marie was able to lean in close and whisper to Sophia without fear of being overheard.

"How are you, really?" Marie asked.

"I don't know, really, if I am being honest with myself," she answered, sighing and wringing her hands together. "Rupert can be so beastly sometimes but... but... but it would make Father so happy for me to marry him. Mother, too, naturally."

"Would it make you happy?" Marie asked. She felt she was taking a risk; she did not want to push too hard, too fast and alienate Sophia, however, there may not be a more opportune moment so she decided it was worth the risk.

"I... I don't know what would make me happy," Sophia admitted reluctantly. Marie took this to be an answer itself, even if Sophia genuinely did not see it. "I so want to make my parents proud," Sophia continued. "And Father does so value Rupert's business acumen. Besides, I have been brought up to put other considerations before love when it comes to marriage."

"Really?" Marie asked, shocked.

"Oh, yes," Sophia answered matter-of-factly. "It is important to marry into the right family, a family with a long, proud history. My family has done it that way for generations. Breeding is very important."

Marie, who was sipping at a glass of water, nearly choked, a fine spray of water flying from between her lips. She coughed and coughed until tears ran down her face. As she drew looks from the others around her, she managed to compose herself.

"Sorry," she muttered with a gasp. "It must have went down the wrong way. Sorry," she said again. "Um, what was it you were saying, Sophia?"

"I was talking about breeding," Sophia answered.

"Breeding?" Marie repeated, feeling her cheeks redden.

"Yes," Sophia answered, oblivious to Marie's discomfort. "It's important to have strong genes, after all."

"Genes? Oh, right, er, that kind of breeding," Marie stammered.

"What did you think I meant?" Sophia asked, puzzled.

"Um, nothing, nothing," Marie said quickly.

"So, it really does not matter how I feel," Sophia said softly.

"Okay, supposing I pretend to understand that kind of thinking," Marie said, "at least, consider how you would like to be treated. I don't mean to pry, but it looks, sometimes, as if Rupert tries to bully you."

Sophia stared down at her hands, biting her lower lip, staying quiet.

"Anyway, that is all I'll say on that subject," Marie said at last. "I just want you to know, if you need to talk, I'm right here."

Haddington-Smythe stopped at the front desk. Emma looked up with a start, dropping her nail file on the desk.

"I do so hate to interrupt," the manager said dryly.

"Oh, um, no, not at all," Emma answered quickly, rearranging some papers on the desk then straightening the keyboard of the computer.

"Calm down," Haddington-Smythe said. "I realise that there is probably very little you can be doing at the moment, except for sitting here in case one of our guests should require assistance."

"Yes," Emma agreed with a nod. "Even if we are not expecting guests, there are usually still phone calls to deal with. But with the phone lines still down and no new arrivals expected, not that they could reach us through the snow, well, it is a bit... quiet."

"Well, in that case, I have some exciting news for you," Haddington-Smythe said in a flat tone that somehow managed to belie the promise of excitement. "Obviously, the band that were due to perform at tonight's ball cannot get here. Luckily, our house DJ was on the premises before this infernal snow descended upon us so he will provide the music."

"So, um, what exciting news do you have for me?" Emma asked.

"I would like you and Ms Franks to be... hosts, of sorts," Haddington-Smythe answered. "Provide the, ah, sound bites, we might have expected from the band's lead singer between songs, mingle, ensure everyone is having a good time, choose the winners of the costume competition."

"Don't we provide all the costumes?" Emma asked.

"Yes," Haddington-Smythe replied patiently. "Still, the guests do have the option of improvising, if they so choose. Regardless, it is all a bit of fun, what? All part of the festive jollities. Of course, I appreciate it will be, in effect, a double-shift, so you will be remunerated accordingly."

"Oh, of course, er, fine," Emma answered, secretly pleased at the prospect of being paid to attend a party. "Who will be covering the front desk?" she asked, not that she particularly cared.

"I will do that," the manager said. He cleared his throat, then said, "It is the least I can do to allow you ladies to help at the ball."

Yeah, right, Emma thought to herself. More likely, you just don't want to go to the ball yourself.

Near the end of lunch, as he started on his third drink, JT decided his attempt at prising information out of Rupert,

103

however discreetly, was a wasted effort. Rupert had gratefully accept the drinks JT supplied him with, grateful for any sort of friendly company. Like JT, Rupert was slightly tipsy by this point and more than eager to talk but none of what he had to say was helpful to JT. Rupert bemoaned the fact that he was 'expected' to marry Sophia, who he considered 'not good enough' for him, in order to do well in his job. Nobody understood the pressure he was under, including Philip who, as well as expecting Rupert to one day succeed him in running the company, expected his soon-to-be son-in-law to be the perfect husband to his oh-so-perfect daughter. Really, is it any wonder if, now and again, the strain starts to show? It would take more than the patience of a Saint to deal with this family, he attested. All these obligations he was expected to fulfil, no questions asked. Did anyone care about him or what he wanted? No. Then, the temerity of that barman! A barman, if you can believe it, thought he could make him look like a fool? Humiliate him?

Suddenly, JT sat up a bit straighter. With the subject turning to Toby and the events of the previous night, and all down to Rupert's drunken ramblings, he instantly became hopeful that he might learn something constructive, after all.

"Tell me about it!" JT said, slurring his speech slightly, deliberately emphasised to encourage Rupert to keep talking. "These... people, nothing but glorified servants and they think they can act like our equals!"

"Exactly!" Rupert agreed, also slurring his words. "I am in line to run a company that makes tens of millions a year and he... he... he pulls pints. Hah!"

"He's not pulling pints any longer," JT reminded him.

"Good riddance, I say!" Rupert whispered harshly.

JT decided to play a hunch, since Rupert was being so forthcoming. "Yes, no one would blame you if you had to sort him out, um, when you went out later."

"Well, that wasn't why I went out..." Rupert stopped, realising what he had inadvertently blurted out. "That is, I didn't... I mean, when I... who told you I went out? Was it Sophia?"

"You did," JT replied, "Just now."

Rupert swallowed nervously, cleared his throat, said, "Er, well, not that it matters, eh? It was an accident, after all." He laughed nervously.

"Why did you lie?" JT asked. "Where did you go? What did you do?"

"Why did I lie?" Rupert repeated derisively. "To avoid questions like these!" JT remained quiet, waiting for him to continue. Finally, Rupert said, "Look, this may all be some kind of game to you but I am not amused. The death of that oik was the result of an accident so I do not have to explain my whereabouts to you or anyone else. Thank you for the drinks."

With that, he stood abruptly, knocking his chair over. As everyone looked on, he tried to compose himself then, swaying slightly, left the ballroom.

"Will we see you tonight?" JT called after him. "At the ball?"

"What's up with that damned fool man, now?" Philip asked testily. "Can he not go one minute without causing a scene?"

"Don't be too hard on him," JT answered casually. "I think it's just the pressures getting to him."

"Pressures?" Philip scoffed.

"I think he doesn't feel appreciated," JT suggested. "Has he shown any signs of stress at all, lately? Any odd behaviour?"

"Until we got here, I would have said no," Philip answered.

"He has always seemed so… organised," Theresa added. "His behaviour lately has been more than a bit strange."

"Well," JT said thoughtfully, "some people can keep all these things bottled up, showing no outward signs of stress, but they keep building and building until…"

"Until what?" Sophia asked.

"Until they erupt," JT answered grimly.

Chapter 9

After lunch, JT suggested to Marie that they spend some time in the library. When Marie queried the reason for this, all he said was, "I like books."

The library, which was one of the original rooms in the old building, was a large room with tall bookcases, stretching up to the ceiling, lining two walls. Several other bookcases, not quite as tall, were placed about the room creating an almost maze-like quality. Some small tables and a scattering of comfy chairs completed the furnishings. The wall opposite the door had two tall, thin windows on either side of a glass double-door which opened onto a large lawn which, at the moment, was a sea of white. The lawn was lined by large fir trees which were also covered in snow.

"Oh, that is a shame," JT said wistfully, looking around.

"What is?" Marie asked.

"I had hoped the library would have one of those fixed step ladders, you know, the kind on wheels that you just roll along until you get to the section you're after." There were step ladders available if anyone required a book from a higher shelf but they were of the more mundane type, much to JT's disappointment.

A vending machine near the door dispensed hot and cold drinks. JT reached into his pocket, found some loose change and slotted a few coins into the machine, punching in his selection. He then repeated this process and got a second cup which he passed to Marie. Wandering into the maze of bookcases, they found a couple of chairs with a table between them.

"So, how much did you have this time?" Marie asked as they sat.

"Ah, two, maybe three," JT answered. "Don't judge me; it was tactical. Plus, it's nearly Christmas."

"Maybe Father Christmas will bring you a new liver," Marie muttered.

Choosing to ignore her, JT said, "I managed to get Rupert to admit he left his room last night."

"After he stormed off, Sophia admitted as much," Marie responded. "She says she doesn't know where he went but says he was gone for about an hour."

"Rupert clammed up as soon as he slipped up," JT informed her. "Does Sophia have any theories at all?"

"If she does, she is not telling me," Marie said.

Magenta and Scarlet wandered into the library, Scarlet looking bored. "Well, isn't this exciting," she said sarcastically.

"I was just curious," Magenta said. "I wanted to see if it was as... boring as it sounded. My goodness, how dull!"

They walked along one of the bookcases staring at some of the books on the shelves. Scarlet stopped and pulled one out, holding it out for Magenta to see. "Can you believe it?" she asked. "Who would want to read 'A History of the Tudors' for goodness sake? Who are they, anyway? Do they have their own reality show?"

"Somehow I don't think so," Magenta answered with a smile.

Scarlet returned the book to the shelf and they wandered round to another bookcase, stopping in front of it as Scarlet idly pulled some books out, flicked through the pages and then put them back.

"Boring," she muttered.

"I know," Magenta agreed. "Hopefully the ball will be a bit livelier."

"I'm sure we can spice things up!" Scarlet said, laughing, then quickly lowering her voice. "What do you think?"

"Well, no one is on to us," Magenta said, "So far, anyway."

On the other side of the bookcase, JT heard the voices of two women. He motioned for Marie to be quiet and they both listened carefully as the conversation continued.

"Why would they suspect us?" Scarlet asked. "We are just a pair of sweet, innocent young ladies spending Christmas in a scenic hotel."

"Of course," Magenta agreed. "As long as they think we are one of them, we will be fine."

"They have no reason to think otherwise," Scarlet said. "You know, this beastly weather does have one glorious advantage; even if anyone had doubts about us, there is no way to look into it."

"We will have to be careful, remember," Magenta said. "As long as the blizzard continues, we are trapped here."

"Yes, yes, yes, I know," Scarlet said impatiently. "Look, can we get out of here? This really is a frightful bore. Say, why don't we go down to the gym? We might see those cute boys who were sitting at that other table!"

"Yes, why not?" Magenta replied. "Then, we need to sort out a couple of costumes for tonight."

"Ooh, yes," Scarlet agreed excitedly.

There was silence after that, except for the faint sound of receding footsteps. Marie opened her mouth to speak but JT held his hand up to silence her. Jumping out of his chair, he hurried to the end of the bookcase behind which they were sitting.

He was just quick enough to catch a glimpse of the two young ladies as they exited the library.

Appearing at his side, Marie asked softly, "Did you see who it was?"

"Yes," JT answered. "I believe it is the two sisters, Magenta and Scarlet."

"What do you think they were talking about?" Marie asked. "What are they up to?"

"Hmm," was all JT said in response as he stared at the empty doorway, a frown creasing his forehead. "Let's go!" he said suddenly.

"Where to?" Marie asked. "Do you have a plan?"

"Yes," JT answered with a smile. "A plan to get a couple of costumes for tonight's ball."

Valentina stood outside the hotel, huddled against the side of the building, trying to get some shelter from the swirling snow. There was a small shelter erected by the hotel for the benefit of staff who smoked but, since it was located round by the car park, Valentina decided she would be as well staying where she was. She was far enough away from the entrance that no one should complain and she figured as long as she discarded her butt properly there would not be any problems,

Here, the snow was about eighteen inches deep although a narrow path had been furrowed by a number of people doing what Valentina was doing now. Stamping her feet to try and keep warm, she held one arm just above and in front of her face to keep her cigarette dry. She had vowed, numerous times, that she was going to quit; this New Year, she resolved to finally do it. The thought of having to do this for another couple of months was a pretty strong incentive to quit.

As she neared the end of the cigarette, Valentina took a last, long drag on it. Exhaling smoke, she turned and stubbed it out on the wall. Turning, she spotted the closest waste bin, with a metal section on top for cigarette butts, which was about ten feet away which, in the current weather conditions, could have just as easily been a mile. Sighing to herself, she wrestled briefly with her conscience; she could just drop the butt in the snow and it would be covered almost immediately. No one would know it was there until the snow thawed and that would be quite some time away. But she would know it was there and she prided herself on always doing things properly, following rules, not cutting corners.

Finally, she decided to do the right thing and dispose of it properly even though it meant trekking through the deeper snow and probably getting wet feet. Leaning into the wind and snow, Valentina trudged through the snow, her feet sinking into the white powder, crunching, slowly advancing forward. She was almost there when, unexpectedly, she lost her footing and tumbled forward. Arms splayed wide, she uttered a cry which was swallowed by the wind and toppled forward into the snow.

Pushing herself to her feet, she silently cursed her conscience. The only consolation, if it could be called such, was she had kept a grip of the cigarette butt. Carefully, she stood up and tossed the butt into the bin but, as she turned, something gold caught her eye. Looking down where she had fallen, she had cleared a small section of snow between her fall and efforts to get back upright and it revealed something tiny protruding from the snow. Valentina reached down and fumbled with her cold fingers, grabbing onto something metal. She pulled it free and was surprised to find herself holding a set of keys. There was a fob bearing the hotel's insignia and six keys on a small metal ring.

Mystified, Valentina trudged back to the hotel's entrance.

Beryl Lambert was seated at one of the tables in the foyer, a glass of sherry on the table in front of her. Beside her, her handbag was open and she was slowly looking through a bundle of old, faded photographs, their edges curled. She wiped at her eye, feeling foolish. It had been quite a few years since her husband died and yet the pain had never really left her. Yes, life goes on, as they say, and her life had continued. She knew that is what her husband would have wanted so that is what she did; continued to live her life. But the loneliness never really went away and sometimes, like now, she felt it more keenly. Christmas was always a special time for them. Neither of them had any family to speak of so they spoiled each other with gifts. Not that it was the material things that Beryl missed; rather it was no longer having someone to share this time with.

Slowly, she returned the photographs to her handbag and gently closed it. She had her memories which, for her age, was something to be thankful for even if, sometimes, those same memories brought as much sadness as joy.

Carefully, she sipped her drink, grateful she was able to spend this time at the hotel. After so many visits, she knew a lot of the staff fairly well and they all treated her with kindness, as a friend rather than an unwanted distraction. Her reverie was broken by the excited cries of Valentina who had just come back into the hotel, hurrying across the carpeted floor, snow shaking itself off her as she went.

"Mr Smythe?" she cried. "Mr Smythe! Look what I find!" She almost bowled over Stanley Lewinski as he entered the foyer with his wife, Gemima. "Oh, I sorry, I sorry!" Valentina cried over her shoulder.

At the front desk, Emma was speaking with Harold and Prunella Weathers who were looking at options for costumes for the ball. Valentina stopped at the desk, breathing hard and, ignoring the two hotel guests, said to Emma, "Where is Mr Smythe?"

"I'm sorry," Emma said to the Weathers. She turned to Valentina and said politely but firmly, "Val, I'm with guests just now."

"But I find these!" she exclaimed holding the keys aloft.

"Look, try his office," Emma said in exasperation. "I must see to these people." Valentina hurried off leaving Emma offering another apology to the Weathers.

"Think nothing of it," Harold said. "Not sure what has got a bee in her bonnet but she seems rather excited."

Beryl Lambert watched all this with fascination. In fact, there were quite a few witnesses to Valentina's seemingly bizarre behaviour. Seated at a table next to the Christmas tree, Pamela Stepford looked up from her book when she heard the commotion; Philip and Theresa Sonnerson, with Sophia in tow, had just stepped from the elevator; Peter and Lucy Tenor had been on their way to the bar; Rupert was heading through the foyer, trying not to be seen by Philip, planning on stepping outside for a moment to clear his head, the snow be damned; Magenta and Scarlet were at another table, close to the front desk, chatting to a pair of young men; JT and Marie had returned from the library and were about to speak to Emma about costumes for the ball.

"I say, old girl, what was all that about?"

Beryl turned and found Sir Henry standing beside her table. "I don't know," she answered. "That nice young lady, the one with the funny hair, seems to have found something, I think."

"Huh, foreigners!" Sir Henry muttered. "Strange lot, very strange lot." As he spoke, Beryl continued to stare, even though Valentina had disappeared from the foyer. "What is it, old girl?" Sir Henry asked, startling her.

"Oh," she said. "I… I just have the strangest feeling but I can't quite put my finger on what it means."

"Well, don't let them rattle you," Sir Henry said, patting her shoulder. "Us Brits are too good for that, what?"

"Yes, of course," Beryl answered, giving a polite little laugh.

Valentina ran up to the office door and urgently knocked, a continual series of loud thumps until she heard a voice from within call, "Come!" She opened the door and hurried inside and ran up to the desk, leaving the door open behind her. Jane Franks was sitting in one of the seats opposite Haddington-Smythe but Valentina ignored her.

"Ms Szbarga," Haddington-Smythe said impatiently. "Is there a problem?"

"Mr Smythe, Mr Smythe!" she said quickly. "I find!"

"What, exactly, did you find, Ms Szbarga?" the manager asked, taking in her flushed face, the remnants of snow still clinging to her clothes, her dishevelled hair (then he remembered, her hair always looked that way) and…. "What is that?"

"Are those…?" Jane asked, leaning forward, peering at the set of keys. "Oh, my goodness!"

"Barman Toby!" Valentina said. "I find his keys! Is important, yes?"

"Ahem," Haddington-Smythe cleared his throat. He quickly glanced at Jane and gave an almost imperceptible shake of his head. So far, other than the detective and his assistant, and the doctor, the only other people who knew Toby's keys were missing were Candace and Jane who he had just been updating as she was an old friend, someone he could trust. "Well," he continued, "it is good that they have been located. Er, where did you find them?"

"In snow," Valentina replied. "I outside have cigarette, put end of cigarette in bin, like we suppose to do, yes?" Haddington-Smythe nodded, encouraging her to continue. "I slip, fall in snow. Find Barman Toby's keys!"

"Yes, well, thank you, um, Valentina," Haddington-Smythe said taking the keys from her. "Um, Toby must have dropped these last night."

"Last night?" Valentina asked, clearly confused. "No possible. How he get in cellar?"

"Ah, I am sure we will work that out," the manager said dismissively. "Thank you," he repeated.

"You tell detective, Mr JT?"

"Of course," Haddington-Smythe assured her.

Valentina left the office muttering to her-self, "How he get in cellar if he lose keys outside? Very peculiars."

Turning to the manager, Jane asked, "What does this mean?"

Haddington-Smythe sat back in his seat, the keys resting in his hand. "I shall speak to Mr Thomas, naturally," he said. "However, it seems obvious the killer threw the keys away, hoping they would be lost in the snow."

As they talked, they paid no attention to the office door which Valentina had neglected to pull closed behind her.

Outside, Philip Tenor stood against the wall, listening to the conversation in the office. Glancing about constantly, since he did not wish to be caught eavesdropping, he listened with interest. Then, sensing the conversation was nearing an end he quietly crept away and returned to the foyer.

"You were gone a long time," Lucy said, as her husband sat down beside her.

"Oh, well," Philip said, faking embarrassment, "you know it can be a bit more... difficult when you get a bit older, eh?"

"Oh, Philip, don't be silly," Lucy said with a smile.

Seeing Valentina hurrying to Haddington-Smythe's office, JT made a mental note to head there next. Right now, however, he was going to sort out their costumes for the ball later that evening.

"Okay," Emma began, "we have an extensive selection of costumes kept in storage. Here is a list of them; the ones highlighted have already been requested so those are not available for selection."

"Oh, I don't think this is a good idea," Marie murmured looking at the list.

"Nonsense," JT retorted. "It'll be fun!"

"I, um, that is, I don't really enjoy... these kind of things," Marie stammered.

"Nonsense!" JT repeated.

"Why don't you ever listen to me?" Marie asked quietly.

"I do," JT said. "But, like I said, it will be fun."

"It's, er, not my... idea of fun, really," Marie said, her anger and frustration building.

"Look, Marie," JT said, turning to face her, "stop 'umming' and 'erring', okay? What is it you are trying to say?"

"What I'm saying is, I suck at balls!" Marie said loudly, her fists clenched by her sides, her face red. "When it comes to balls, I suck at them, all right?"

JT stared at her, then looked around. It was as if, just seconds earlier, a mute button had been pressed as everyone, it seemed, had paused for a second. Even the background noise, the music played at a low volume to add to the ambience, had quietened as one song faded out before another was ready to begin.

It was in that brief moment of quiet that Marie had her outburst, loud enough for everyone in the foyer to hear her. As one, all heads turned in her direction, some with puzzled expressions, others smirking. The two Weathers children were giggling and pointing as their mother tried to shush them.

"Um," Marie mumbled wishing the ground would open up and swallow her.

"You know, that is why you should not dress like my Grandmother," JT said absently.

"What?" Marie demanded, feeling her eyes moisten. She quickly rubbed at them.

"Well, because you dress like you are about eighty years old, well, it just makes what you said a moment ago so much funnier."

"You think this is funny?" Marie whispered harshly.

"Not as much as those two children over there," he replied pointing.

"Oh, God, there are times I feel like I could kill you!" Marie said through gritted teeth.

"Funny, I do seem to have that effect on people," JT said calmly. "Anyway," he continued, turning back to Emma, "I think we will take these." He pointed to a couple of costumes.

"Of course, sir," Emma said, as she ran one of her perfectly manicured (fake, Marie thought again) nails along the page. "I must say, I think you will look quite dashing in this one." She flashed a smile at JT as she gave her hair a little flick with her other hand.

"Why, thank you," JT replied, almost subconsciously sucking his gut in just a little bit. "I did wonder if I was perhaps too old to make it work?"

"Oh, not at all," Emma said, another smile dazzling JT. "I will arrange to have these sent up to your room."

"Thank you," JT said. "I hope to see you tonight, at the ball, that is."

"Oh, I wouldn't miss it," Emma answered. "I love balls," she said, licking her lips.

"Ahem, quite, well, see you later," he said. Gently pulling at Marie's arm, he headed for Haddington-Smythe's office. Tugging at his collar, he said, "Is it just me, or is it rather warm in here?"

"'I love balls'," Marie whispered in a high-pitched imitation of Emma. "Please!"

"You know, I think that young lady really does like me," JT said almost to himself.

"She must see you as a father-figure," Marie suggested bitterly.

"Stop it," JT said harshly. "First of all, I am not that old…"

"Hah!" Marie scoffed.

"Second," JT continued, "why are you getting jealous?"

"Jealous?" Marie demanded. "Is that what you think?"

"It is the only reasonable explanation for your behaviour!"

"Well, Mr Detective, if I were you, I'd stick to investigating murders because you don't have a clue when it comes to women!"

They reached the office door, which was still open, and JT peered in.

"Ah, the very chap," Haddington-Smythe said looking up. "Come in, come in." He introduced them to Jane Franks then updated them on Valentina's discovery. "What I wonder," he said when he had brought them up to date, "is why the killer did not just keep them, hide them in the hotel."

"He, or she, maybe figured there was a risk, however small, that they might be found in the hotel," JT speculated. "Burying them out in that blizzard possibly seemed the easiest way to safely dispose of them. It was a million to one chance that Valentina fell on them."

"A stroke of luck for us?" Haddington-Smythe wondered.

"It does confirm what we already suspected," JT answered. "Unfortunately, it does not help us identify the culprit."

"Are the guests safe?" Jane asked.

"Safer in here than outside," JT said, gazing closely at her. For a moment, he fell silent, a faraway look in his eyes then, with a barely noticeable shake of his head, he returned to the present. "Look, most likely, Toby was targeted. Therefore, it is highly doubtful any of the other guests are in danger."

"You hope," Jane said.

"Don't worry," Marie muttered sarcastically. "We will be at the ball tonight to keep an eye on everyone."

"Ah, yes," Haddington-Smythe said. "We, ah, heard your… statement."

Feeling her cheeks redden, Marie said, "Um, sorry about that. Er, I, ah, didn't mean to be quite so… loud."

"Well, ah, no harm done, eh?" he offered with a forced smile.

Stanley excused himself and shuffled off towards the bar leaving Gemima sitting at the table with Harold and Prunella Weathers. The two children were running round the Christmas tree, laughing and giggling. Gemima had a large ball of wool sitting on her lap and was nimbly working two knitting needles, the rhythmic click-clicking sound of metal on metal.

"They are adorable," Gemima said. "So precocious."

"They can be quite a handful," Prunella said with a smile.

"Little dynamos," Harold agreed.

"If only things had been different," Gemima said softly, a sad look descending upon her.

"Oh, Gemima," Prunella said leaning forward. "Whatever is the matter? Did you not say you and Stanley never had children? Do you regret that?"

"Now, Pru, don't pry," Harold said.

"No, no, it is quite all right," Gemima said, patting Prunella's hand. "The truth is, I do wonder how things might have turned out if, well, things had been different."

"Oh, I am sorry," Prunella said.

"Thank you, dear," Gemima said. "I sometimes wonder what might have been. Would we have had grandchildren now? Oh, ignore me. I don't mean to get so maudlin. It is Christmas Eve and I should be thankful for what I have."

"As should we all," Harold added, looking at his children.

Vanessa was supervising the work required to prepare the ballroom for later. All the balloons had been blown up and tied and were now suspended in several nets hanging from the ceiling. The tables had been rearranged slightly to maximise the dance floor space, fresh table linen had been laid out and the tables adorned with Christmas crackers and party poppers. A couple of people were now going round the tables setting out cutlery and glasses.

The DJ had set his equipment up on the small stage and was testing the microphone as another two people were climbing ladders at either side of the stage so they could hang a brightly coloured banner. Beneath the Christmas tree, several new presents were being added to the ones already there. These ones, unlike the existing ones, were real and would serve as prizes at the climax of the ball.

Vanessa approached one of the people placing presents under the tree and said, "That's right, good. Just slide it back slightly but make sure the number label is firmly attached."

Candace had wheeled in a trolley and was going round putting a small floral arrangement on each table. When she passed Vanessa, Vanessa stopped her. "Hey, how are you feeling?" she asked.

"Oh, much better, thanks," Candace said. "It was a bit of a shock but I think I'm okay now."

"Glad to hear it," Vanessa said. "Listen, if you need anything, just let me know, okay?"

"To be honest, I think the best thing is just keeping busy," Candace said. "That way, I don't think about... well, you know. So, I am looking forward to the ball, tonight!"

"You and me both," Vanessa said. "After recent events, it will be good for everyone, I think. A bit of fun for everyone."

Candace smiled, nodded, and resumed her job and Vanessa went back to surveying the ballroom.

After leaving Haddington-Smythe's office, Marie decided she needed to have some time to herself. JT could be so infuriating, it made her blood boil. Why? Why did she put up with him? She spoke to Sophia about the way Rupert treated her yet she was subjected to as much abuse, verbal if not physical, and kept going back for more. Maybe this little getaway would turn out to be a good thing, after all, she thought. I am stuck here with him and forced to put up with his cruel comments. Well, maybe I need this to finally realise that I am better than that! Yes, she thought, as soon as this 'holiday' is over, I am quitting. JT will just have to find some other doormat to walk all over, do his bidding and write his bloody book because it won't be me!

Having resolved to do that, Marie felt like a weight had been lifted off her shoulders deciding that she had just given herself the best Christmas present ever.

"Penny for them?"

The voice startled Marie and she realised she had been grinning inanely.

Vanessa was standing there, holding a clipboard. "Sorry," she said. "I didn't mean to startle you. You looked like you were a million miles away."

"Um, I was, er, just, ah, daydreaming," Marie said, flustered. She had been so wrapped up in her thoughts that she had not realised she had wandered into the ballroom.

"Are you looking forward to the ball?" Vanessa asked. "What, did I say something wrong?"

"Uh, no," Marie said, embarrassed. "You will hear all about it, I'm sure."

"What?"

"Um, nothing, it, er, doesn't matter," Marie said. "The truth is, I don't really enjoy these kind of things."

"What's not to enjoy?" Vanessa asked, surprised. "There will be music, dancing, fun."

"Music, dancing, fun," Marie repeated, her heart sinking. "Yes, that about sums up what I don't enjoy about them. I just don't handle balls well." Suddenly, realising what she had just said, Marie blushed and said, "Um, I, er, didn't mean... that is, er, I..."

"I'm sure it won't be that bad," Vanessa said kindly, trying to save Marie from further embarrassment. "What will you be wearing?"

"I... I... I don't know," Marie said, just realising that she had been so angry with JT that she had not paid attention to what he picked. "JT made the selection. Emma seemed to think it would a good choice," she added drily. "What is her story, anyway? She seems very... friendly, sometimes, if you know what I mean."

"Just between us," Vanessa said, lowering her voice, "the popular rumour is she is on the look out for a nice, rich, older man to take her away from this place."

"Huh, well JT meets one of those requirements, I suppose," Marie muttered.

"What do you mean?" Vanessa asked, puzzled.

"Well, he is older," Marie responded. "As far as being rich, well, don't believe his stories about the 'family money' because he is here on someone else's dime! And nice? Don't get me started on that topic!"

"Okay," Vanessa said with a wince. "Obviously a touchy subject. Sorry."

"Oh, just ignore me," Marie said with a sigh. "Let's just say that, if I wasn't working for JT, I would not want to be anywhere near him. I think this current confinement has made me realise how bad it is. Actually, I have just decided, as soon as we are done here, I am quitting."

"Wow, things must be bad," Vanessa said sympathetically.

"You honestly have no idea," Marie said. "Look, could you do me a huge favour?"

"Sure," Vanessa told her. "Name it."

"Please, please, please don't tell Emma any of this," Marie said smirking.

"My lips are sealed," Vanessa promised.

Chapter 10

Following Emma's list, two ladies were pushing trolleys along corridors, knocking on doors and handing over large dry-cleaning bags to the guests containing their costumes for the ball. Rupert, looking anxious and tired, opened his door and, without a word, took the bag from the woman and closed the door. "You're very welcome, sir," she muttered under her breath as she approached the next door. This one was opened by Philip Sonnerson.

"Excuse me, sir," she said. "I have your costumes for this evening."

"Thank you very much," Philip said taking the bags from her. "Gosh, this will be fun!" The other lady was on the floor above doing the same thing. She knocked on a door which was opened by Magenta.

"Your costumes?" the lady said.

Magenta, who was peeking round the door which had only been opened a crack, said, "Oh, yes, thanks. Um, I've just stepped out the shower. Could you just leave them at the door and I will get them after I have thrown some clothes on. Thanks awfully."

As Magenta closed the door, the lady briefly wondered why she was not wearing a bathrobe but decided that the guests at the hotel could afford to be eccentric. She left the two bags against the door and carried on.

Further along the corridor, JT was just returning to his room. Maybe Marie should just stay in the room tonight, he thought. Honestly, if she is going to make such a fuss, she would be better spending the time going over my case notes.

He dropped into a seat and sat back. He replayed in is mind all the facts he had learned concerning the death, well, the murder, of Toby. Unfortunately, the facts did not amount to much and certainly did not point to any viable suspects. The obvious suspect, Rupert, was just too obvious. And, no matter how much of an ass he appeared to be, JT just could not imagine him having the stomach for murder.

Apart from Rupert, nobody was aware of anyone having any issues with Toby. Obviously, someone did, but how to identify him or her? When Marie returned, he would suggest she speak to Gerald to find out as much as she could about his time at the hotel. There must be something, JT thought.

And, something else was nagging at the back of his mind. Frustratingly, it remained elusive, no matter how hard he tried to identify what it was. The knock at his door interrupted his thoughts. Opening the door, he took the proffered bags with a smile, thanked the lady and dropped the bags on the sofa.

"No," he said to himself, smiling. "I think Marie should go to the ball."

Beryl Lambert sat alone in the foyer. Sir Henry had left a short time ago to get ready for the ball.

She would not be wearing a costume, as such, feeling she was too old for that kind of thing. However, to make a token effort she would have a domino-style mask which she could hold up to cover her eyes. Much more elegant than trying to wear some garish outfit at her age.

While she had been with Sir Henry, her subconscious was busy trying to highlight something she had seen but not noticed. Now, as she was ready to return to her room, it hit her what had puzzled her earlier, when she was telling that nice young man about when she last saw Toby and why she had had a strange feeling just after that, then again this afternoon just after that strange comment from the young man's companion.

It was clear in her mind now, yet, how could that be? It made absolutely no sense. Although aged, she was confident all her faculties were intact but, this time, could she be wrong? Could she have been mistaken, no matter how sure she seemed? Perhaps if she shared her thoughts with someone, but what if they thought she was 'batty' or whatever the current vernacular is?

Looking about, there were a few people milling about but no one she knew. She glanced over at the front desk but it was unattended at the moment. Not that she would have felt particularly comfortable sharing her thoughts with the young lady on the desk. Beryl was sure she was perfectly nice but, really, what was it about young ladies and their obsession with make-up? When she was young, women who used that much make-up, well, they acquired… reputations. It was just not the done thing, not for a proper lady.

Best to keep her thoughts to herself. She would attend the ball; maybe that would give her a chance to have a proper look. She wanted to be certain before she told anyone.

Marie had been wandering around the hotel, exploring the building's layout, for about an hour after her conversation with Vanessa. As she roamed around, lost in her thoughts, she eventually found herself back in the library.

Absently, she wandered along the path of bookcases, gazing at the books. This reminded her of what she was supposed to be doing for JT, fictionalising some of his cases, turning him into a literary hero. A literary hero who wanted to have a catchphrase, she recalled.

For a moment, she started to think of possibilities, from the case notes she had studied so far, until she reminded herself of her plan to quit.

"Maybe," she said softly to herself, "he could hire Emma and her fake nails. Hah!"

"Ssh!" a voice reprimanded from nearby.

Marie blushed and hurriedly left the library. Eventually, her wanderings brought her back to the foyer. It was nearly 5pm and it was dark outside. The snow was still falling although it was quite light and more sporadic now. Pulling her cardigan tight around herself, she walked through the revolving door and stepped out into the night. Out here, it was peaceful, everything covered in white. The wind had dissipated, although it was still bitterly cold, and everything seemed… calm. Marie guessed the snow was about two feet deep now; apart from a small section in the front of the hotel which staff had managed to keep reasonably clear of snow, everything else was covered. Looking up at the night sky, Marie could see there were fewer clouds, leaving most of the sky clear. Stars sparkled like diamonds and Marie marvelled at the wonders of the universe. It made everything around her suddenly seem insignificant. As her breath fogged in front of her, Marie decided it was time to get back inside. She turned and found herself facing Valentina.

"Oh!" she said with a start. "You surprised me."

"Sorry, I no mean frighten you," Valentina said. "I just come out for cigarette. You smoke cigarette?"

"Er, no, no," Marie replied. "I… I suppose I just wanted a moment to myself. Now that the blizzard has passed, it is quite peaceful out here."

"Peaceful, yes," Valentina agreed. "But cold, yes?"

"Yes," Marie agreed with a shiver. Unlike Valentina, Marie had not planned on going outside so was not dressed accordingly. Realising how cold she was, she gave Valentina a brief smile and stepped back into the hotel. As she walked through the foyer, she did not notice Peter Tenor lurking off to the side, watching her as she headed towards the elevator.

Now that she had cooled off, figuratively and literally, Marie felt ready to return to her room. She rode the elevator up to her floor, stepped out into the corridor and walked along and stopped at the door. Steeling herself, she turned the handle and entered the room. JT was sitting on the sofa, nursing a drink from the mini bar.

"Ah, there you are," he said happily.

"Um, yes," Marie replied, wondering why he was not mad at her after her outburst.

"Come and see your costume," JT said beckoning her over. Of course, the reason he was not mad at her, she realised, was because her thoughts, feelings, opinions were barely a blip on his emotional radar. He really did think the universe revolved around him.

Marie walked over and looked at the two bags.

"Here," JT said, "this one is yours."

Marie pulled the zip down and was lost for words.

"Well?" JT asked expectantly. "What do you think?"

"Um, you, er, want me to, ah, wear that?" she stammered.

"Yes!"

"And you will be wearing…"

"Of course!" JT said, sounding delighted. "We will be fantastic!"

Marie could not think of anything else to say. She just reminded herself that she would soon be finished with JT.

"Listen, I have a little job for us, before we get dressed up for tonight," JT said. "It shouldn't take too long."

Quickly, he explained he wanted Marie to speak with the manager and find out anything she could relating to Toby's employment at the hotel while he got some background on the guests from Emma. "Are you sure that's wise?" Marie asked innocently.

"What do you mean?" JT asked.

"Well, it's obvious you have some sort of… effect on that girl," Marie said, emphasising the last word. "What if she can't think clearly in your presence? Perhaps I should speak with Emma and you can interview Mr Haddington-Smythe?"

"Ahem," JT cleared his throat. "I'm sure, whatever feelings Emma might have won't stop her from… assisting me."

Marie turned away so JT could not see her rolling her eyes. Keeping her tone neutral, she said, "Of course. She does strike me as being a… pro, um, a professional, that is."

Moments later, Marie and JT exited the elevator and turned and walked off in opposite directions. Marie stopped at the office door and gently knocked on it. A voice from within beckoned her in so she opened the door and stepped inside. "Sorry to, er, bother you," she began.

"No, no bother at all," Haddington-Smythe answered. "Please, take a seat. Now, how can I help?" Marie explained what she was after. "Ah," he said, nodding, "of course. I suspected you would come asking about that sooner or later so I took the liberty of getting his personnel file."

"Oh, Mr Thomas, you just caught me," Emma said, dazzling JT with one of her smiles.

"Please, call me JT," he said. "I insist."

"Well, of course, JT," Emma purred. "If you insist. And you can call me anytime," she said, giving a little laugh at the end.

"Heh, yes," JT said suddenly feeling quite warm. "I was wondering if you could perhaps help me."

"Any way I can," Emma answered sweetly (and did she just flutter her eyelashes or was JT imagining things?).

"Yes, right," JT croaked. Quickly clearing his throat, he continued, "I am looking for as much information as possible on the guests here."

"Oh," Emma suddenly looked unsure. "I'm not sure Mr Haddington-Smythe would like that."

"Don't worry," JT said. "Nothing personal, honest. I am just looking for a bit of information about any guests who have been here before, perhaps a few times. You never know, maybe there's something that could shed a little light on what happened to Toby. Listen, can you keep a secret?" he asked, lowering his voice and leaning closer to her.

"For you, honey, sure," Emma whispered back.

For a moment, JT let Emma's perfume fill his nostrils, the sweet scent making him almost lightheaded. Forcing himself to concentrate, he said, "Gerald, Mr Haddington-Smythe, is trying to keep this quiet but Toby's death was not an accident."

"You think a guest murdered Toby?" Emma squeaked loudly.

"Shh!" JT said quickly, looking around and relieved to see they were alone. "Honestly, I don't know. But anything you can tell me might be helpful. And, remember, don't breath a word of this to anyone, right?" Especially Haddington-Smythe, JT thought.

Half an hour later, JT and Marie were back in their suite. They each went to their own bedroom to shower and get dressed for the ball. With their doors slightly ajar, they shouted back and forth to update each other on their respective interviews.

"Did Gerald have anything worthwhile to report?" JT called.

"Not really," Marie called back. "I mean – ugh, who designed these? – I mean, Toby worked here for about five years. There has been some staff turnover in that time but nothing major. Most of the people here have been here for at least that long."

"Any problems?"

"None," Marie replied. "It seems he was well-liked, got on really well with everyone, staff and guests, and didn't cause any problems."

"Hmm," JT said.

"What was that?" Marie shouted.

"I said, 'hmm'," JT called back.

"Him?" Marie queried. "Him who?"

"Not 'him', 'hmm'," JT said loudly.

"Oh, right, hmm," Marie answered. There was another thud from her room.

"Are you okay across there?" JT called.

"Uh, yes," Marie said. "Just, ah, lost my footing for a second. So, was Emma helpful?"

"About as helpful as Gerald," JT retorted. "Similar story; a few guests have been staying here, on and off, for years; Toby, like most of the staff, got to know them; he seemed to get on well with them, never any issues, no complaints from the guests. He was Mr Popular, it seems."

"Somebody had an issue with him," Marie said. "Look, do I really have to do this?" she asked.

"Ah, you're ready, then?"

"As I'll ever be!"

"Come on, then!"

Marie stepped from her bedroom and met JT as he entered the lounge part of the suite. He was dressed as Father Christmas, large, black boots, red suit, black belt to hold in the padding provided with the costume, fake beard and moustache, hat to match the suit, and a large sack.

"Ho, ho, ho!" he said heartily.

Marie was dressed as an elf, her green costume adorned with little bells and other trinkets, her shoes long and curled at the tips, a waistcoat, pointed hat and a mask which covered her face and reached back so that it looked like she had pointed ears. "I look ridiculous!" she muttered.

"You look like one of Santa's little helpers," JT said.

"I'm just glad I have a mask to wear," Marie grumbled. "It should be slightly less humiliating, at least."

"Part of the fun of this will be trying to guess who everyone is," JT said.

"Yay! Fun!" Marie said flatly.

"Come on, then," JT said. "It's time Father Christmas and his helper elf faced the music."

With every step she took, Marie could hear tiny jingling noises. No matter how tightly she wrapped her arms around herself, she could not silence the sounds. Above the entrance to the ballroom, a sign advised guests that tonight, for one night only, there would be no ordered sitting arrangements; people could sit wherever they chose and, as most people wore some sort of mask, they would probably not know who they were sitting next to, unless that person chose to identify themselves.

Keeping in the spirit of it, JT had announced to Marie that she was only to address him as Father Christmas or Santa Claus.

"And what about me?" Marie demanded. "What will you call me?"

"Hmm," JT said, tugging gently at his beard. "I think, perhaps, you should be called Trixie." Behind her mask, Marie rolled her eyes, stifling the groan threatening to burst out of her. Now, as they entered the ballroom, their senses were assaulted by loud music courtesy of the DJ on the stage, flashing lights lighting up the dance floor and a rainbow of colours from the different costumes being worn by everyone.

"Um, JT, I mean, Santa?" Marie practically shouted. "Don't we eat first?"

"Oh, my poor, little Trixie!" JT replied, adding a 'ho, ho, ho' after it, jiggling his padded belly.

"First, we dance. Later, we eat."

"Oh, goody," Marie muttered, too quietly to be heard.

"Hey, Santa!" a voice cried.

JT turned and saw Emma (he would recognise those... nails anywhere, he thought) standing beside him. She was dressed up as a French maid, complete with feather duster.

"Bon soir, ma chere," JT said.

"Oh, Monsieur speaks French!" Emma purred.

"Well, you know, Santa travels all around the world," JT said. "It pays to be multi-lingual."

"I'm also good with tongues," Emma cooed.

"Ahem," Marie cleared her throat loudly. "Hi," she said to Emma.

"Oh, you must be Santa's little helper," Emma said, looking over Marie. She turned back to JT and said, "You know, Santa, I could give you all the... help you'll ever need. Would you like me to come sit on your knee later and tell you what I want for Christmas?"

"Yes," JT answered enthusiastically. "Most definitely, ye...!"

He did not get to finish as Marie suddenly grabbed his arm and pulled him away, shoving him towards the dance floor, not because she particularly wanted to dance but she was not going to let herself be abandoned here because some gold-digging… harlot thought JT was a prize catch. As much as she was looking forward to seeing Emma's face when she found out the truth, tonight was not the time for it.

On the dance floor, they were surrounded by all sorts of colourful characters, cartoon characters, superheroes, famous pop stars, even a tree!

"Look at that," she said, giggling, pointing. "Who 'wood' come dressed as a tree? Wood. Get it?"

"How droll," JT answered, having to lean closer to make himself heard. The song currently blaring out from the speakers was 'Step Into Christmas' by Elton John. "Do you mind telling me why you dragged me off like that?"

"You made me come here," Marie shouted back. "You are not going to abandon me at the start, okay? At least let me have dinner, then Santa can go and see as many people as he likes."

"Fine," JT said. "I'm sure I'll find her. Hopefully standing under the mistletoe!" Marie tried to put that particular image out of her mind less it spoil her appetite.

At the front desk, Haddington-Smythe could hear the music coming from the ballroom. He accepted that Christmas was a popular time for the hotel and, accordingly, Christmas parties were to be expected. However, at the risk of being labelled a humbug, he had no wish to subject himself to the festive excesses which invariably seemed to occur.

Offering to man the front desk made Haddington-Smythe look like he was doing a kind act for his staff and he was spared the ball. A win for everyone, in his mind. He was pleased to know he was not the only person who did not find the idea of this evening's festivities to their liking; he knew (everyone within earshot, which encompassed quite an area, knew) of Marie's feelings towards this event; he had witnessed a family heading towards the ballroom, mother and father (presumably) bickering away about something or other as the two children jumped up and down oblivious to the tension in the air; then there was Sir Henry Fitzroy and Beryl Lambert who would attend the ball but more for appearances sake than any desire to 'party', as the younger generation put it.

The phone lines were still inoperable and, outside, the snowfall had increased again. Other than the occasional hardy soul willing to brave the Arctic conditions in order to satisfy a nicotine craving, the foyer was generally quiet. Haddington-Smythe had settled back in the chair, and picked up the book he had retrieved from the library earlier; 'Sir Hubert Investigates: A Christmas Mystery', a Victorian-set detective thriller. Haddington-Smythe thoroughly enjoyed the 'Sir Hubert Investigates' series of books. He enjoyed the romanticised depiction of Victorian England which appealed to him on a subconscious level. He liked that the crimes, by today's standards, were relatively 'tame' (today's generation, obsessed with gore and violence on television and film, seemed to be entertained by the most horrific of acts!) and that, the main character, Sir Hubert, was a gentlemen who relied on his intelligence to solve the mystery, never resorting to violence or profanity, always dignified.

Haddington-Smythe emitted a contented sigh as he opened the book and resumed reading, allowing himself to be absorbed into this world which, for all its obvious shortcomings, had so many redeeming features.

As Marie glanced around, she spotted a 'criminal' (the stereo-typical striped top, full face-mask depicting a snarling, old man, missing a couple of teeth, hiding behind a lone ranger-type mask, large sack-cloth bag labelled 'swag' draped over his shoulder, gloved hands) and wished she had gotten that costume. She also spotted 'Spider-Man', Dennis the Menace, a former U.S. President and Marilyn Monroe. As well as that, there were also pirates, at least two other elves, a snowman, a couple of cowboys and much more.

"Hey, how come there are other elves?" Marie shouted to JT.

"Some costumes, they have more than one, I guess," JT answered.

Beneath the mask, her face hot, Marie wondered if she could somehow sneak off. If JT was not paying too much attention, he would see other elves in the ballroom and, perhaps, assume Marie was mingling. Okay, he may not believe that but, unless he confronted the elves and removed their masks, he could not be certain. After all, they looked about the same size as her. "Trixie!" JT said, waving his hand in front of Marie's face.

"Oh, um, er, sorry," Marie answered. "What did you say?"

"I just asked if you wanted a drink," JT called back. "I think they will be serving food soon and I thought I would just get myself an aperitif to, you know, get in the spirit of things."

Marie thought to herself that the kind of spirit JT was trying to get into was probably about 12% proof. She said, "Um, maybe just a soft drink, thanks."

"Okay," JT replied. "Look, grab a couple of seats at that table over there and I will be right back." JT fought his way through the crowded dance floor, shouting "Merry Christmas!" and "Ho, ho, ho!" as he went.

A moment later, the song faded and the DJ spoke into his microphone, "Well, I hope all this partying has made you hungry as the food is about to be served. Why don't you all find yourselves a seat, pull a cracker, if you haven't already done so, and rest your legs. I promise you, the rest of the evening will be even more exciting!"

As people wandered to tables, the DJ played music, at a lower volume, as the ballroom lit up. Marie went to the table JT had indicated and sat down, making sure the seat next to her was kept available for him when he returned from the bar.

Food was now being served and Marie noticed how most people, in order to try and maintain their anonymity, only pulled their masks up to just above their mouths in order to eat or drink, then dropped the masks back into place so they could see again.

JT reappeared at that moment carrying two drinks; a fruit juice for Marie and his favoured double vodka.

"I see Santa plans on getting very jolly," Marie said sardonically.

"It's a party," JT replied. "It's Christmas!"

At their table, they were joined by Albert Einstein, one of the Teletubbies (Marie did not wish to ask which one), a mime artist, a cowboy and Abraham Lincoln.

JT introduced himself as Father Christmas and Marie as one of his little helpers, Trixie. Everyone else followed suit and avoided using their real names. Between the music, the hubbub of conversation and everything else, Marie could not even be sure if the people were male or female. She might have assumed

'Albert Einstein' was male but the greatly-exaggerated, cod-German accent made it impossible to know for sure.

As the ball was underway, a shadowy figure had crept through the hotel until it reached a door marked 'staff only'. Seemingly undeterred by this, it produced a lock pick and, holding it between gloved fingers, worked the lock until a soft 'click' indicated the door was now unlocked. A quick glance around to make sure it was unobserved and the figure passed through the doorway, softly closing the door behind it. It ascended a flight of steps and reached another door, this one unlocked. Opening the door, the figure found itself in a large attic, used as storage for all sorts of stuff. In one corner, there were piles of boxes marked 'Records' while, in another, there was an old, dented filing cabinet. There were some crates as well as a couple of chests which were overflowing with old clothes.

Ignoring the clutter, the figure crept past everything, a tiny flash-light providing enough illumination to avoid tripping over anything. At one end of the attic there were three small skylights. The figure stopped at the nearest one and unlatched it, giving it a small push. It refused to move, probably never having being opened in years, the wooden frame slightly warped after years of exposure to the elements. The figure pressed both hands against the bottom of the skylight and pushed as hard as it could, straining, until, finally, there was a slow, groaning creaking noise as it lifted up. Locking it in place, the figure reached down into the bag it had been carrying, pulling from it a length of rope with a grappling hook affixed to one end.

Near the skylight, there was a wooden beam, one of several which criss-crossed the apex of the attic. The figure approached the beam, then, satisfied at its sturdiness, wrapped the end of the rope around it, the grappling hook securing it in place. Once done, the figure strode back to the skylight and threw the rest of the rope through the opening. Finally, it dragged a crate across and climbed onto the top of it so that it was able to more easily climb through the skylight.

There was no wind at the moment and the snow was still falling, the thick, lazy snowflakes drifting down from the sky above. Shivering slightly, the figure sat on the edge of the skylight, the rope between its fingers, slowly turning, careful not to slide on the snow covered roof slanting down.

Finally, happy that the rope was secure and its footing was steady, the figure slowly lowered itself down the roof until it felt the guttering beneath its feet. Pausing briefly, the figure glanced over the edge of the roof and saw the snow-covered ground far below. If nothing else, if this went horribly wrong, the snow would provide a softer landing than the ground beneath it.

Holding its breath, it lowered itself over the side, hands firmly clasping the rope, inch by inch for what seemed an eternity until it reached a window ledge. With its feet wedged at each end of the ledge, the figure released one hand, reached into a pocket and produced a pen-knife. Slotting the blade into the small gap where the top half of the window met the bottom half, the blade was wiggled about until it dislodged the clasp keeping the window shut. That done, the figure reached down and pulled up the bottom half of the window, grateful that it moved much easier than the skylight window.

Kicking back slightly, the figure stretched its legs forward as it swung back towards the open window, letting go of the rope as its body crossed the threshold, landing with a slight thump. Jumping to its feet, the figure waited a few seconds, letting its eyes adjust to the dark room. Happy the room was empty, the figure produced the tiny flash-light again and, keeping the beam pointing to the floor, crept across the room. Passing a mirror, it paused briefly as it saw its reflection; the striped top, the mask with the face of a hardened crook, minus a couple of teeth, wearing a lone ranger-type mask. All that was missing was the swag bag which was currently up in the attic. Turning away from the mirror, the figure shone the beam of light slowly across the floor, stopping at the side of the bed. Now, if the information was accurate, this would be a piece of cake. On the bedside cabinet, there was a small safe provided by the hotel but the figure ignored this choosing instead to drop to its knees and reach under the bed. It moved its arm about until it hit something.

A bit of fumbling and it grabbed onto a handle and pulled a small attaché case from beneath the bed. It had a combination lock, however, like the safe, the figure was hoping this would not be an issue. Clicking the latches on the case, the figure was rewarded with a satisfying sound as the latches popped up, allowing the attaché case to be opened. The figure shone the light inside and was pleased to see the sparkling diamond necklace, bracelet and pendant. Their combined value was rumoured to be in seven figures, even allowing for fencing them on the black market. The figure reached in and scooped up the jewellery and slipped the items into a small pouch it took from beneath its striped top. Stuffing the pouch in its pocket, the attaché case was closed and slid back under the bed. The figure hurried back to the window, grabbed onto the rope and pulled itself out, carefully closed the window behind it and proceeded to haul itself back up the rope, hand over hand. Naturally, the figure could not cover all its tracks; there would be damp footprints in the room and it was impossible to close the latch on the window once outside. Still, by the time the theft was discovered, the figure would be nowhere near the scene of the crime and would be no more suspected than anyone else.

With a grunt, it pulled itself up over the guttering and got back to the skylight, lowered itself through the window and onto the crate then pulled the rope in behind it. With an effort, it pulled the skylight closed. Hurriedly bundling the rope into the swag bag, and checking the pouch was still safely tucked in its pocket, the figure left the attic, pausing at the door, listening carefully for any sounds from the other side before letting itself out.

With the corridor empty, the figure hurried away, thinking what a merry Christmas it was going to be.

Chapter 11

Beryl Lambert held her mask up to her eyes and peered through it, looking at the people on the dance floor. No one seemed to dance properly nowadays, she thought wistfully. It was all just jumping about and waving arms.

"Blasted youth, eh?" Sir Henry said.

Beryl turned to look at the man who, honestly, was not much older than some of the people dancing. He liked to affect an air of… colonialism, for want of a better word, Beryl thought, as if the British Empire was still a force to be reckoned with. Like Beryl, he was not wearing a costume but did have his old military uniform on, the buttons polished to perfection, a row of medals hanging proudly.

"I fear those days are far behind me, Sir Henry," the old widow replied. "In fact, even watching them is tiring me out!"

"Poppycock, old girl!" Sir Henry declared. "I am sure you could show these young pups a thing or two about proper dancing."

"You are too kind, Sir Henry," Beryl said with a smile. For a moment, she grew thoughtful. She still wasn't sure about her earlier revelation but, perhaps, Sir Henry would be a good sounding board. Yes, he has a sensible head on his shoulders, she thought. He will advise me what is best. She was about to speak when there was a screech of feedback as someone spoke into a microphone.

"Good evening, Alpine Lodge!" Emma squealed from the stage. "Are we having a good time?" There was a chorus of agreement and applause which seemed to fuel Emma's enthusiasm. "I don't know about you but I just love balls, right? The bigger the better!" She giggled into the microphone. "Great big, extravagant balls. I just love them!"

At that moment, Jane Franks hurried on to the stage and quickly removed the microphone from Emma's hand. With a forced smile, she said, "Thank you, Emma. So, as Emma was saying, we are all having fun so let's have some more. The DJ will work his magic and we want to see everyone back on the dance floor. And, just for a bit of fun, we will pick out some people; it may be for your costume, your dancing, who knows? But there are some prizes up for grabs! Good luck, everyone!"

As Jane passed the microphone back to the DJ and tactfully dragged Emma off the stage, there was more cheering and applause from the audience.

"Okay, let's have another Christmas classic," the DJ announced as 'Merry Christmas, Everybody' burst from the speakers.

"Sir Henry?" Beryl said loudly.

"What's that, old girl?" he asked, leaning over.

"I wonder if I could get your advice on a… delicate matter," Beryl said.

"Certainly," Sir Henry replied. "Only too happy to help."

"Oh, good, thank you," Beryl said. "Perhaps later, when it is a bit quieter."

"Of course," Sir Henry answered. "Listen, you sit here and enjoy yourself. I will toodle along to the bar and get us a libation. Sherry?"

"Please," Beryl said.

Sir Henry got up and walked off leaving Beryl alone at the table. She sat and watched all the colourful characters dancing, or mingling, moving between tables. Without realising it, she found herself tapping her foot in time with the music.

At the bar, there was a queue of people waiting to be served. Behind the bar, Vanessa and two other people were taking orders, somehow managing to do their job amidst the chaos of loud music and multiple conversations, moving back and forth behind the bar without bumping into one another or spilling any drinks.

As Sir Henry waited, he could hear the conversation taking place immediately in front of him.

"What can I get you, sir?" the man behind the bar asked.

"Oh, please, you don't need to call me sir. I'm Stanley," the customer, dressed like Friar Tuck said jovially. "I will have a glass of tonic water and a carrot juice, if you would be so kind."

"Of course, sir, I mean, Stanley," the barman said, reaching for glasses.

Stanley turned and saw Sir Henry. "Good evening," he said with a smile. "It is quite an event, is it not?"

"Yes, I'll say," Sir Henry agreed.

Stanley introduced himself then collected his drinks and excused himself as he carried the drinks back through to the ballroom where his wife was waiting for him.

After a couple of minutes, Vanessa came across to Sir Henry.

"What will it be, Sir Henry?" she asked.

"A gin and tonic and a sherry, please," Sir Henry replied.

"Coming right up," Vanessa said quickly sorting the two drinks. Sir Henry handed over a £10 note and told Vanessa to put the change in the charity tin sitting at the bar. "That's very kind of you, Sir Henry, thank you," she said.

"Well, it is Christmas, after all," he replied with a wink.

He lifted the two glasses and weaved his way back through the sea of bodies to the table where Beryl was waiting, still on her own. Her head was slightly drooped. Sir Henry marvelled at the way some people could just nod off no matter how much noise there was.

"Here you go, old girl," he said, sitting the glass on the table. "This should help you get your second wind."

Beryl did not respond. Goodness, a right sound sleeper, Sir Henry thought. He leaned across and gently shook her shoulder. "Wakey-wakey, old girl," he said. "Here is your…"

He did not finish his sentence. Instead of waking her up, shaking Beryl's shoulder resulted in her tipping forwards and sideways, falling to the floor. A startled scream nearby drew more attention to the scene and seconds later the music was silenced as it became apparent there was something wrong.

"Beryl!" Sir Henry said frantically kneeling down beside the elderly woman, cradling her head. Looking up, he cried, "We need help here! Is there a doctor here?"

As people stood watching, someone stepped forward. "I'm a doctor," a woman's voice said as she lifted her mask off. It was

Pamela Stepford. She knelt down beside Beryl and reached for her wrist, checking her pulse.

Beryl's eyes flickered open and she looked up at Sir Henry.

"Oh," she said weakly. "Sir Henry."

"Don't speak, old girl," he replied. "Save your strength."

"No, please… important," Beryl murmured.

"Oh, my God!" Pamela said as she pulled her other hand back which was covered in blood which was pooling beneath Beryl. "I… I think she has been stabbed!"

"Sir Henry…" Beryl whispered.

"What is it, old girl?" Sir Henry said, leaning down, putting his ear to Beryl's mouth.

"Toby," she murmured. "Toby…"

"Toby? What about him?"

"It's Toby," she said again, barely audible. "He's… not fat…"

There was a last exhalation then her body went limp. By now, Jane Franks had rushed up carrying a first aid kit but Pamela just shook her head slightly.

Sir Henry sat in Haddington-Smythe's office, along with JT and Marie, still in their costumes.

Marie had removed her mask and JT had removed his beard and hat. Haddington-Smythe sat in his chair, his complexion white, his hands shaking slightly.

Jane stepped into the office and said, "All the guests have returned to their rooms."

"Thank you, Jane," Haddington-Smythe said. "What about Dr Stepford?"

"She is cleaning herself up," Jane informed him. She should be here shortly."

"Okay, thank you," the manager said. "Um, I am aware that Emma is rather… merry. Could you be so kind as to cover the front desk? If any guests do come down, please ask them to return to their rooms until morning. Don't say anything about what has happened."

"Of course," Jane said and left the office.

Silence filled the room. Haddington-Smythe was tapping nervously on his desk, Sir Henry was scowling, Marie was biting her lip and JT was lost in thought.

A minute later, Pamela Stepford entered the office. She had washed the blood off her hands although there were flecks of it on her costume.

Sitting in one of the empty seats, she said, "It appears she was stabbed with a long, thin object."

As Pamela folded her arms, JT spotted something on her costume. "Excuse me," he said as he stepped closer to get a better look at the mark.

"What's the matter?" Pamela asked, puzzled.

"That mark, how did you get it?" JT asked.

"Oh, I have no idea," Pamela said, surprised. "I'm sure it wasn't there earlier. Maybe I brushed against something when I was trying to help Mrs Lambert. Why?"

JT did not answer, except to mutter, "Hmm."

"But why?" Marie asked. "Why would someone want to kill a harmless old lady?"

"She was trying to say something," Pamela said, looking at Sir Henry.

"Really?" JT asked quickly. "What?"

"I don't know." Sir Henry sighed. "It did not make much sense."

"Sir Henry, please, it might be important," JT said.

"Well, it was something about Toby," Sir Henry said.

"What about Toby?" Haddington-Smythe asked. "Was it about his death?"

"She, er, well, she, ah, said he's not fat," Sir Henry said uncertainly.

"What?" Marie asked, confused.

"Those were her exact words," Sir Henry said. "I'm sure of it."

"We know he wasn't fat," Haddington-Smythe said, puzzled. "What an odd thing to say."

"I'm afraid the old girl may have been a bit batty, after all," Sir Henry said grudgingly. "However, I would appreciate if this was kept quiet. She does not deserve to have her good name tarnished by cruel comments from people who did not know her."

"Of course, Sir Henry, of course," Haddington-Smythe quickly agreed.

"Look, I don't care if she was batty or not," JT said bluntly. "I don't believe in coincidence."

"What are you saying?" Pamela asked.

"I'm saying," JT answered, "that this murder is obviously connected to Toby's."

"I was only gone a few minutes," Sir Henry murmured. "Just a few minutes."

"All those people," Marie said. "People coming and going, everyone dressed up, disguised. It could have been anyone."

December 25th

"Um, that's midnight," Marie said hesitantly. "Merry Christmas?"

"Ahem, yes, of course," Haddington-Smythe said. "Merry Christmas."

There was a muted echoing of this sentiment from the other people in the office. Under the circumstances, none of them were feeling particularly merry but no one wanted to be rude by ignoring the customary festive salutation.

"Well, now that is out of the way," Pamela said, "can someone please tell me what on Earth is going on here?"

"I would also like to know the answer to that question," Haddington-Smythe added. "One can safely assume now that the cat is well and truly out the bag. Everyone will know Mrs Lambert was the victim of foul play."

"It is not too much of a leap of logic to assume Toby's death was also the result of foul play," Marie said.

"Young Toby was murdered?" Sir Henry asked, shocked.

"I'm afraid so," the manager conceded.

"You mean to say, there is a murderer prowling the corridors out there and you never said a word?" Sir Henry's voice got progressively louder as he spoke.

"Please, Sir Henry," Haddington-Smythe implored. "You have to understand, we did not want to cause a panic."

"What was more concerning for you; causing a panic or damaging the Alpine Lodge's reputation?" Haddington-Smythe looked beseechingly to JT for some kind of support.

"Okay, listen," JT said to Sir Henry, "Gerald was acting on my advice. It was of no benefit to anyone for Toby's murder to become common knowledge."

"Excuse me," Sir Henry sneered at JT, "but who exactly are you?"

"Jack Thomas, private detective, at your service," JT answered. "Perhaps you have heard of me?"

"No, I'm afraid not," Sir Henry answered. As Marie stifled a giggle, Sir Henry continued, "I have heard some chatter from one or two people, something about 'new money' from investments? There was some talk of solving a murder but I just assumed you were some kind of dilettante."

"I take offence at that!" JT said indignantly. "I have never indulged in that kind of lewd behaviour!"

"He means amateur," Marie whispered in his ear.

"Oh, right," JT mumbled. Then he turned to Sir Henry and said, "I take offence at that! I am a highly-respected, widely-known investigator. I specialise in murder investigations and have yet to take on a case I could not solve."

"And how many people have to die before you catch the culprit?" Sir Henry asked snidely.

"The average is about three," Marie answered without thinking.

"Not helping," JT muttered softly to her.

"Well, good," Sir Henry said. "So, as soon as someone else gets bumped off, we can expect you to reveal the killer, eh? Jolly good show, what?"

"Sir Henry, please," Haddington-Smythe said. "This is not helping…"

"Helping? This isn't helping Beryl, old boy, is it?" Sir Henry glared at Haddington-Smythe. "You know I play golf with the Trustees of this place? Rest assured, I will be making my feelings known to them once this debacle is over. Do not be surprised if you find yourself looking for new employment in the New Year, Gerald."

With that, he turned and stormed out the office, slamming the door behind him.

"Well, er, that could have gone better," Haddington-Smythe said, wiping his brow.

"Try not to worry, Gerald," JT said brightly. "Things might turn out okay in the end."

"Really?" the manager asked sceptically. "How, pray tell, is that even remotely possible?"

140

"Well, the killer may bump him off next," JT said with the barest hint of a grin.

"I'm sorry, Mr Thomas, JT," Pamela said. "I do not find that funny in the least. This is a very serious matter and should not be treated so… frivolously."

"Sorry, Pamela," JT replied. "In my line of work, you find it helps to have a gallows sense of humour."

"Well, not in my line of work," Pamela responded.

"Um, now that, uh, that is settled, shouldn't we get back to the question of why someone murdered a defenceless, old lady?" Marie asked, trying to steer things back on track.

"Okay, let's see," JT said, thinking aloud. "What, if anything, connects Toby to Mrs Lambert?"

"The Alpine Lodge," Haddington-Smythe answered immediately.

"Anything else?" JT prompted.

"I really can't imagine them mixing in the same social circles," Haddington-Smythe said. "Sorry, don't mean to sound like a snob."

"No, it's a fair point," JT agreed. "But the Alpine Lodge could link a lot of people, if that were the connection. Hmm, what else?" He paused, thinking. "Okay, let's try a different tack; forget about Toby, is there any reason someone would want to kill Mrs Lambert?"

"Ah, well, um," Haddington-Smythe said, awkwardly fidgeting in his seat.

"Come on, Gerald," JT said sharply. "I can't solve this if I don't have all the facts."

"Well, there is her jewellery," he answered.

"Jewellery?" Marie repeated. "What kind?"

"Her late husband, before his passing, had acquired for her a diamond necklace, bracelet and pendant," Haddington-Smythe explained. "They are quite valuable, I believe."

"Seven-figures valuable?" JT asked.

"Ahem, yes, I believe so."

JT whistled in appreciation. "Well, that's a helluva motive, I guess. And she had them here, at the hotel?"

"I believe she took them with her everywhere," Haddington-Smythe answered. "It was the last gift her husband bestowed upon her. My understanding is that they held more sentimental value, for that reason, to Mrs Lambert than monetary value."

"Does the hotel have some kind of safety deposit facilities for high value items?" Marie asked.

"Yes," Pamela answered, before the manager could speak. "All the rooms have their own safes for the guests' use."

"Oh, yes, I remember now." Marie nodded. "We have one in our suite, a small, steel box with an electronic keypad, like an ATM keypad. Sorry, I don't have to, er, worry about high value things."

"And, if the guests wish to use it, they are given the pass code," Haddington-Smythe explained.

"So, you have a record of all the codes?" JT asked.

"Well, not exactly," Haddington-Smythe replied. "Naturally, for security, the guests are encouraged to change the PIN. They would then inform us of the new PIN when they check out so we can provide this to the next guest using it."

"Hmm," JT said again.

At the front desk, Jane handed Emma another cup of coffee. Still dressed in her French maid's costume, Emma sipped at the coffee. "Urgh!" she said in protest.

"Drink it," Jane ordered.

"It's vile," Emma objected.

"It's strong, bitter and black," Jane replied. "Just like my heart. Now, drink up. It will clear your head. How much did you have, anyway?"

"Uh, I'm not sure," Emma admitted. "I was kind of letting my hair down. God, did I really say all those things?"

"About balls?" Jane asked innocently. "'Fraid so." She smirked, then patted the younger woman's shoulder. "Don't worry, after what happened to poor Mrs Lambert, I don't think anyone will remember your performance!"

"Do you know what's happening?" Emma asked.

Jane stared across the foyer in the direction of the manager's office. She had seen the people going in. So far, apart from Sir Henry who had stormed out about ten minutes earlier, everyone was still in there. She said, "I have no idea. They are still in there, though."

"I can't believe there's been a murder," Emma said, taking another sip of coffee and scrunching her face in revulsion.

"Murders," Jane said. "Don't forget Toby."

"You mean, that wasn't an accident?" Emma asked.

"No, I'm afraid not," Jane answered. "Mr Haddington-Smythe had hoped to keep it quiet so as not to alarm the guests. I guess that won't be possible, now."

At that moment, the elevator dinged and Valentina stepped out. She walked over to the desk. She was fully dressed, wearing a thick coat, and was holding a packet of cigarettes.

"Oh, hi," Emma said. "Trouble sleeping?"

"Yes, I have troubles," the young woman replied. "I tell Mr Smythe very peculiars when I find keys. Now, this. Nice old lady killed dead in front of everyone!" She shivered as she recalled the murder of Beryl Lambert. "I too scared to sleeps!" she proclaimed. "Maybe I killed next!"

"Uh, right," Emma said uncertainly. "Well, ah, I'm sure Mr Haddington-Smythe is dealing with the situation."

"I not sure," Valentina said with a shrug. "I hopes detective man, Mr JT, catch killer but maybes killer too clever for detective man. I was going to stop smokes but my nerves are tight like piano string."

"Piano wire," Jane corrected but Valentina had already turned away and was headed for the door.

"Huh, I doubt Valentina is in danger from the killer," Emma muttered.

"Unless the killer is Mr Nicotine," Jane added with a smile.

Nearby, at the entrance to the stairwell, a figure lurked. Peter Tenor stood listening to the three women talking, standing unobserved in the shadows. As Valentina walked off, he lingered for another moment then crept back up the stairs before he was spotted.

Rupert paced in his room, back and forth, worriedly wringing his hands together. He had already felt under suspicion after the incident with the barman and, now, a murder in the middle of the ballroom! Those people who perhaps had their doubts about him would be quick to point the finger of blame, he was sure. He had finally changed his mind about going to the ball, feeling isolated, instead sulking in his room.

At least, that is what he wanted everyone to think. Unfortunately, unless he admitted what he did he was left without an alibi. Even if he did admit it, it still did not give him an alibi. The only thing that might help him was the fact that most people were wearing masks so others may also find it difficult to prove where they were. He had heard Philip, Theresa and Sophia discussing Beryl's murder loudly when they returned to their room. Damn Sophia, why did she have to say he had been out of the room the night of the barman's death? This was all her fault. If she could just do what was expected of her, for once in her spoiled little life!

Okay, he would just try and behave normally and deal with any suspicions as and when he encountered them.

"I think we need to see Mrs Lambert's room," JT decided.

"Can't it wait until morning?" Marie said, stifling a yawn. "I'm beat."

"We need to know if the jewellery is there," JT replied. "Gerald, could you take us there, please?"

"Of course, uh, anything to help," Haddington-Smythe said getting to his feet.

"Did Mrs Lambert get a note of the previous PIN for the safe?" JT asked.

"Yes, naturally," Haddington-Smythe responded. "However, I think it highly unlikely she will have availed herself of it."

"In that case, can you tell us what it is, please," JT said. "If she hasn't changed it, we should be able to open it up."

A few minutes later, Haddington-Smythe led JT, Marie and Pamela, who had decided to tag along, to Beryl Lambert's room, which was located on the top floor at the opposite side of the building to the suite JT was occupying.

Taking out the master electronic key card, Haddington-Smythe swiped it and they heard the click as the door unlocked. Turning the handle, he entered the room, switched on the lights and beckoned the others in.

Glancing around, Marie observed it was similar to JT's suite. The main part of the suite, apart from the standard furniture, was quite bare. They walked into the bedroom and immediately spotted the small safe. As Haddington-Smythe entered the PIN,

Marie had opened the wardrobe and was peering in but could not see much other than a small selection of clothes hanging there and one medium sized suitcase sitting on the floor.

There was a clacking sound and the safe door swung open and Marie turned to peer into it along with everyone else. "Empty," JT muttered.

They started looking around and it was not long before they found the attaché case which opened to reveal it was also empty. JT peered closely at the small combination dials next to the clasps. "Hmm, dusty," he murmured. "I don't think these have been used in a long time, if ever." He studied the clasps, holding the case close to his face. "Tweezers!" he said, waving his free hand.

"I don't have any on me," Marie answered. "I'm not exactly dressed for this, you know."

"Right, right, sorry," JT murmured.

"Here, I have some," Pamela said, passing them across.

Taking the tweezers, JT carefully pulled at two tiny threads which had been caught in one of the clasps. "There," he said, holding them up, squinting at them. "Looks like black and white, or possibly charcoal and white. Marie, check all her clothes, see if you can find something in these colours. We know she wasn't wearing black and white earlier."

"You think these came from the murderer?" Pamela asked.

"Maybe from the thief," JT answered.

"Surely the murderer and the thief is one and the same man," Haddington-Smythe protested.

"What do you mean, man?" JT asked, suddenly turning to face the manager.

"Well, er, that is, ah, it is just, uh, this is not the kind of behaviour one expects from a lady, is it?"

"Maybe, maybe not," JT answered. "As for your other assertion, you may be right. On the other hand, if the thief was successful in stealing the diamonds, why bother killing her? Why draw more attention to yourself?"

"And what does any of this have to do with Toby?" Haddington-Smythe asked, frustration evident in his tone.

"JT, nothing here which matches those colours," Marie announced.

JT started pacing about the room, lost in thought. Then, staring at the carpet, he looked at the impressions left by their footsteps. Unfortunately, because they had all been stepping back and forth, he could not be sure if any impressions belonged to the thief. He turned to HaddingtonSmythe and asked, "Is it possible to gain access to a room without having the key card?"

"I suppose the door could be forced," the manager answered.

"No other way?" JT persisted.

"Naturally, the master key card opens every lock but I assure you that is either in my safe or on my person!" Haddington-Smythe said indignantly.

JT looked about then walked over to the large window which, he noticed, was unclasped. He raised the window up, ignoring the chill and snow outside, and spotted what looked like partial footprints in either corner of the window ledge, the snow only just starting to cover them.

"I'll be damned!" he whispered, then closed the window and turned and faced the group. "This is how he got in, through the window. Marie…?"

"Don't tell me, you want me to go down and check the ground beneath the window and see if there are tracks in the snow?" Marie said.

"If you hurry, you won't have too much time to feel the cold," JT said with an encouraging smile. "Go and work your magic, Trixie!"

As Marie crossed the foyer, she saw Emma and Jane sitting at the front desk, drinking coffee and chatting. Marie quickly banished the thought of the steaming hot, rich coffee from her mind and braced herself for her foray outside. She had stopped briefly at their suite and grabbed a small torch and a thick coat.

She pushed the revolving door and felt the temperature plummet. Regretting the lack of gloves, she switched on the torch and started walking round the building. At first, the going was relatively easy as there had been a path of sorts cleared along the front of the building. However, as she rounded a corner, she found herself faced with snow which was almost two feet deep. With difficulty, she waded into it thankful she did not have much further to go. Looking up, she could see JT leaning out the window looking for her. Nearing the spot directly beneath the window, she shone the torch around but could not see any impressions left in the snow from feet, ladders or anything else.

With her feet starting to get numb, she turned and trudged back to the hotel's entrance.

"Brrr!" she said through chattering teeth as she stepped back into the foyer, stamping her feet and brushing snow off her clothes. With a puzzled look from Emma and Jane, Marie hurried to the elevator and returned to Beryl's room. "Nothing!" she declared, her cheeks red.

"How can that be?" Haddington-Smythe asked. "If they gained egress through the window, surely they would have needed some sort of ladder."

"Unless they climbed down from the roof," JT reasoned.

"They are still on the premises, then?" the manager asked, a worried look on his face.

"Look outside, Gerald," JT said simply. "They, whoever 'they' are, have been here since before the blizzard started."

Haddington-Smythe gulped.

"Well, I don't think there is much else we can do at the moment," Pamela decided. "I think we should try and get some sleep." She glanced at her wrist watch. "They will be serving breakfast in a few hours."

Chapter 12

The atmosphere in the ballroom was quite subdued. There had been various exchanges of festive greetings but, with the events of the previous night still dominating the conversation, a dark pall seemed to hang over everyone. One or two people had approached Sir Henry and offered their condolences. Sir Henry had learned from Haddington-Smythe about the theft which only increased his ire towards the manager. As he made his feelings known, rather loudly, some people had overheard some of it. As a result, as well as Beryl's murder, mostly everyone now knew about the theft. Along with the various conversations speculating on the person or persons responsible, people were starting to query the death of Toby. They were now more suspicious and less inclined to believe it was an accident. Feelings ranged from indignant to fearful as people eyed each other with distrust.

When Rupert entered the room, several people fell quiet. Heads turned and stared as he crossed to his table and sat down. Sophia was already at the table, along with her parents, Peter and Lucy Tenor, and JT and Marie.

"Good morning, everyone," Rupert said. Then, trying to force a small smile, added, "Merry Christmas, too, I suppose, although it does rather seem the festive spirit has bypassed this place." Peter and Lucy returned Rupert's 'Merry Christmas', but Sophia, Philip and Theresa pointedly ignored him. Maria mumbled something which may have been 'Merry Christmas', but Rupert could not be sure. JT was more enthusiastic.

"So, er, you're the detective," Rupert said with forced cheer. "Maybe you can explain what the blazes is going on in this place, eh? Look at everybody, they are all scared to touch their food in case it has been poisoned!" He forced a small chuckle.

"That is wholly inappropriate, Rupert," Philip spoke up. "A woman died here last night, was murdered, in fact. Is it any wonder people are on edge? And you make jokes!"

"Rupert, I deal with these situations using humour, too," JT said reassuringly. "As to your question, well, as much as I hate to admit it, I am still in the dark."

"Now, no need to be coy," Rupert persisted. "I mean, surely you must know something?"

"Where were you last night?" Marie asked suddenly.

"Ahem," Rupert said, clearing his throat. "Well, it is like this, since you helped poison my fiancée against me, I did not feel like attending last evening's little soiree. I stayed in my room and got rather well acquainted with the mini-bar. Not that it is any of your business!"

"So, you were alone?" Marie asked defiantly.

"Now, you listen here, young lady," Rupert began, raising his voice.

"Don't listen to her," JT said kindly. "Father Christmas left her a lump of coal in her stocking and she has been in a foul mood all morning!"

"I should not have snapped," Rupert said, "however, there is only so much one can take, you understand? The whispers as I pass by people, the not-so-subtle stares…"

"It's Human nature to think the worst," JT said sympathetically. "People jump to conclusions, without having all the facts, and that's it, their minds are made up. Honestly, I would be surprised if any jury rendered a verdict based solely on evidence."

"You may be right," Rupert said. "I suppose that makes it even more important to me that you get to the bottom of this."

As people ate their breakfast, and the muted conversations continued, Marie whispered to JT, "I still think he is involved, somehow."

"Who, Rupert?" JT whispered back. "There is something… off with him, I'll admit. Like a pair of ill-fitting boxer shorts, he rubs me up the wrong way, but murder? I don't think so."

As Marie tried to purge her mind of the image of JT in boxer shorts, ill-fitting or otherwise, she accepted that JT was more qualified in these matters but reserved the right to hold onto her doubts in the meantime.

At a nearby table, Magenta and Scarlet were engaged in a whispered conversation of their own. Like a lot of other people, they had noticed Rupert enter the ballroom and, immediately, he had become the focus of talk.

"Just look at him!" Scarlet said. "He's just too smooth, in fact I'd say he's smarmy. Look at his eyes, too. Definitely shifty."

"I agree," Magenta replied softly. "Honestly, what that girl sees in him, I have no idea. Mind you, she does not exactly look like a catch, does she?"

"Probably can't afford to be too choosy," Scarlet said with a cruel smile. "Anyway, I hear they are no longer talking."

"Tres awkward," Magenta smirked looking across at Rupert and Sophia.

"Girls, please," Gemima said. "I am sorry to interrupt, and I don't mean to eavesdrop, but is that kind of talk really necessary? Passing judgement on other people's lives and sounding as if you are enjoying it. At this time of year, especially."

"Well, excuse us!" Scarlet said mockingly.

"Scarlet," Magenta said in a warning tone.

"No, Magenta," Scarlet said stubbornly. "I am fed up being criticised by this woman! Telling us off for judging other people? Is that not what she is doing with us?"

"Now, please," Stanley began.

"No," Scarlet said. "If you and your wife disapprove of us, well, fine, that is your opinion and I suppose you are entitled to it. However, I am entitled to have a private conversation with my sister without being lectured by some old woman who is stuck in Victorian times!"

"Really!" Stanley said.

"Oh, don't you 'really' me," Scarlet said, getting to her feet. "You are just as bad. You are both nothing more than hypocrites, actually!"

With that, she stormed off leaving Stanley and Gemima speechless. Harold and Prunella both fixed their attention on their breakfast while their two children were listening to the heated outburst and giggling.

Calmly folding her napkin and placing it on the table, Magenta stood up and said, "Well, when she's right, she's right."

With an insincere smile, she excused herself and followed her sister out of the ballroom.

Stanley was patting Gemima's hand. "It's all right," he said. "Considering how they have gossiped about other people, it is not surprising they are so ill-mannered."

"Oh, Stanley," Gemima said, wiping at her eyes. "What is it with the youth of today? Why are they so cruel?"

"Now, now, dear, it is not all the youth," Stanley said. "I think, with these two young ladies, they are nothing more than spoiled girls. Look, you are upset. Come on, let's go back to our room and you can rest for a while."

Gemima and Stanley stood up and, holding hands, they walked slowly out the ballroom.

After breakfast, JT decided to take another look at the cellar.

"What are you looking for?" Marie asked.

"Nothing in particular," JT replied. "I just want to see if anything jumps out at me, something that may help join the pieces together."

He sent Marie back to their suite so she could continue looking over his case notes and told her he would join her shortly.

At the cellar, one of the hotel's staff was in the process of bringing supplies up to restock the bar. JT explained why he was there and asked the man if he could have perhaps ten minutes alone just to study the cellar.

Now, standing at the top of the stairs, beside the open door, JT looked down and tried to imagine the scene. Toby would have come to the cellar, as he had done numerous times before, unlocked the door then... JT looked to his left and could see the front desk and part of the foyer. He could not see who was sitting behind the desk therefore that person could not see him. So, unless they happened to stand up, they would not have seen Toby or noticed if someone else was there. On his other side was the open door blocking his view of the corridor. Unless he stepped back, he could not see if there was anyone there. Was that how the murderer caught Toby unaware? Did he or she approach from that side, unobserved, and surprise him?

Suddenly, the door swung into JT and, before he could react, he was flung forward, arms flailing, losing his balance. He felt himself tipping forward, unable to halt his momentum, saw the stairs rushing up at him as he tumbled down. Everything spun around him as he crashed off the stairs, his legs twisting as he landed on his back. Unconsciously, his hands reached out and he managed to grab onto the handrail with one hand, stopping his tumbling descent.

Breathing heavily, his legs pointing up to the doorway, holding tightly to the handrail, JT remained motionless for several seconds, his heart thumping in his chest. Slowly, carefully, he started to pull himself to his feet. At the top of the stairs, the door was opened by the man who had been bringing supplies up. When he saw JT, he hurried down and helped him up.

"Are you all right?" he asked. "What happened?"

"I… I'm not sure," JT answered, wincing in pain. "I was standing up there and the door…"

"Someone must have bumped into it," the man said. "I've warned management about that. They should have the door opened inwards or sort the hinges so it can swing round all the way to the wall."

"Did you see anyone up there?" JT asked.

"No, I was just coming back from the bar," the man replied. "Look, are you sure you are okay?"

Slowly, JT started hobbling up the stairs. "Yes," he said through gritted teeth. "Just a few… bumps and bruises."

JT entered the suite, still limping, looking slightly dishevelled and found Marie sitting on a sofa with sheaf of paper scattered around her as she scribbled notes on another sheet of paper. "Oh, that was quick," she said. "Listen, I was thinking about a catchphrase and… JT! What happened?"

She jumped to her feet and helped JT onto the sofa. He filled her in on his accident.

"My God!" she gasped. "You could have been killed!"

"The thought had crossed my mind," JT said. "Just like Toby."

"You think it was deliberate?" Marie asked.

"I told you, I don't believe in coincidence," JT answered. "Of course, I have no proof, but I suspect someone just tried to kill me."

"And there was no one else there?"

"According to the man working in the cellar, no," JT said doubtfully.

"Could he be lying?" Marie asked.

"I don't know," JT answered. "It might be worth speaking to Gerald about him, see if there is anything remotely dubious or suspicious."

"Does this mean you are getting close to solving this?" Marie wondered.

"It doesn't feel like it," JT said. "However, it does look like someone wants me off the case."

Sir Henry stood facing Haddington-Smythe, leaning forward, hands flat on the manager's desk, a determined look on his face.

"It's the only way!" he said angrily.

"I don't think I have the right…" Haddington-Smythe began.

"Don't talk to me about rights!" Sir Henry snapped. "We are stuck here with no chance of outside help for goodness knows how long. I, for one, am not content to sit here and let a murderer and a thief roam freely amongst us!"

"But…"

"No!" Sir Henry said emphatically. "Look, get that detective fellow to assist you, if you like."

"And if people object?" Haddington-Smythe asked desperately.

"If they have nothing to hide, they will be happy to co-operate," Sir Henry replied.

"But searching all their rooms?" the manager said.

"Look, you agree the thief is still here," Sir Henry said forcefully. "Therefore, Beryl's diamonds are here. You find them, you find the thief and the murderer. Case closed!"

"Er, perhaps we should speak to Mr Thomas about this," Haddington-Smythe said.

"Quite," Sir Henry agreed. "Get him down here, right now." Haddington-Smythe sighed.

Magenta and Scarlet sat in the bar, occupying a corner booth which afforded them a good view of everybody coming and going. It seemed as if the 'shell shock' was starting to wear off; people were livelier, more relaxed, behaving the way you would expect them to at Christmas. There were a few other people in the bar, either at tables or sitting at the bar. The bar staff were serving drinks, sharing laughs with the guests.

"It is a good thing that interfering old lady isn't here," Scarlet said archly. "Gosh, people enjoying themselves, having fun, have they no respect for the dead?"

"You shouldn't let her get to you, Scarlet," Magenta said.

"Oh, don't you worry your pretty little head, Magenta, honey," Scarlet said with a big smile. "She does not get to me in the least. In fact, I think I was getting to her! I definitely enjoyed sticking a pin in her sanctimonious balloon. Now, if we are lucky, they will request a different table."

"Here's to that," Magenta said, raising her glass.

"Another?" Scarlet asked, holding her now-empty glass aloft.

"Don't mind if I do," Magenta replied, tipping her glass back and swallowing the last of her drink.

In the next booth, Peter and Lucy Tenor sat with drinks but neither was drinking.

"What are you up to?" Lucy asked plaintively. "You keep disappearing without explanation."

"It's nothing you need to concern yourself with, Lucy, I swear," Peter said. "Honestly, it's nothing."

"Then why won't you tell me?" Lucy demanded. "You have been acting strange almost since the moment we arrived here. Now, people are getting murdered, diamonds have been stolen…"

"You can't think I had anything to do with any of that nonsense, surely?" Peter protested.

"A few days ago, I would have quite confidently said 'no' but now, well, now I am not so sure." Lucy sighed. "I'm afraid, Peter. Afraid for us, if I feel I can't trust you."

Peter gripped his glass tight, his knuckles turning white. His jaw moved as he opened then closed his mouth, unable to find the words Lucy needed to hear. He stared down at the table, giving his head a slight shake. "Listen, I promise you, I am not involved in murders or jewel thefts. You must believe me!" he said desperately.

Lucy opened her mouth to speak but Peter continued, "As for the other... stuff, I will explain everything, I promise. I just need some time, that's all."

With an exasperated sigh, Lucy stood and hurried out the bar leaving Peter staring into his glass. After a few seconds, he pushed his glass away, stood up and also left the bar, his shoulders slumped and a worried frown upon his face.

As he went, Scarlet turned to Magenta. "Well, well, well," she said. "What do you make of that? It would appear somebody has secrets."

"Very interesting," Magenta agreed. "Very interesting, indeed. Get the drinks in, there's a good girl, and we'll see if we can't use this to our advantage."

Jane Franks had returned to her room earlier that morning, after sitting with Emma for a while.

With everything that had been happening, all the normal routines had been thrown out of kilter. Emma, having been fortified by Jane's coffee, had offered to cover the front desk until noon. Jane had sat while Emma hurried to her room to freshen up. When she returned, Jane went to her room and caught a few hours' sleep.

She awoke at 10:30 am and decided to go for a swim before she went back to work. As she had hoped, the pool was empty, all the guests elsewhere. Removing her bathrobe, revealing her swimming costume beneath, she lay the robe over a wicker chair near the pool. She walked to the ladders at one end of the pool and climbed down into the water. Although it was a heated pool, it still felt cold at first but it only took a few seconds for her to become acclimatised to it.

Jane dunked her head under the water and lifted it back out. She ran her hand through her hair and wiped water from her eyes. A pair of goggles hung around her neck which she fitted into place. On one wall, a large clock displayed the time and, from speakers hidden along the walls, music played.

"Right," she said to herself, looking at the clock. "Twenty laps."

She kicked off, her body gliding through the water, her arms stretched out in front of her then, before she could lose momentum, she kicked with her legs as her arms started pulling her along.

The knock at the door startled Marie. She opened it and found herself face to face with the manager, Haddington-Smythe.

"Ah, is Mr Thomas available?" he asked nervously.

"JT, it's for you," Marie said, swinging the door fully open so JT, sitting on the sofa, could see the man standing in the doorway.

"Gerald, what is it?" JT asked.

"Goodness," Haddington-Smythe said, noticing JT's bruised face and somewhat dishevelled appearance. "What happened to you?"

"Just a little… accident," JT answered. "Nearly took a tumble down some stairs. I really must be more careful."

"Er, yes, of course," Haddington-Smythe agreed uncertainly. "Um, I am sorry to bother you but, well, you see, I have Sir Henry in my office."

"Best place for him," JT muttered.

"Er, quite, quite. The thing is, ah, well, er, he has made a suggestion. Of sorts."

"And you came up here, in person, to share this with me?"

"Emma is working at the front desk," Haddington-Smythe explained. "I would have asked Jane to deliver this request, rather than leave Sir Henry alone, however, I believe she is currently availing herself of the swimming pool before her next shift is due to start."

Listen, Gerald," JT said. "I know I am not exactly busy at the moment but is there any chance you could get to the point? Maybe before New Year's?"

"Ah, yes, of course. Ahem, well," Haddington-Smythe said, "perhaps it would be best if you came down to my office so Sir Henry can explain himself?"

"Oh sure, why not?" JT said, getting to his feet. "Listen, let me, ah, freshen up. I'll be down in half an hour, okay?"

Haddington-Smythe left and Marie said, "Well, if you are going, do you need me to tag along?"

"No, I should manage this on my own," JT said.

"In that case, I think I will maybe go down to the bar for a coffee," she said. "See you later." Marie had hurried out the room before JT had a chance to respond. He stared at the door for a few seconds then gave a slight shrug.

Sophia was sitting in the foyer with her parents having an intense conversation. Philip had been reluctant at first to go to the foyer preferring instead to have the conversation in their room. However, Sophia was feeling she had been cooped up for too long, in more ways than one, and had insisted they find a seat in the foyer.

They had ordered coffees and, with Sophia enjoying a view of outside, had sat in silence for a few minutes. Finally, Sophia spoke. "I will get right to the point," she began. "This break has highlighted what I have known for a while but been reluctant to face up to; I cannot marry Rupert."

"Now, dear," Theresa said, trying to sound sympathetic. "I know you are upset but I am sure Rupert has just been under a bit of pressure, that's all."

"Yes, Sophia, dear," Philip added. "I admit, his behaviour has been a bit... off but I'm sure once we are home, we can get back to normal."

"Daddy," Sophia said. "I don't love him!"

"Oh, you're far too young to know about love," Philip said dismissively.

"And Rupert does not love me!" Sophia angrily added.

"Don't be silly, Sophia," Theresa said. "He positively dotes on you."

"Do you think I am blind?" Sophia demanded. "The only thing he dotes on is Daddy's company! And, Daddy, I know the reason you thought Rupert was such a 'catch' is because you want a man to take over your company when you retire!"

"Sophia," Philip protested, although it sounded half-hearted, even to his own ears.

"It's true, Daddy!" Sophia said, wiping at the tears running down her face. "Well, you know what? I may be a woman, but I know more about the company than he ever will. All the major decisions he has made in the past year, every single one, he has discussed the matter with me and taken my advice and passed it off as his own."

"Sophia, I… I don't know what to say," Philip stammered, flustered. "I had no idea…."

"You did not want to know!" Sophia said.

"Oh, darling," Theresa said, taking her daughter's hand in hers and shooting an unkind look towards her husband. "That is terrible. I believe your father has some thinking to do."

"Er, yes, I suppose I do," Philip muttered.

It was then that Rupert appeared, looking apprehensive. He tried forcing a smile, hoping to be ingratiating, but this quickly wilted under the stony stares from Philip and Theresa.

"Well," he said. "I'm glad everyone is here. I believe there has been a bit of a… stormy time over the past day or two. Having said that, Philip, I am more than willing to let bygones be bygones, wipe the old slate clean and start afresh." He paused hoping someone would say something but no one spoke. "I am even willing to forgive you, Sophia," he continued. "You'll understand about women getting hysterical, Philip, eh?" He gave a little laugh but quickly stopped when no one, least of all Philip, joined in.

"So, er, what do you say? New Year, new start?"

"Rupert," Philip said slowly. "How long have you worked for me?"

"About a year?" he answered slowly.

"And how long have you been engaged to my daughter?"

"Um, perhaps eleven months?" he answered. Quickly, he added, "Yes, it was a quick engagement but, what can I say? It was love at first sight."

"And do you discuss business matters with Sophia?"

"Um, er, ah," Rupert mumbled nervously.

"It has just come to my attention," Philip continued, "that all the decisions you have been making, the decisions which so impressed me and made me think of you as my business heir, were in fact made by Sophia. Is that correct?"

"Ah…"

"Rupert," Philip said. "Let me make this simple; you are fired."

"But…"

"You will, of course, receive a salary to cover your notice period but you will not, under any circumstances, be required to return to work. Do I make myself clear?"

Rupert stood, dumbfounded, looking from Philip to Theresa to Sophia. "Is this a joke?" he asked at last.

"Do I look as if I am joking?" Philip asked sternly.

"I… I… I, ah, understand," Rupert said slowly. He paused, made to turn away, then turned back and said, "You know what your problem is, Philip? You're a chauvinist! As for you," he said, turning to Theresa, "you were so desperate to see a man, any man, want to marry your daughter that you happily embraced me as a 'son' and made sure Philip promoted me, to keep me around!"

"You vile, horrible man!" Sophia cried. Rupert turned and stormed off.

It was slightly over a half hour later that JT entered the manager's office and found Haddington-Smythe sitting behind his desk, looking flustered, while Sir Henry paced back and forth.

"At last!" Sir Henry said.

JT was wearing a fresh set of clothes and his hair was damp. "I would apologise, Sir Henry, but, honestly, I am not in the mood," JT said brusquely. "You may think you are important but you are no different than the rest of us, I assure you. If some crazed maniac decides to target you, all your money won't make a bit of difference."

Sir Henry stopped, taken aback. His face turned red as he opened his mouth to reply.

"Please, please, gentlemen," Haddington-Smythe interjected quickly. "Naturally… tensions are running a bit high. Perhaps if we just take a breath, compose ourselves, we can begin anew?"

Sir Henry harrumphed before dropping into an empty chair. "Damned impertinence," he muttered.

"Okay," JT said. "Sir Henry, Gerald was saying you have an idea?"

"Yes," Sir Henry said sullenly. "What we… you need to be doing is searching everyone's room, looking for old Beryl's diamonds. Find them and you find your killer."

JT stood quietly, pondering this suggestion. Eventually, he said, "I understand your reasoning, Sir Henry, but it is not as simple as that."

"Really?" Sir Henry scoffed. "Please enlighten me."

"First of all, no one is obliged to consent to a search," JT explained. "We have no legal right. Second of all, there are far too many rooms in this hotel where the diamonds could be hidden. Only a rank amateur would keep them in his room."

"Who says we are not dealing with an amateur?" Sir Henry persisted.

"This was not some opportunistic crime," JT replied smoothly. "They knew when to strike, they planned it in advance and had the necessary equipment. They knew they were trapped here with the rest of us but still carried out the theft so they are confident they won't get caught."

"Or just bloody desperate!" Sir Henry said angrily.

"Finally," JT said, ignoring the outburst, "if you begin searching rooms, the thief will be made aware immediately and, if necessary, move them. How many staff are employed here? How long would it take to search every room? Also, what if the thief works here? No, Sir Henry, there are too many problems for that to be a practical idea."

"Hmph!" was all Sir Henry said.

"Um, what would you suggest?" Haddington-Smythe asked.

"For the moment, we wait," JT responded. "I continue to look into things and, I am sure, we will get to the bottom of this sooner rather than later."

"Blast it!" Sir Henry cried. "Surely someone must have seen something!"

"Of that, I have no doubt," JT said. "Unfortunately, seeing is not the same as observing."

"What do you mean?" Haddington-Smythe asked.

"I mean, someone probably did see something," JT explained. "However, they may not have realised what they were looking at. Take Mrs Lambert, for instance."

"A crying shame, what happened to the old girl," Sir Henry said sadly.

"Yes, quite," the manager agreed.

"But think about it," JT said, almost to himself. "Of course, why didn't I see it before? I'm getting sloppy in my old... well, middle years."

"What are you babbling about, man?" Sir Henry demanded.

"Mrs Lambert, Beryl," JT replied, "told me she saw Toby yesterday morning which, of course, was impossible since he was already dead. She also saw him the previous night."

"So?" Sir Henry asked. "The old girl got confused, happens to the best of us, what?"

"Perhaps," JT answered thoughtfully. "But, suppose she wasn't confused? At least, not totally?"

"You're not making any sense!" Sir Henry said angrily. Haddington-Smythe was looking confused over the whole conversation.

"Beryl had been coming here for years, correct?" JT asked. "She recognised Toby, of course. But what if she saw someone from a distance that she assumed to be Toby? Her mind reaches this conclusion and she doesn't question it. But then, she learns Toby has been found dead and suddenly she wonders, did she really see him like she thought? When I spoke to her, she had a faraway look in her eyes and I just assumed she was a bit…" JT glanced at Sir Henry and decided it would be best to keep his opinions of Beryl Lambert's state of mind to himself. "The point is, maybe her mind wasn't drifting. Maybe, when she realised she couldn't have seen Toby yesterday morning, she saw something, or someone, which made her realise what it was she actually saw?"

"That is an awful lot of speculation," Sir Henry retorted. "If that were the case, she would have spoken up."

"Would she?" JT asked. "Tell me, Sir Henry, you knew Beryl Lambert quite well? What do you think?"

"I, er, I mean, the old girl, she would have, ah, wanted to be certain," Sir Henry admitted. "The old girl hated the idea of anyone thinking she was batty. Blast it!" This last comment was said softly, almost a whisper. "Could that have been what she wanted to discuss with me?"

"What?" JT asked quickly.

"You never mentioned this before," Haddington-Smythe added.

"Sorry, old boy," Sir Henry said sheepishly. "I was rather shocked by the old girl's death, must have slipped my mind."

"When was this?" JT asked. "When did she mention wanting to discuss something with you?"

"Last night," Sir Henry answered. "At the table. Just before I went for drinks. And there was the funny thing she said just before she died," he continued, his mind drifting back to that terrible moment. "She said something about Toby, about him not being fat."

"I don't understand," Haddington-Smythe said, clearly puzzled. "Toby isn't.... wasn't fat. What a strange thing to say."

"Yes," Sir Henry said ruefully. "I must confess, I thought it was some kind of delirium."

"Hmm," JT murmured. "What did she see?"

He continued murmuring to himself, scratching his chin thoughtfully, seemingly forgetting there were two other people in the room with him.

Haddington-Smythe was about to interrupt JT's musings when the office door was flung open and Emma, looking panic-stricken, cried, "Jane's dead!"

Chapter 13

Haddington-Smythe stood and stared at the body of Jane Franks, floating face-down in the swimming pool. Beside him, JT looked thoughtful. There was a tiny stream of blood drifting from a wound on the body's head, slowly dispersing in the water.

"God, this is a nightmare!" Haddington-Smythe moaned. "Is there any chance it could have been an accident? Could she have slipped and hit her head on the side of the pool as she fell?"

"Under other circumstances, I would say yes," JT answered. "You'll forgive me if my suspicious nature leans towards foul play initially, though, I expect."

Haddington-Smythe had enlisted the help of a couple of people to retrieve Jane's body from the pool. Dr Stepford had been located and was waiting to examine the body. Another member of staff had been posted at the entrance to keep away any onlookers as, unsurprisingly, word had spread fast that someone else was dead.

Marie suddenly appeared at JT's side, looking flustered, out of breath, her shoes and clothes looking damp. "I just heard," she gasped. "I was, er, outside, um, looking for, uh, clues. I got here as quickly as I could."

"Are you okay?" JT asked. "You look a bit... anxious."

"Of course I look anxious!" she retorted. "I feel anxious! People are being killed by a bloody maniac! Is there a reason I shouldn't be anxious?"

"Okay, calm down," JT said placatingly. "I was just saying. Anyway, don't jump to conclusions; this may have been nothing more than a terrible accident."

"Wanna bet?" Marie asked.

"You sound very sure," JT said carefully. "Is there something you know that I don't?"

"Just call me cynical!" Marie said. "I know now is maybe not the best time to bring this up, er, but, um, I've been thinking and…"

JT turned to her and said, "What? What have you been thinking? Just spit it out already!"

"I'm quitting!" Marie snapped. "Honestly, the way you treat me, making me feel useless and insignificant, well, I have had enough, okay? And, you know what else? I am not like you, I don't get a thrill out of investigating murders, especially when I could be next on the killer's list!"

"You are being dramatic," JT said. "And when have I ever treated you badly?"

Marie scoffed derisively. "Are you serious? Do you really not see anything wrong with the way you talk to me? God, you are so full of yourself I… I… aargh, I quit!" She turned and hurried out, ignoring the startled looks from everyone around her.

"Sorry about that," JT said calmly. "I really don't know what has gotten into her. Hormones, probably."

Biting her tongue to stop herself saying something she might regret, Dr Stepford took a breath then said coldly, "Mr Thomas, if you would care to look here, please." JT knelt down beside her as she examined the dead body which had been lifted onto the side of the pool. "Look there," she said pointing to a gash in the head. "And there," she added pointing to a tiny smear of blood at the edge of the pool. "From the look of everything, Mr Haddington-Smythe can rest easy this time. I would guess that, as he speculated, Ms. Franks, Jane, was at the side of the pool, perhaps walking along or getting ready to dive in, when she slipped, lost her balance and fell. There is where her head collided with the edge of the pool. Looking at the wound, I would surmise she lost consciousness immediately and, unfortunately, drowned as a result."

"Hmm, yes, it does look like it could have happened that way," JT agreed. "And there is nothing else to suggest anyone else was involved?"

"Nothing that I can see," Pamela replied. "There are no bruises on the body, or cuts or abrasions, to suggest any kind of struggle. No, this time it was nothing more than a terrible accident."

"Oh, thank goodness," Haddington-Smythe said with a smile which he quickly lost under a stern look from Pamela. "I mean, ah, a tragedy, of course, but, er, well, I'm sure you can understand why I am, ah, relieved it wasn't murder, eh?"

As the body was covered then removed, JT waited until Pamela had also left then said quietly to Haddington-Smythe, "Listen, can I trust you?"

"Of course," the manager replied. "Um, with what, exactly?"

"It may be nothing," JT said, "and I feel awful for even thinking this but…" He paused, rubbed a hand through his hair, sighed. "Look, Marie has been a bit… off since we got here."

"You mean her outburst just now?" Haddington-Smythe asked.

"Among other things," JT answered. "It's just… I know Pamela was sure this was an accident but, well, when you were up at my suite earlier you mentioned Jane was taking a swim."

"Yes, what of it?"

"Right after that, Marie left in quite a hurry," JT explained. "Now, this story about her being outside looking for clues? I am not sure I buy it."

"Surely you are not suggesting she killed Jane?" Haddington-Smythe asked, horrified.

"Did you see her clothes?" JT asked.

"Yes, they looked wet," the manager responded. "Which they would if she had been out in the snow."

"Possibly," JT said. "Or…"

"Or what?"

"If she killed Jane," JT said softly, "then she could have gotten wet committing the crime and needed an excuse to explain it."

"I… I… I don't believe it," Haddington-Smythe stammered.

"I'm not sure I do, either," JT said with another sigh. "It's just… the way things have happened here, I just can't be sure."

"But what do you want me to do?" Haddington-Smythe asked nervously.

"Nothing!" JT answered quickly. "I guess I just needed someone to confide in. Normally, that person would be Marie but I can't tell her about this, obviously. Listen, I'm sure I'm just being silly. A lot has happened in the past couple of days, everyone is on edge, myself included, and the pressure keeps building. I really need to get to the bottom of this, huh?"

"For all our sakes," Haddington-Smythe agreed.

"Thanks for listening, Gerald," JT said, patting him on the shoulder. "Remember, mum's the word."

Magenta was frantically searching through a pile of clothes, discarding items as quickly as she could pick them up, behind her another pile forming of the searched-through garments.

"Where is it?" she asked, her voice a mixture of anger and fear. "It has to be here!"

"Of course it is, silly," Scarlet said. "I put it in the…" Suddenly, her voice trailed off and the colour drained from her face.

"Oh, please tell me you were not that stupid!" Magenta shrieked as she realised what had happened.

"I… I thought it was the safest place," she answered. "But, then…"

"You let them take the wrong one!" Magenta cried.

"Oh, my God!" Scarlet said, dropping to her knees and frantically searching through the clothes again. "Oh, my God!"

Outside, the snow was no longer falling as the sun shone down from the clear, blue sky. All the guests had been informed a short time ago that phone lines had been re-established. It was only a matter of time before the roads were made passable and the authorities could be summoned to deal with the events of the past few days.

"How much time do you think we have?" Scarlet asked.

"Not much," Magenta answered. "Quick, gather up all your things. We need to get out of here as soon as possible."

"Won't that look suspicious?" Scarlet asked.

"Of course it bloody will!" Magenta snapped. "What choice do we have? Do you want to stick around and wait for the police? Well, do you?"

At the front desk, Emma was busy with the phone. Per Mr Haddington-Smythe's instructions, once the phone lines had been reconnected, she called the authorities and explained that there had been three deaths at the hotel. She said that a private detective was on-site assisting the hotel but, naturally, the sooner the police got here, the better. The dispatcher, when informed there was no immediate danger to anyone, advised that it would still be another few hours before the roads were cleared but, as soon as they were, police and paramedics would be dispatched.

Now, she watched as people milled about, everyone seemingly using mobile phones to make calls, excited whispers as they explained what had been happening at the hotel. In between, she had been dealing with queries from guests who, now that the weather seemed to be improving, were enquiring about the possibility of curtailing their stay at the hotel and leaving as soon as possible. To these guests, she politely explained that it would still be some time before it would be safe to travel while hoping they did not realise that this also served the purpose of trying to keep everyone in the hotel when the police were finally able to get there. Unfortunately, quite a few guests had enquired about leaving so Emma's theory about the killer giving themselves away in this fashion proved useless.

At least now internet access had been restored and Emma was able to trawl through holiday websites and gaze longingly at sunny beaches and tropical paradises.

JT and Haddington-Smythe returned to the manager's office. JT had been informed that phone services had returned and was eager to avail himself of the internet to do some research. He was convinced that the key to all this lay in the past, Toby's past, but had been severely limited as to what he could dig up, relying solely on what was in Toby's employment file (nothing much of interest) and what the other staff could tell him (even less of interest).

Occupying the manager's seat, JT started accessing news websites, typing Toby's name into the search fields, looking for something, anything, to explain why he was killed. At first, his search proved futile, finding nothing relating to Toby on any of the news sites. Then, he expanded his search, covering the full country.

"Is there anything I can help with?" Haddington-Smythe asked, standing off to one side.

"Ah, no, no thank you," JT murmured without looking up from the screen.

"Well, erm, in that case, I will, ah, see how Emma is getting on. No doubt, a lot of guests will be trying to leave."

"Uh-huh," JT muttered as Haddington-Smythe left the office. JT lost track of time as he searched different sites then, finally, he found something. Peering closely at the screen, he read the text, frowning, scrolling down the screen and looking at the accompanying photographs. "Well, I'll be damned!" he muttered.

Finally, something that could explain what had happened. Yet, there was still a piece missing. If what JT had just learned explained the motive, it did not help with identifying the suspect. Perhaps there was more to the story than had been reported in the press, he thought. The police would have all the details and JT had a friend on the force who could perhaps shed some more light on this particular puzzle. He pulled his wallet out to retrieve the card with the contact number of his friend and a scrunched up napkin fell out and dropped to the floor.

Puzzled, JT leaned down and picked it up. How did that get in here? He wondered. Noticing the small stains on it, he peered at it thoughtfully. The stains were beige in colour, just like… Wracking his memory, he managed to retrieve a slightly distorted, fragmented image of pulling money from his wallet, dropping it, Marie retrieving it and stuffing it back in…

He turned back to the computer screen and read the story again. Leaning closer to the screen, he gazed long and hard, absorbing the details.

He reached for the phone on the desk and pushed a button labelled 'reception' and heard Emma answer. JT quickly explained he wanted to call his suite and speak to Marie but he was not sure how to operate the phone. Emma said she would deal with it.

Five minutes later, Marie walked into the office, looking sullen and dejected.

"Emma said you needed to speak to me?" she said.

"Here, look at this," JT said. "Quickly."

He stepped aside to allow Marie to sit in front of the monitor and read the story he had found. After a few minutes, she looked up and said, "Okay, I understand the first part but, how does this help you identify the murderer?"

"Remember Beryl claimed to have seen Toby the night he was killed," JT answered. "And, crucially, the next morning."

"So?" Marie responded. "Obviously, she was mistaken."

"Obviously," JT agreed. "However, what if she was also correct?"

"You're losing me, now," Marie said with a sigh. "That makes no sense."

"I know," JT admitted. "It's just… a theory that's starting to form."

"But what about the theft?" Marie asked.

"Nothing to do with the murders," JT answered confidently. "I think it was just rotten luck for our thief that poor Beryl was murdered when she was. The thief, like the murderer, did not plan on being snowed in here."

"So, why do it, then?" Marie wondered. "Knowing you are trapped here, why risk it?"

"I think the killer was more concerned about revenge than escape, to be honest," JT answered. "As for the thief, I can only assume greed overcame common sense."

At the front desk, Stanley and Gemima were talking with Emma, enquiring about the prospect of leaving. Emma told them the same thing she told everyone else.

"No matter, dear," Gemima said with a smile. "It is not for us. I know some people have got themselves a bit worked up over the murders but, well, at our age, we expect the Grim Reaper to come visiting at any time so we are not worried. We have had long, happy lives, and have no reason to think we are likely to be targeted by a killer. I just hope the police get here before the killer escapes."

With that, they shuffled off to be replaced by Magenta and Scarlet. "Um, we would like to check out, please," Magenta said.

"I'm sorry, that is not possible, just now," Emma said.

"But, the snow…" Scarlet began.

"The snow has stopped falling, yes," Emma said. "However, the roads are still blocked. I assure you, as soon as it is possible to travel, we will let you know."

"But there is a murderer here!" Magenta snapped. "What about our safety?"

Haddington-Smythe had been nearby and heard this last part. Walking over to the desk, he said, "Now, ladies, please, I understand how you feel but, er, it would be foolish to risk your lives out there, don't you think?"

Exchanging worried looks, Magenta and Scarlet turned and left.

"They are just the latest in a long list of guests desperate to leave," Emma said with a sigh.

"I fear the hotel may never recover from this," Haddington-Smythe said sorrowfully.

"Mr Haddington-Smythe!" a frantic voice cried from behind him.

Turning, he almost collided with the woman who had been running towards him. It was a member of staff, a young woman who had been gathering back all the costumes which had been issued to the desk. She was holding a small, cloth bag.

Thrusting the bag into the manager's hands, she said, "I found this amongst the costumes!" Haddington-Smythe peered into the bag and gasped with surprise. There, nestled at the bottom, was the missing jewellery.

Haddington-Smythe threw his office door open and excitedly declared, "We've found them!" Marie and JT both looked up and saw the cloth bag in the manager's hands, clasped tightly to his chest, a smile of delight spread across his normally stoic features. He closed the door behind him and brought the bag across to his desk and, carefully, tipped the contents out in front of Marie and JT. Marie gasped as the diamond jewellery lay before her, the precious stones sparkling and twinkling. Carefully, she lifted up the pendant and held the silver chain between her fingers, letting the pendant swing gently from side to side in front of her face.

"Oh, wow," she murmured.

"Where were they?" JT asked.

"They were found amongst a pile of costumes which had been collected for laundering," Haddington-Smythe answered. "Unfortunately, we cannot say with certainty which costume they were with."

"Hmm, I suppose that would have been too easy," JT murmured.

"However," the manager continued, "we can narrow it down to one wing on the third floor."

"How many rooms does that cover?" Marie asked, her eyes still fixed on the large diamond.

"Six," came the prompt response.

"So, we know the thief is in one of those rooms?" JT said. "We need to see the costumes. Quickly."

"Of course," Haddington-Smythe said, nodding. "But, er, have you made any progress in the, er, other matter?"

"Quite a lot, as it happens," JT said, taking the pendant from Marie and returning it to the bag. "You better put these in your safe," he said to Haddington-Smythe. "I can see why diamonds are a girl's best friend."

"I would never have described myself as shallow," Marie said, shaking herself out of her diamond induced trance. "Certainly, I never obsessed over size. But, my goodness, did you see the size of that? Oh, how I wish it was my friend!"

"Erm, quite," Haddington-Smythe mumbled, suddenly feeling embarrassed. He walked behind his desk and stood in front of the small safe mounted on the wall, entered the PIN on the keypad and opened the safe. Placing the bag inside, he closed the safe, making sure it was locked. "Well, Sir Henry should be pleased with this," he said, hoping this would help to temper any comments Sir Henry intended to pass on to the Trustees.

"Okay," JT said. "Where are these costumes?"

Haddington-Smythe led them out of his office and a few minutes later they passed through the hotel's kitchen and found themselves standing in the laundry room, a large room filled with industrial washing machines and driers, presses and various other items.

The woman who had found the bag was standing with a trolley piled with costumes next to a washing machine where she had started piling in the garments she had collected from the guests' rooms before her discovery had stopped her in her tracks. Haddington-Smythe had instructed her to do nothing further until he came down so she had been waiting there for him to arrive with the detective.

"This is Sonja," Haddington-Smythe said introducing the young woman. She looked to be in her early twenties, had short brown hair and wore a worried expression. She was biting at her finger nails, nervously eyeing the new arrivals.

"Hello, Sonja," JT said.

"Hi," Marie added with a friendly smile. She knew that a lot of people got nervous when being questioned, even when they had done nothing wrong so tried to put the young woman at ease.

"Hey," she said.

Without another word, JT started sifting through the clothes. "This is where you found the bag?" he asked.

"Uh, yeah," Sonja answered. "I was just emptying them into the washer, you know? Then I sees this bag lying there. Well, at first, I figgered one of the guests had got it wrapped up in their outfit without knowin' and so I had a look, you know? So's I could find out who to return it to, you know?" She sniffed. "Well, let me tell you, I bloody near shit myself when I saw what was in it, you know? Oh, beggin' your pardon, Mr Haddington-Smythe!"

"No, no, ah, it's okay," the manager said, gesturing for the woman to continue.

"Well, like I says, I got the fright of my life, you know?" Sonja said. "Anyways, I took them straight to Mr Haddington-Smythe here and, well, that's it, really."

"Look at this," JT said holding up a black-and-white striped jumper.

"Isn't that part of the 'cat burglar' costume?" Marie asked.

"Yes," JT replied. "And it is the same colour as the fibres caught in the attaché case clasp."

"Well done," Haddington-Smythe declared. "It should be easy enough to find out who it was issued to."

"Only one problem," Marie interrupted.

"What's that?" JT asked.

"I remember seeing someone wearing that costume," she answered. "I'm pretty sure they were there all night, until Mrs Lambert was killed, anyway. After that, they would hardly have had time to carry out the theft and certainly would have been seen by somebody."

"Plus," JT added, "if they weren't responsible for the murder, I doubt they would risk it. They'd have no way of knowing how long her room would be empty. No, this would have been carried out before Mrs Lambert died."

"But if they were in the Ballroom all evening?" Haddington-Smythe asked, clearly puzzled.

"Is there more than one costume like this?" JT asked.

"No, I'm certain we only have one of that particular costume," Haddington-Smythe replied. "Emma can tell us who it was issued to but if your assistant is already providing an alibi, what can we do?"

"I don't know," JT answered, frowning. "I do know we need to be quick because it is only a matter of time before the roads are cleared and people start leaving, including a thief and a murderer."

It took only a moment for Emma to get the name of the guest who got the 'cat burglar' costume. "It was one of those sisters, Magenta Porter."

"Thank you, Emma," Haddington-Smythe said.

"Oh, my pleasure," she answered, her eyes fixed firmly on JT, her long finger nails brushing against his hand. "I'm always happy to help."

Oh, I just bet you are, Marie thought. Happy to help yourself to some rich, old fool's fortune, given half a chance!

As they turned away, Emma said, "Oh, Mr Haddington-Smythe, they were trying to check out earlier, remember?"

"Yes, I recall," the manager said. "They did seem rather anxious. Of course, half our guests have tried to check out recently and every single one of them looked exactly the same."

"Still, I think we need to speak to them," JT said. "Listen, Emma, could you check something out for me, please?"

As he whispered a request to the young woman, Marie asked Haddington-Smythe, "Should we go to their room? If they are even still here, that is."

"No one has left. Not yet, anyway," Haddington-Smythe said. He glanced at his watch and realised it was still not noon. "Lunch will be served soon. Perhaps we should look for them in the bar area, first," he suggested.

JT stepped over to them. "Right, let's go," he said.

"I was just saying, perhaps we should check the bar area first," Haddington-Smythe told JT.

"Good idea," JT agreed.

They crossed the foyer and entered the bar. Stopping in the threshold, they glanced around and Marie spotted them sitting in a corner booth.

"Good day, ladies," JT said, offering a smile. "Season's greetings with all the trimmings, eh?"

"Oh, hello," Magenta said warily. "Um, can we help you with something?"

"Funny you should ask that," JT said sliding into the booth and forcing Scarlet to shuffle along before he bumped into her. "Mind if we join you? Here, budge round a bit so we can all be seated." Too surprised to object, the two ladies slid closer together to allow Marie and Haddington-Smythe to sit down.

"Look, what is this about?" Scarlet asked.

"Something sparkly," JT replied. "Something valuable. Something missing."

"Now, listen here," Magenta said, trying to sound forceful. "We are feeling rather below our best, what with everything that has happened here recently. If you are going to talk in riddles, we will just leave."

"Diamonds," Marie said simply. "The guest who was murdered last night, Mrs Beryl Lambert, had some incredibly valuable diamond jewellery which was stolen."

"Obviously the thief is the same person who killed her," Magenta suggested.

"No, I don't think so," JT answered. "I won't bore you with my theories but let us just proceed on the assumption that the theft occurred before Beryl was bumped off."

Haddington-Smythe winced at JT's choice of words. Clearing his throat, he said, "The stolen items have been recovered. Perhaps, if the culprit confessed it might mitigate against any... legal repercussions."

Magenta and Scarlet exchanged brief, nervous glances then, composing herself, Magenta said, "I do not understand why you are telling this to us. Are you trying to imply we had something to do with the theft?"

"Okay, let's throw subtlety out the window," JT declared. "The diamonds were found amongst some costumes, including yours," he said to Magenta. "Some fibres were found in Beryl's room which match your costume," he continued. Admittedly, it was only the colours which matched, however, JT figured he was on fairly safe ground. "Finally, someone spotted a suspicious-looking character, wearing that costume, lurking about near Beryl's room." Okay, that was a complete fabrication but, again, JT was confident in his suspicions so hoped this bluff would work.

"This is preposterous!" Scarlet exclaimed. "We do not have to sit here and be accused of this. You are not with the police, you have no authority. Mr Haddington-Smythe," she said, turning on the manager, "my sister and I find this harassment quite distressing. Needless to say, we will not be staying here again. In fact, when Daddy hears of this, well, let's just say, he is very well connected!" As the manager nervously fidgeted in his seat, Magenta said, "Besides, I was in the Ballroom all evening. There are a number of people who can confirm this. So, whatever you think you know, you are mistaken! Actually, perhaps you should speak with that Peter Tenor, chap, or his wife. Apparently, he has been acting a bit oddly, disappearing without explanation. Now, if you will excuse us?"

She stared at JT for a few seconds, as if challenging him, before he gave a slight nod of his head and motioned to Marie and Haddington-Smythe to stand up. They watched as the two sisters walked through to the Ballroom.

"They seem quite confident," Haddington-Smythe said. "Unless they confess, and they have no reason to do so, how can you prove they were involved? And what did she mean about Mr Tenor?"

"Leave that with me," JT said.

"All right, if you are sure," the manager said doubtfully. "So, what progress have you made with regards the murders?"

"I found a news story," JT explained. "It is from several years ago, involving Toby, and could explain why he was murdered."

"Goodness," Haddington-Smythe said. "What happened?"

"To cut a long story short," Marie said, "Toby was involved in a car accident. He and a young woman by the name of Sarah-Louise Hampton were driving in a car, returning from a party, when they took a corner too fast, lost control and the car crashed into a tree. Toby survived, Sarah-Louise was not as fortunate. An inquest was held and, as Sarah-Louise was driving, it was ruled as death by misadventure. The girl's distraught parents did not accept this verdict, blamed Toby for the death of their daughter and vowed they would get justice, one way or the other."

"Goodness," the manager repeated.

"Unfortunately, none of the articles carried photos of her parents," JT said. "All we know are their names, Sidney and Germaine Lewis, and their ages which, then, were forty-eight and forty-five respectively. That would put them in their early fifties now."

"We have many guests who are about that age," Haddington-Smythe said. "I can ask Emma to check our bookings but I do not suppose they would book in under their real names?"

"Probably not," JT agreed. "Ask Emma to check it out, anyway. We might get lucky."

Haddington-Smythe left to speak to Emma and JT and Marie returned to the foyer in time to see Peter Tenor walking towards the hotel's entrance.

"Ah, the very man," JT muttered. "I wonder where he is going? Why don't we find out?"

With Marie beside him, he stepped through the revolving door into the cool, crisp air and saw Peter standing about twenty feet away, staying close to the side of the building, watching another figure who was about the same distance away again.

"That's Valentina," Marie whispered as she recognised the woman Peter was staring at. "Why would he be following her?"

"Hmm," JT murmured. "Let's get back inside. I need to do some thinking and I think better in the warmth."

Unseen by Peter or Valentina, they turned and hurried back in the hotel.

JT and Marie returned to the Ballroom for lunch although neither of them ate much, instead spending most of the time trying to discreetly observe the other guests, hoping to see something that would reveal the killer.

During lunch, Haddington-Smythe appeared at the table and whispered to JT that, as suspected, there were no guests registered under the names Sydney and Germaine Lewis. He went on to say that Emma was quite keen to speak to him about something JT had asked her to look into. "She seems rather excited by it," Haddington-Smythe said. "She would not say what it is as she wishes to speak with you directly."

"Wait here," JT told Marie. "This should only take a minute."

JT walked briskly to the front desk where Emma was speaking with Rupert. When he saw JT approach, Rupert said, "Come to arrest me?"

"Now, now, Rupert," JT said. "Is that a guilty conscience I hear?"

Rupert scowled and walked off. JT turned to Emma. "Well?" he asked.

"I checked our records, like you suggested," she answered almost breathless with excitement. "You were right! It was about two years ago when it happened and a replacement had to be ordered."

"Two years?" JT repeated, whistling. "Talk about long-term planning. Did you get a list of the people staying here when it happened?"

"Yes," Emma answered, her smile dazzling JT. "Here, I printed a copy."

JT studied the sheet of paper Emma handed him, scanning down the list of names to see if any of them stood out. Spotting two names, his brow furrowed as he considered the theory forming in his mind. "Yes," he said to himself. "That might explain it. Thank you, Emma." He turned to walk away then swung back round to the desk. "Listen, could you check one other thing for me, please?"

As Marie waited on JT's return, she absently pushed the food on her plate with her fork. She was thinking about the incident with Toby and this girl who died; even if the report of the accident was right, and the verdict correct, Marie could understand how grief might consume the poor girl's parents to the point where they would consider murder as the only way to get justice.

She casually glanced around the large room, looking at the people who were potential suspects, either through their own behaviour or because of things other people said. Rupert was sitting at the table, having just arrived a moment before, with a rather unpleasant expression clouding his face. Sophia still appeared to be shunning him as she carried on a conversation with her parents. Rupert seemed to have a temper and could not account for his whereabouts the night Toby was murdered but was his minor scuffle with Toby sufficient motive to kill him?

Marie watched Peter and Lucy Tenor. He was trying to appear relaxed but Marie thought she could detect an air of anxiety hanging over him. As he turned to speak to Philip Sonnerson, Marie saw Lucy glance at him, a look of worry on her face. If Magenta was telling the truth, Peter was hiding something from Lucy but what? Did it have something to do with Valentina? Marie found it hard to imagine somebody like Valentina being interested in a middle-aged man like Peter Tenor but it would certainly explain his furtive behaviour and evasiveness with his wife.

At another table, Magenta and Scarlet were sitting engaged in a whispered conversation. As Marie was watching them, Scarlet looked up and, for a moment, their eyes locked. If looks could kill, Marie would have probably dropped dead at that moment, so fierce was the glare from the other woman.

Averting her gaze, Marie looked at the other people sitting at that same table; an elderly couple, another middle-aged couple and two young children. While JT seemed confident the two sisters were involved in the theft, but had yet to prove it, he did not think they killed Toby or Mrs Lambert.

Did they tell JT about Peter Tenor just to draw attention away from themselves?

Meanwhile, all this speculation did not take into account the article JT had discovered. Were the parents of the girl who died in the accident responsible for Toby's death? If so, why kill Mrs Lambert? More importantly, how could they be identified? With only names and ages to go on, any and all middle-aged couples could be potential suspects. Or, Marie thought, it could be just the father or just the mother. Did the dead girl have any siblings? The article did not say.

Pressing her knuckles against her temple, Marie massaged her head to ward off the impending headache all this thinking was going to induce. How does JT do it? Marie wondered.

As if on cue, she spotted JT walking towards her. He sat down beside her and she said, "I hope you have been struck by inspiration because I have been thinking about this and all I'm doing is getting a headache."

"I have warned you before about thinking," JT said solemnly. "You know it always leads to trouble."

"Not for much longer," Marie said. "Remember, after this, I'm through."

"Yes, well, who knows, maybe you'll change your mind after this," JT said.

Don't bet on it, Marie thought.

"Anyway," JT continued, "I think I now have enough information to prove our two favourite sisters are responsible for the theft."

"That's good, I guess," Marie said. "But what about the murders? This place is full of middle aged people, any one of them who could be our killer."

"Yes," JT agreed. "Still, the pieces are falling into place. I think I know who is responsible."

Chapter 14

"What?" Marie asked, stunned.

"Yes, the pieces all fit together now," JT replied, a hint of a smile tugging at his jowls.

"Well, who was it?" Marie asked excitedly.

"Ssh, ssh," JT whispered. "Not yet."

"Oh, please don't tell me you are going to do your 'thing'!" Marie exclaimed. "It's cliché, you realise that, right?"

"Indulge me my little pleasures, please," JT replied with a wink.

"Wow, that's quite the bombshell!" Marie said, shocked. "Are you sure?"

"There were a few little things that didn't quite… add up," JT murmured in response. "However, I can see now how things fit together."

"So, what are you waiting for?" Marie demanded. "Let's get this over with."

"Not so fast," JT replied. "I am waiting on one final piece of confirmation."

As if on cue, Emma entered the Ballroom and hurried across to their table. She leaned down to whisper in JT's ear, one of her manicured hands resting lightly on his shoulder, the other brushing against his hand on the table. JT's face broke into a tiny smile with the news from Emma and he patted her hand as he thanked her.

"My pleasure," she purred sweetly before turning and leaving.

"Well?" Marie demanded. "Did you get what you hoped for?"

"Oh, I think I might…. Ahem, I mean, ah, yes, I have the, um, information," JT answered, flustered. "Also, it seems the road to the hotel is almost clear. The authorities are on their way.

Time to wrap this up."

"So, now are you going to do your 'thing'?" Marie said with a sigh. This would be the part where JT would make himself centre of attention and milk the situation for all it was worth. Honestly, he made such a performance out of it, Marie wondered if he was some kind of frustrated actor.

He sprang from his seat and made a beeline for the small stage, meeting Haddington-Smythe enroute. They exchanged a few words, JT quickly explaining what he was about to do and what he needed the manager to do. Haddington-Smythe turned and headed to the Ballroom entrance and spoke to a couple of staff before standing discreetly in the doorway with Emma by his side.

JT bounded onto the stage and picked up the microphone from the DJ equipment still sitting there. He tapped it once, twice but, when nothing happened, flicked a small switch he found on its side. Tapping the end of the microphone again, there was a small burst of feedback and, satisfied it was now working, JT held it to his mouth and spoke.

"Ladies, gentlemen, please, if I could have your attention for a few minutes," he began as people replaced their cutlery, exchanging puzzled looks with one another. "I am sorry to interrupt your lunch but I have something to say which might make dessert more palatable. For most of you, anyway."

Marie tried to watch people's reactions to see if anyone was looking especially anxious just now. It was hard to tell as most eyes were facing the stage.

"My name is Jack Thomas," JT continued. "You may have heard of me." He paused but there was no reaction from the people seated. "Well, er, no matter, that is not really important, right?" he continued awkwardly. "What is important is that I am a private detective. I make my living this way and I deal with a lot of murders. I may have, er, given some of you the impression that I am wealthy and just dabble in this sort of thing to relieve the boredom. Not true, I'm afraid. I am not wealthy and I take my job very seriously."

Marie looked over to Emma and saw the young woman look disappointed then angry. Oh boy, Marie thought. JT might be in for some fireworks, just not the kind he anticipated. She smiled to herself at the thought of it.

"Over the past couple of days," JT was saying, "there has been a series of events involving murder, theft and more besides."

"At Mr Haddington-Smythe's behest, I set about trying to unravel these events and make some kind of sense out of them. Well, I believe I now have done that."

There were a few murmured whispers now being exchanged as people grew more attentive, sitting forward in their seats eager to hear what JT was about to say.

"Okay, let's start with the most straight forward issue," JT announced. "As you all know, Mrs Beryl Lambert was murdered last night in this very room. What most of you will not be aware of is that, probably about the same time she was being murdered, a thief broke into Mrs Lambert's room and made off with some very valuable jewellery.

"Mrs Lambert was very fond of her jewellery but was reluctant to use the safe in her bedroom or even properly lock her attaché case. I think we can safely assume, because of her age, she was the type of person who would sooner stash her cash beneath her mattress than put it in a bank. This made her an easy target for someone who knew her habits. I believe the thief planned the robbery with the intention of leaving before Mrs Lambert even realised a theft had occurred. Unfortunately, they had not planned on being snowed in nor, more importantly, they could not have anticipated Mrs Lambert being murdered and leading to the theft being discovered much sooner than planned.

"So, the killer did not take the diamonds?" This was from Sir Henry whose table was near the stage and he was now standing. "Then why was she killed, blast it!"

"Please, Sir Henry," JT said calmly. "If you will take your seat, I will explain. I promise." With a disgruntled 'harrumph', Sir Henry sat back down. "Yes, the obvious conclusion was to assume the theft and murder were linked. After all, it would be quite a coincidence otherwise." JT paused, letting this hang in the air. "Still, coincidences happen, good and bad, and that is what this was; a coincidence, pure and simple.

"The thief entered the room from the roof," JT explained to his captive audience. "Took the diamonds, left by the same route and left almost no trace of their presence. There was one tiny clue; a couple of threads, barely noticeable, caught in the clasp of the attaché case which didn't match any of Mrs Lambert's wardrobe. What they did match was one of the costumes provided by the hotel. Appropriately enough, it was the costume of the burglar, complete with swag bag. This costume was worn by you, Magenta Porter!"

There were gasps and whispers as everyone turned to the table JT was pointing towards. With all eyes upon her, Magenta could feel her cheeks turning red. Marie was not sure if it was embarrassment or anger.

"This is slander!" she said defiantly, rising to her feet. "You know perfectly well that I was at the ball all evening with witnesses to verify it. And the hotel only has one costume like it!"

"Ah, yes, that," JT replied. "Yes, you are correct but, well, how did you know that? I mean, it's not really the sort of thing people would concern themselves about, is it? And yet, you seemed unusually concerned, to the point where you actually made a point of reserving this particular costume six months ago."

"Well, er, I like to be… organised," Magenta answered. "That is hardly a crime!"

"No, not a crime, just highly unusual," JT told her. "But why so keen to get that particular costume?" JT paused but Magenta stayed silent. "Did you know that in all the years this hotel has been hosting costume balls, only one costume has ever been stolen? Care to guess which one?" Magenta's jaw seemed locked as she glared at JT. Turning back to the rest of his audience, JT continued. "One costume stolen, ironically, the burglar costume. Heh, almost enough to make you laugh, right? Remember I was speaking of coincidences, the time that costume was stolen, there were two guests registered at the hotel, two young ladies claiming to be sisters. Only, this time it was not a coincidence. Two years ago, having learned of Mrs Lambert's diamonds, as well as her lack of safety precautions with them, two young ladies set in motion a long-term plan.

"First, they stole the burglar costume. Then, much later, they arranged to return to the hotel, using different names. Making sure the stolen costume had been replaced, they made sure to reserve it for their own use. Which brings us almost to the present. You, Miss Porter, if that is in fact your name, did attend the ball, as you said. You made sure you were noticed by as many people as possible so you would have an ironclad alibi, if required. However, you, Scarlet, did not attend the ball."

"Rubbish!" the other young lady said angrily as she rose to her feet.

"Were you in costume?" JT enquired innocently, already knowing the answer.

"I… that is, er, well," Scarlet stammered.

"Don't bother lying," JT said. "The hotel did send two costumes up to your room, however, only one was worn. Before you deny it, you forgot to remove the tags. Very sloppy. Still, that wasn't the worst part, was it?

"You, Scarlet, wearing an identical costume to Magenta, stole the diamonds. You both knew you were snowed in and you might not be able to leave before the theft was discovered but you had been planning this for years! You weren't going to let this chance slip away, were you? Greed forced your hand, did it not?

"And then Mrs Lambert was murdered and, unsurprisingly, the theft was quickly discovered. Was that when you started to panic? Because you became even sloppier when you returned your costumes, didn't you? You returned the wrong costume, the one that had the diamonds hidden in it. Amateurish, to say the least," JT scoffed.

"That is a very… fanciful tale," Magenta said, trying to hide her fear. "Unfortunately, you have no proof. We will be leaving as soon as possible and you cannot detain us!"

"I have good news ladies," JT said. "The roads are almost cleared. In fact, the authorities are on their way here as we speak. I am sure that they will wish to speak to you in more detail, probably search your room, too, where they will, I am sure, find the other costume and learn your true identities. I'm sorry, ladies, it is most definitely over for you both."

"Damn you!" Magenta snarled. Then, she whirled round on Scarlet. "You imbecile! How could you be so stupid? I planned this for years and you mess everything up by sending the wrong bloody costume back!"

With a shriek, Magenta hurled herself at Scarlet, kicking and scratching her as they tumbled to the floor. Quickly, they were separated, Magenta fuming while Scarlet remained tight-lipped and sullen.

"Damn you, you stupid bitch!" Magenta fumed.

"Without me you wouldn't have known about the old bag's bloody diamonds!" Scarlet shouted back. "I was the one who worked with her for all those months, having to pretend to like her and her inane stories! Me! Not you, me! Without me, you would have had nothing!"

"Thank you, ladies," JT interrupted. "It's always appreciated when, during my big reveal, you let anger cloud your judgement and completely incriminate yourselves. Makes the job of the police so much easier."

"Jolly good show, old chap," Sir Henry said with a broad smile. "Let the blighters hang themselves."

As both women were seated back at their table, a couple of the hotel staff nearby to keep an eye on them, JT resumed, "Anyway, that was the easy one. Honestly, my assistant could probably have solved that one!" He chuckled to himself oblivious to the glare from Marie. "However, that was not the worst crime committed here lately.

"Over the past couple of days, there has been three deaths; two hotel employees and one guest," JT said, enjoying the rapt attention he was receiving. "At first, Toby's death looked like it could have been an accident, a simple, yet tragic, fall down a flight of stairs to the cellar. But then we learned that the door at the top of the stairs was locked and Toby's keys were later found outside. So, no longer an accident, definitely foul play.

"Except…" JT paused here. "Except, a witness claimed to have seen Toby that same night, leaving the cellar, locking the door, and, crucially, the following morning. But how could that be? His dead body was lying in the cellar all night so there was no way he could have been seen the next day.

"Then, to further murky the already-muddied waters, this witness was herself murdered the next night. No doubts, this time, definitely murder. Mrs Beryl Lambert was stabbed to death here in this very room in front of everyone and no one saw a thing. With her dying breath, she spoke to Sir Henry, here, but what she said seemed to make no sense. She spoke of Toby, said he wasn't fat. Well, obviously, Toby wasn't fat but why would those be her final words? Delirium due to blood loss? Shock? Was she simply… batty?"

"Here, old boy, there's no need for that!" Sir Henry called out.

"Please, Sir Henry, allow me to finish," JT responded. "No, those final words seemed nonsensical yet, her death, her last words, too much of a coincidence, even for me!

"So, it seemed logical to assume both murders were connected but how? Everything seemed to centre round Toby, his was the first murder, after all. So, what was the motive? He seemed well liked, popular. There was an… incident that night involving Toby and one of the guests." At this, Rupert fidgeted in his seat and refused to look at JT. "A minor scuffle which finished with threats being made against Toby by Rupert over there." JT pointed, just in case there was anyone who had not witnessed or heard about the altercation, although it seemed everyone had. "Later that night, Rupert left his room. He has no alibi and has pointedly refused to discuss his whereabouts. He also has no alibi for when Mrs Lambert was murdered. Care to enlighten us now, Rupert?" There was silence as everyone looked towards Rupert waiting for some kind of response.

After a few seconds, he looked up at JT and said, "I… I, ah, well, um, you see, when I, ah, get stressed I, um, well, the only way I can seem to unwind is to… to… to, er, dress as a woman."

This last part was said softly but, because of the blanket of silence, was still heard by most people. "Thank you for that brave admission," JT said kindly. "Not that it is important. I was just curious."

"Damn you!" Rupert cried. "You humiliated me!"

"Oh, don't get your panties in a twist," JT replied with a smirk. "So, one suspect in the clear. During the course of investigating the theft, it was suggested that another guest had been acting suspiciously, isn't that right, Mr Tenor?"

All eyes turned to Peter Tenor who looked startled. "I'm sorry, what?" he asked, trying to effect an air of nonchalance.

"Is it not true that you have been disappearing lately?" JT asked pointedly. "You and your wife were overheard having an argument about it. Any comments, Mrs Tenor?" Lucy looked towards her husband then back at JT but remained silent.

"Maybe this will help, Mr Tenor," JT said. "You were seen following a member of staff, Valentina. In fact, you have only started staying at this hotel since Valentina came to work here. Is it not true you are having an affair with her? Did Toby find out and, perhaps, try to black mail you?"

"Peter!" Lucy cried, shocked.

"No!" Peter said. "No, that's a lie. I can... I can explain."

"Please do," JT said.

Ignoring JT, Peter turned to his wife and said, "I was going to tell you... I mean, I haven't even told her yet... I... Oh, God! Look, it's not what you think, I promise. It's... Valentina is my daughter. I found out a while ago but I didn't want to believe it. I started bringing us here so I could see her, try to find out if it was true. But, I've been too scared even to speak to her."

"Oh, Peter," Lucy said, tears running down her face. "Why didn't you say?"

"I'm sorry, I'm such a fool," Peter whispered.

"Oh, um, right, not an affair," JT said, coughing slightly. "Well, no matter, because I also know you are not our killer."

Marie rolled her eyes as JT again paused for dramatic effect. He seemed to take delight in this performance, not caring what effect it might be having on those people he was putting in the spotlight. Hopefully, he would get to the punchline soon.

"Then, we made a breakthrough," JT announced. "Thanks to the wonders of the internet, that is less wonderful when it is snowing, I learned that Toby had been involved in an accident a few years ago, an accident which resulted in the death of a young woman.

"There was nothing to suggest Toby had done anything wrong, an inquest ruled the woman's death as an accident, however, her parents, no doubt wracked with grief, held Toby responsible and vowed to seek justice. Unfortunately, all we know about the parents are their names and that they are middle-aged. Obviously, we checked the hotel register and there is no one here registered under their names, Sydney and Germaine Lewison, so all you middle-aged couples sitting here are potential suspects." Now, people started glancing around, looking and wondering if they were looking at a killer. "Now, I was getting somewhere," JT said. "Then, a couple of seemingly-random events helped drop the pieces into place.

"The other night as I was leaving the Ballroom, I, er, dropped some money and my assistant was good enough to retrieve it for me. She placed it back in my wallet along with a napkin which she had accidentally picked up. I only discovered this the next day. The napkin had a small stain on it, beige. Seeing that reminded me that there was a similar stain found on Toby, as well as the hand rail leading down to the cellar.

"Then we come back to Mrs Lambert's final words; Toby wasn't fat. That made me think that, perhaps, she was not meaning Toby wasn't fat. No, what she meant was the person she saw, who she assumed was Toby, could not have been Toby because she saw this person the next day and realised she recognised him as who she had thought was Toby except this person was fat so this could not have been who she thought she saw, right? No doubt, this is what kept her silent, her confusion, doubting herself. If she had only spoken up earlier, she would still be alive, isn't that right, Mr Lewsinski?"

Now, all eyes focused on the elderly man.

"I hate to burst your bubble, old boy," Sir Henry said, "but that chap was in the bar when poor Beryl was murdered. Friar Tuck, if I recall."

"Heh," Stanley gave a small laugh. "Not to worry, nobody's perfect. Me, a killer!" Beside him, Gemima smiled.

"Oh, sorry," JT said.

"No apology necessary," Stanley assured him.

"No, you misunderstand," JT said. "I am apologising because I am getting ahead of myself. You see, the stain on the napkin, and the one on Toby, was make-up. Theatrical make-up, as it happens. When I thought about it, it made sense; the killer disguised himself."

"It would take more than make-up to disguise that stomach," Sir Henry said, quickly adding, "no offence, old boy."

"Yes, it would," JT admitted. "Unless, that stomach was the disguise! Who would suspect an elderly, borderline-obese, man of committing murder? However, a middle-aged man, with a strong motive to kill, might disguise himself, make himself look older, fatter, then shed this disguise to carry out the crime. You, Mr Lewsinski, wearing a 'borrowed' hotel uniform, followed Toby to the cellar, pushed him down the stairs and made sure the fall killed him. However, in order to make sure you weren't implicated, you had to make sure the body wasn't discovered too soon so you took Toby's keys, locked the door as you left and, sometime thereafter, threw the keys away outside. Unfortunately for you, Mrs Lambert spotted you, called out to you, thinking you were Toby. That could have been a problem but then you saw a way to take advantage of it by making sure she also spotted you the next morning. That would confuse the issue of when, precisely, Toby died. So, what went wrong? Did Mrs Lambert start to put two and two together after Toby's body was discovered? Did she start to wonder if it really was Toby she saw? Maybe, the more she thought about it, she recognised something in you, Mr Lewsinski. What, did you find her gaze lingering on you when she thought you weren't watching? You could not be certain but why take a chance? You, like the rest of us, were stuck here until the roads were cleared and the longer you were here, the more chance that Mrs Lambert would piece together what you had done. So, she had to die."

"But I have already said this man was being served in the bar when the old girl was murdered," Sir Henry said again. "Unless you are questioning my faculties?" he challenged.

"No, Sir Henry," JT replied. "You did see him in the bar. It was maybe even planned that way, you know, when they saw you leaving Mrs Lambert alone when you went for drinks. Yes, Mr Lewsinski was in the bar, but Mrs Lewsinski was not."

There were a few audible gasps as the implication of that statement sank in. The Lewsinski's sat in silence, impassive.

"Mrs Lewsinski, I have noticed, as I am sure most other people have, that you are rather fond of knitting," JT said matter-of-factly. "You always have your bag with you and, unless dining, usually are sitting knitting. If you don't mind my saying, for an elderly lady, you are rather adept with the knitting needles. Age has definitely not slowed you down.

"Last night, when your husband went to the bar, how long would it have taken you to casually approach Mrs Lambert, lean down as if in conversation with her, then stab her with one of your knitting needles? Dr Stepford confirmed Mrs Lambert was stabbed by a long, thin, pointed instrument; I am willing to bet when the authorities examine your needles, they will find traces of blood on one of them, correct?"

There was a deathly quiet as everyone stared at the elderly couple, almost afraid to breathe in case they missed another revelation. JT stood, waiting, watching.

Finally, Mrs Lewsinski spoke. "He killed our daughter," she said, her voice trembling. "I don't care what the inquest ruled, that man killed our daughter, our only child."

Mr Lewsinski pulled at his scalp and removed the bald cap which had covered his head. Using one of the napkins, he started rubbing at his face, removing some of the make-up which he had used to age himself by a couple of decades. Then, he unbuttoned his shirt to reveal the body suit he was wearing beneath it. "Bloody make-up," he murmured softly. "It gets everywhere, doesn't it?"

"But, why kill Beryl?" Sir Henry asked. "She was harmless."

"That was my idea, I am afraid," Mrs Lewsinski answered. "I was consumed with making that man pay for what he had done and I could not stand the thought of anything ruining our plans. When I saw her staring at us, I knew she knew. I'm sorry, I… I… I was not in my right mind."

"So," Haddington-Smythe spoke up from where he was standing, "Mr and Mrs Lewsinski are actually Mr and Mrs Lewis?"

"Yes, Sydney and Germaine Lewis," JT confirmed, "Parents to Sarah-Louise Hampton."

"Hampton?" Haddington-Smythe queried. "Not Lewis?"

"No, most assuredly Hampton," JT replied. "Which brings us to the final piece of the puzzle. Now, this was quite clever, really, a most impressive performance. You see, there was an attempt on my life; as I was standing at the top of the stairs where Toby fell, someone deliberately bumped the door in an attempt to send me to a similar fate. Now, I don't think Sydney or Germaine would have broken character and risk being seen exerting such force for elderly people, nor would Sydney risk being seen dressed in the hotel uniform again. So, I concluded there was a third party."

"Someone else?" Marie asked, surprised.

"Yes, someone else," JT confirmed. "Isn't that right, Rupert?"

"What?" Rupert said, flustered. "I don't know what you mean!"

"Really?" JT asked. "You are registered here as Rupert Harcourt but you real name is Rupert Hampton, correct? Husband to the late Sarah-Louise Hampton. You see, the articles I found contained a photograph of the young woman and her husband, a slightly fuzzy photo, granted, and her husband had a beard but I recognised your eyes. There is just no hiding that shifty look, is there?

"I have to commend you, I really do. How much planning was involved to inveigle your way into Sophia's life? Get engaged, plan for the wedding here, now? And then your performance here, wow! Acting like a complete ass, being rude and obnoxious, getting into a fight with Toby, making yourself look like a suspect, leaving yourself with no alibi then culminating with the fake admission of cross-dressing? Bravo!"

Rupert sat glaring at JT. "Why did you have to interfere?" he snarled. "I knew you would work things out, that is why I took the chance when I saw you at the top of those stairs. It was just a spur of the moment thing, you know? Just too good a chance to pass up."

"I suppose I can take it as a compliment," JT told the man. "So, the three of you conspired together. Well, you got your revenge, I hope you are happy."

"He got what he deserved," Rupert said, walking over to stand beside Sydney and Germaine. "I have no regrets."

"What about Mrs Lambert?" JT retorted but he was greeted with silence.

A short time later, with the roads cleared, the authorities arrived and Sydney, Germaine and Rupert were taken into custody while the bodies were loaded into ambulances.

In Haddington-Smythe's office, the manager sat with JT and Marie and a police detective. JT had finished explaining everything to the police detective.

"So, the death of," the policeman looked at his notes, "um, Ms Franks, was unrelated to all this other business?"

"Yes," JT confirmed. "It was, as Dr Stepford surmised, nothing more than a tragic accident." As the police detective, satisfied, closed his notebook and stood to leave, JT thought back...

From the first time he met her, JT knew there was something about Jane Franks which bothered him. He could not put his finger on it immediately so decided it was best to simply focus on other matters and let his subconscious deal with this problem.

It took several hours but, finally, the memory coalesced; nearly thirty years earlier, an incident occurred which was a major factor in JT's career choice, something he had not thought about in a very long time. Until now.

As soon as he had been informed of Jane Franks' whereabouts, he decided on a course of action. Taking the stairs, he made his way to the swimming pool, taking care to not be noticed by anyone. It was surprising sometimes how little attention people generally paid and, in his line of work, often frustrating. However, on this occasion, it worked to JT's advantage as he reached his destination unnoticed.

He stepped through the door and walked along the short corridor which connected to the changing rooms. At the end of the corridor, he could see one end of the swimming pool, the water gently undulating, casting flickering reflections of pale light on the walls, the smell of chlorine assaulting his nostrils. As he walked along the tiled surface at the side of the pool, JT heard his footsteps echoing. In the water, he saw Jane Franks gliding beneath the surface then kicking with her legs, her hair trailing behind her. As she reached the opposite end of the pool and turned, she spotted JT.

"Oh, hello," she said, then swam over to where he stood. "Is there a problem?"

"You know, it took me a while to remember," JT said.

"I'm sorry, remember what?"

"Where I had seen you before," JT answered.

"Oh?" Jane said. "I don't recall meeting you before."

"We haven't met before, not exactly," JT said cryptically, crouching down so he was closer to the woman in the pool. "Your hair's different, naturally you have a few more wrinkles but thirty years will do that to anyone, and, perhaps not surprisingly, you changed your name."

"Look, I don't have time for games," Jane said annoyed. "I am due on shift soon so if you don't mind..."

"Please, hear me out," JT said reaching out and taking one of her wrists in his hand. "I will explain everything. You see,

there was an... incident, over thirty years ago now. It was quite a big deal at the time, you might remember it; twin toddlers, a boy and a girl, aged three, were murdered by their sociopathic nanny, a young woman who smothered the children for no obvious reason and felt nothing. Not guilt, remorse, regret, hell, not even pleasure.

"*I was a young man back then, following the case with interest because I knew the family. It seemed a slam-dunk case but, unbelievably, the woman got off on a technicality. Her lawyer, who had taken on the case for free, pulled a master-stroke. In the aftermath, the young woman had to get police protection, if you can believe that, before, finally, receiving a new identity and disappearing.*

"*The family was crushed. The verdict was like a hammer blow to them, one they never recovered from. The mother finally overdosed on tranquillisers, the father drank him-self into oblivion.*"

"*Why... why are you telling me this?*" *Jane asked, trying to pull her arm free but unable to break JT's grip.*

"*There are some faces you just don't... can't forget,*" *JT answered calmly. "The passage of time confused me briefly but then I realised where I had seen you before.*"

"*Look, I don't know what you are....*"

"*Don't bother lying,*" *JT said, still sounding calm. "I know who you are.*"

"*Look, that was a long time ago,*" *Jane said quickly, panic building within her. "I was young, troubled... I got help. I... I... I managed to get my life sorted.*"

"*Well, good for you,*" *JT said. "You know, seeing you being acquitted is what made me become a private detective. I was determined, in a way only the young can be, to see that no other murderer escaped justice because of some legal technicality or incompetence on the part of the authorities. I suppose I should thank you.*"

"*Listen,*" *Jane began.*

Whatever she was going to say, JT never heard. Quick as a flash, his other hand shot out and grabbed Jane's head from behind and, in one short, sharp motion, pulled her head forward, smashing it on the edge of the pool. Before she knew what had happened, before her mind had time to register the pain, Jane was stunned into unconsciousness, her limp body floating in the water. Careful not to smudge the blood that had appeared on the tiles, JT pushed Jane's head down, keeping it beneath the surface of the water. At first, there were bubbles as Jane breathed then they stopped. JT remained where he was for a moment longer in case the woman was faking until, finally satisfied Jane was dead, he carefully stood up and left, satisfied no one had seen him. It had been over thirty years but, at last, justice had been served.

JT shook himself out of his reverie and noticed the police detective had left the office. Looking at Haddington-Smythe, he said, "I guess that concludes our business, Gerald. The authorities can take care of everything else from here."

"Well, Mr Thomas," Haddington-Smythe said extending his hand. "I am not sure what the long term impact of these events will have on the hotel but the quick resolution can only be a good thing. You can now relax and enjoy the rest of your stay here. Also, once I inform the board of your sterling work, I am sure they will be inclined to reward you in some manner."

"I was stuck here along with everyone else," JT replied, "so I don't feel I can charge my usual fee. However, if they were to, say, permit me a two-week stay, every year, well, I would not be ungrateful."

"Ahem, er, I will be sure to pass that along," the manager said.

The two men shook hands then Haddington-Smythe turned to Marie and asked, "And what of you? Will you be continuing your stay with us?"

"Of course," JT answered before Marie could open her mouth. "We still have lots of work to do, notes to transcribe, catchphrases to develop, eh?"

"Sorry, boss," Marie answered with a smile. "I told you, as soon as this case was done, so was I. I meant it."

"Well, of course we all say things in the heat of the moment," JT said. "But then we calm down, come to our senses, realise the error of our ways, know when we are on to a good thing, right?"

"Wow, you really are unbelievable," Marie said, rolling her eyes. Before, this would have annoyed her but, having made her decision, Marie was no longer bothered by JT's somewhat narcissistic outlook. "You know, JT, that kind of attitude used to get me really annoyed but, now that I have made my mind up, it doesn't bother me anymore. I feel more relaxed and confident than I have done in a very long time."

"But… but… but what about my book?" JT stammered.

"You'll just have to find someone else to work for you," Marie answered. "But, here is some friendly advice; try to be less condescending, consider other people's feelings, maybe pay a bit more attention and, who knows, you may find someone happy to work for you."

"Great steaming nutsacks!" JT exclaimed.

"And I think you have just found the catchphrase you have been looking for," Marie said, smiling. "Come on, I have to pack. I want to get out of here before it starts snowing again!"

Outside the office, JT and Marie were heading towards the elevator when JT spotted Emma sitting at the front desk.

"Listen, Marie," he said, "you go on ahead. I think I have maybe found the ideal candidate to replace you."

Without waiting for a response, JT headed towards the desk. Marie had pressed the button to summon the elevator but, seeing JT approach Emma, decided this would be too good to miss so, discreetly, she inched towards the desk.

"Hello, there," JT said smiling at the young lady behind the desk.

"Hello, Mr Thomas," Emma replied coolly. "How may I help you?"

"Funny you should ask," JT said, leaning forward, resting his hands on the desk. "There has, um, been an opening, one might call it an opportunity, in my, ah, business."

"What business would that be?" Emma asked. "The one you 'dabble' in to relieve the boredom of your privileged existence courtesy of your family's shrewd investments?"

"Ah, well, funny story that," JT replied, forcing a chuckle. "I'm sure you, er, heard what I said earlier, you know, about, ah, being a bit… creative with the truth, as far as my financial situation is concerned."

"By creative, you mean lying," Emma retorted.

"Well, you say tomato," JT said nervously. "Still, what's money, eh? I am offering you the chance to meet interesting people, record for posterity my achievements, um, keep track of my appointments…"

"Mr Thomas," Emma interrupted and if she sounded cool before, she was positively frozen now, Marie thought. "What possible reason could persuade me to give up my job here, in this hotel, to go and work for you? I am guessing that financial incentives won't win the day!"

"Um, well, er, I, ah, thought… that is, I got the impression that, well, I thought you, you know, liked me?" JT murmured.

"Mr Thomas, I 'like' cheese and pickle sandwiches," Emma replied. "And, to be honest, at this precise moment, that is infinitely more tempting than you, or your offer!"

JT stood for a moment, mouth opening and closing, as he struggled to think of something to say. Eventually, he cleared his throat and said, "Um, okay, well, ah, sorry to have bothered you." With that, he turned and almost fell over Marie who had been listening to the exchange.

"Oh, ah, there you are," Marie said quickly. "I was just, uh, coming to look for you."

"Let's go," JT muttered. "I, ah, am finished here."

"How'd you get on?" Marie asked innocently.

"Um, you know, after talking to her, I don't really think she is what I am looking for," JT said quickly. "I, er, I will just have to transcribe my notes myself. Probably better that way, to be honest. After all, who knows these cases better than me, eh?"

As they walked off, Marie smiled to herself. Despite everything that had happened over the past few days, Christmas had turned out to be not so bad, after all.

THE END

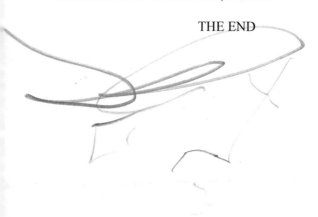